Advance praise for Cameron Abbott's
To the Edge

"This is an excellent and highly readable coming-of-age romance, and a legal thriller as well. . . . Combines the vitality of early feminist ideals and erotic longings with today's issues of courage and power in the life of one heroic woman."

–Phyllis Chesler, PhD, author of *Women and Madness*
and *Letters to a Young Feminist*

To the Edge

Alice Street Editions

Judith P. Stelboum
Editor-in-Chief

To the Edge, by Cameron Abbott

From Flitch to Ash: A Musing on Trees and Carving,
by Diane Derrick

Treat, by Angie Vicars

Yin Fire, by Alexandra Grilikhes

*His Hands, His Tools, His Sex, His Dress: Lesbian
Writers on Their Fathers*, edited by Catherine Reid
and Holly K. Iglesias

Weeding at Dawn: A Lesbian Country Life,
by Hawk Madrone

Façades, by Alex Marcoux

Inside Out, by Juliet Carrera

Past Perfect, by Judith P. Stelboum

Forthcoming

Egret, by Helen Collins

Back to Salem, by Alex Marcoux

Your Loving Arms, by Gwendolyn Bikis

*A Donor Insemination Guide: Written By and
For Lesbian Women*, by Marie Mohler, MA,
and Lacy Frazer, PsyD

Extraordinary Couples, Ordinary Lives,
by Lynn Haley-Banez and Joanne Garrett

Foreword

Alice Street Editions provides a voice for established as well as up-and-coming lesbian writers, reflecting the diversity of lesbian interests, ethnicities, ages, and class. This cutting-edge series of novels, memoirs, and non-fiction writing welcomes the opportunity to present controversial views, explore multicultural ideas, encourage debate, and inspire creativity from a variety of lesbian perspectives. Through enlightening, illuminating, and provocative writing, Alice Street Editions can make a significant contribution to the visibility and accessibility of lesbian writing, and bring lesbian-focused writing to a wider audience. Recognizing our own desires and ideas in print is life sustaining, acknowledging the reality of who we are, our place in the world, individually and collectively.

Judith P. Stelboum
Editor-in-Chief
Alice Street Editions

To the Edge

Cameron Abbott

Alice Street Editions

Harrington Park Press
New York • London • Oxford

This is a work of fiction. All of the locations are fictionalized or products of the author's imagination, and no reference to actual persons or incidents is implied or should be inferred.

Published by

Alice Street Editions, Harrington Park Press®, an imprint of The Haworth Press, Inc., 10 Alice Street, Binghamton, NY 13904-1580 USA (www.HaworthPress.com).

Cover design by Thomas J. Mayshock Jr.

Library of Congress Cataloging-in-Publication Data

Abbott, Cameron
    To the edge / Cameron Abbott.
        p. cm.
    ISBN 1-56023-222-6 (alk. paper) – ISBN 1-56023-223-4 (pbk. : alk. paper)
    1. Women lawyers–Fiction. 2. Coming out (Sexual orientation)–Fiction. 3. New York (N.Y.)–Fiction. 4. Lesbians–Fiction. I. Title.

PS3601.B36 T6 2001
813'.6–dc21.

2001024995

for Michele

With heartfelt appreciation to Judith Stelboum, Helen Mallon, Julie Ehlers, Tom Mayshock, and the rest of the incomparable staff at The Haworth Press and Alice Street Editions.

THE SEVENTIES

Chapter One

"What is it about the hair on these women? How come every time we see a woman go mad onstage, her hair is all messed up?"

Silence around the seminar table as the students pondered Jenna's question for a moment. Anne Henderson started a doodle sketch of Lady Macbeth in the margin of her notebook, and wondered for the umpteenth time why she had signed up for this Women's Studies class. Hell, she wasn't even sure what Women's Studies was. Shirl Porter, the grad student teacher, slowly smiled during the silence, but the quick dart of her eyes betrayed her excitement. Shirl was always excited about something.

"Now there's an interesting question," Shirl said. Her eyes came to rest on Anne near the end of the table. "Any thoughts, Anne?"

About a million, but none had anything to do with this class. Anne had figured it would be a gut when she'd first signed up for it, but it was now proving to be somewhat of a challenge just to figure out what was going on. Shit, she thought as twelve sets of eyes turned to her. I don't need this. "Well–" Think, damn it. She looked up at Shirl. "I guess a woman's hair is just very theatrical." Shirl nodded her on, so she continued, warming to the subject. "I mean, they're always having to wear wigs and different hairstyles to convey a period or style. So if you mess that up, in a sense you're bucking the system, going outside the norm. And when women do that, I guess, the rest of the world considers them crazy."

Whatever it was she'd said, it must have been acceptable because she saw out of the corner of her eye that Rae Sheldon beside her was writing it down. Unlike Rae, Anne rarely wrote notes in this class because, frankly, so much of the discussion took place several yards over her head and she was never entirely clear about the point that everyone else seemed to grasp intuitively. She wished that the only vacant seat today hadn't been beside Rae, who for some reason always made her feel a little uncomfortable. Self-conscious. Rae was one of the beautiful people whom Anne usually tended to avoid, for no real reason. Just an instinctive distrust on some level that Anne never bothered to explore too closely.

"So, in a way," Rae piped up, "it's really just turning the perception of madness back onto the audience."

Shirl's enthusiasm was infectious. "What do you mean?" The question gave Anne an excuse to turn and look fully at Rae. She saw there a face that was beyond attractive. Something off a magazine cover, but no makeup, nothing artificial to mar the perfect olive complexion, cherry-red lips–could they really be that red? Yes, they were–and long dark lashes framing green eyes that even from this angle Anne could see were flashing with each insight. Weird, it suddenly stuck Anne that the depth of Rae's attractiveness had never really registered before–she'd never looked too closely. Rae delivered her words between puffs on a Vantage cigarette, embellished by hands that seemed to sculpt the air in front of her, assisted by a pen twirled in one and a cigarette tipped with an impossibly long ash in the other. Too bad Anne had no idea what she was saying. Anne regularly tuned in and out in her classes, her thoughts usually occupied by a mental review of the previous night's rehearsal or a run-down on all the reading she had to do. As a freshman last year she'd perfected the art of the minimal-effort A, and classes at this point had become somewhat of a chore. Especially this one. But here at least she liked Shirl, and the discussions were lively.

They had been in this seminar twice a week for a month now. All women–what were the guys afraid of?–all cheerfully self-proclaimed feminists, most decked out in the feminist uniform of the day: long hair; jeans; peasant blouses or tee shirts; sneakers, sandals, or hiking boots, depending on the weather; and the ubiquitous backpacks. Anne couldn't get into it. Sure, she had the backpack and requisite long blonde hair down her back, but the comparison ended there. She wore khakis sometimes instead of jeans, preferred penny loafers to sneakers, and refused even to own a peasant blouse.

Anne had not noticed Rae at all when the semester had begun–not until she'd spoken up sometime during the second week. Even after Rae had opened her mouth that first time, she was just an attractive woman, noticeably attractive for certain, but nothing more. As pretty as she was, it was the voice that really did it–husky, deep, smoky.

". . . and isn't it a function of sexuality anyway?" Rae was asking. The way she said it caused Anne's stomach to clench for an uncomfortable instant–sex-u-*al*-ity–her tongue caressing the word, her lips punctuating it with a crooked smile at the end.

Shirl glanced at her watch. "We'll have to take this up next time," she said, "we've already run over."

At that moment, Rae turned and caught Anne staring at her. Rae looked her boldly in the eye and smiled–not crooked this time, a genuine, full-face smile–and Anne felt a blush start to warm her cheeks. Shit.

Rae put her hand on Anne's arm, emphatic, clutching. "Anne, right?" she said quietly amid the clatter of closing books and scraping chairs.

"Yes." Anne wanted to pull her arm away, but didn't.

"Listen, come to the Dragon if you don't have a class now. We'll probably meet up with Shirl there for coffee."

Rae's eyes never left Anne's, the smile never wavered, as Anne considered it for a moment. She had a shitload of work to do, but what would one cup of coffee matter? She'd already finished her can of Tab, and could use the extra caffeine. Besides, there was something intriguing about this woman. Maybe Rae was someone worth getting to know.

"Sure," Anne said as she rose to load her books into her backpack. She made her way to the door and waited for Rae, who remained at the table for a moment, engrossed in a conversation with Jenna. "I just can't tonight," she overhead Rae saying. "He's playing, and I have to be there." Anne watched as Rae gracefully swept her long brown hair behind her shoulder in a move that seemed almost choreographed. She could be a dancer. When Rae turned, she caught Anne staring again and gave her a small smile that curiously made Anne's heart skip a beat. For a second,

Anne reconsidered going to the Dragon, but by the time Rae had joined her at the door, Anne knew she would go, and walked into the hall with Rae limping beside her and Jenna bringing up the rear. Funny, Anne had never noticed the limp before.

The steady drizzle of the past five days had finally abated by the time Anne made her way downhill to her dorm many hours later. Ithaca had a special weather all its own, which included the ever-popular precipitation known as "Ithacating"–not quite rain, but more than a mist, it was such a complete saturation of the air that everything got wet and stayed that way. Her roommate Jane had a friend majoring in meteorology who had conde-scendingly informed them one night that there was no such thing as "Ithacating," but Anne and everyone else she knew at Cornell persisted in calling it that.

This October had seen rain, however. Real rain. The footpaths all over cam-pus were covered by enormous ground worms that had crawled from the sod-den turf in search of air, some dead, some smashed underfoot, but most alive and wiggling. Anne sidestepped the worms as best she could as she ap-proached her neo-Saxon-looking dorm at the bottom of the hill. The building was charming in a way, with heavy stone masonry and rounded Romanesque portals covered two-thirds by ivy, but Anne noticed none of it today as she plodded toward the entrance. Her mind was spinning from the past three dizzy-ing hours of coffee, Tab, and Rae. She didn't even notice Joey waiting for her on the wall beside the dorm until she was nearly upon him.

"Where have you been?" He jumped down as she approached. "We have to be at rehearsal early tonight. I'm starving."

"I was busy," she said as she hurried past him through the heavy outer door and up the stairs to the third floor. "Shit, I wish they'd put an elevator in this place."

"Oh, get over it," Joey said, following her upstairs. "This is the only walking you do. You even hitchhike up the hill to get to phys ed."

Anne reached the landing and pulled out her room key. "Joey, I have to change. Wait out here." She shut the door in his face, and heard his snort just before it closed.

"You weren't busy," he said through the door. "You were just hanging out in the Dragon."

"I needed coffee. And if you knew where I was, then why did you ask?"

"Didn't you have dyke class today?"

"Would you mind not shouting through the door while I change? You can come in in a minute."

"I guess the classes are starting to work?"

She stopped with her shirt mid-chest over her bra, and pulled it back down before opening the door. "I don't know what you think you know, but I think you should just keep it to yourself. And I'm getting tired of you calling it dyke class, too."

He opened his mouth and pulled in his jaw to smear a what-do-you-mean innocence over his face. She wanted to punch him, but she knew he was only teasing her because he had no idea of the turmoil she was feeling from the afternoon. He was her best friend, after all, and she was planning to talk to him about it anyway–about her afternoon with Rae, as she thought of it, even though there were four other people there. She just wasn't ready to get into it with him now. Not until she really knew what she thought about it all.

She sighed with resignation. "Okay, come in, I don't care. But shut the door."

He perched himself on her desktop, feet on her chair, and started pulling on his pubic-hair-looking beard. She turned her back to change her shirt, mulling over how best to begin, but before she'd settled on an approach, he saved her the trouble.

"I saw you going into the Dragon with Rae Sheldon. Awfully cozy." He paused. "She's pretty."

"She has a boyfriend. It's not what you think. And she has a plantar's wart on her foot. It hurts, so she limps sometimes. She needs to hold onto someone when she walks, okay?"

"Uh huh." He was looking at the salt shaker that Jane had inexplicably put on the circuit breaker by the desk the other night.

"Really." As in period, that's the end of it. But it wasn't.

"You can't walk around campus with some woman's arm around you and not have people notice, you know."

This was getting out of hand. Just discussing it was making it more of an issue than it really was.

"She was holding onto my arm. What's the big deal?"

"If you say so." He was really enjoying this way too much. Time to set him straight.

"Look Joey, we've talked about this gay thing a million times, and I'm not going to give you the satisfaction of getting into it again. Just because someone takes a Women's Studies class doesn't mean she's gay. I think you're obsessed."

"It's not like you've never had a crush on a girl."

She pushed her long hair behind her shoulder. "I should never have told you about that. You totally missed the point. It was nothing, okay? I was just a kid, and I wish you'd just forget about it. It doesn't mean I'm gay."

"Uh huh."

"Really. I promise you'll be the first to know."

"She's bi, you know."

"Who?"

"Rae Sheldon."

"Bullshit." That was news. Anne leaned over to tie her shoes, pushing that little morsel to the back of her mind to devour it later, when she could think. "I thought you didn't even know her."

"I don't. But I know who she is. Everybody does. She stands out, you know, kind of exotic looking–people notice her. Just like people notice you."

"People don't notice me."

"Sure they do. You've got this all-American cheerleader thing going, all the jocks are into it."

"I don't know why you make up this stuff. And I really resent being called a cheerleader. If anything, I'm a jock myself."

"Aw, c'mon, it's a compliment. Every girl wants to be a blonde bombshell like you."

"You know, that's really demeaning. And I think I know what girls feel better than you do. Women, I mean."

Joey laughed at her.

"Oh, shut up."

"Anyway," he said, "I heard some stuff about her. Last year."

"She has a boyfriend." Anne was getting annoyed. "And P.S., so do I."

Joey was quiet for a minute. He took down the salt shaker and sprinkled some onto his hand. Poking a wetted finger into the small pile of granules, he lifted his salted finger to his mouth, licked, and repeated the process for a few moments. "I just don't want you to get hurt," he said between licks.

"I don't know how on earth I could get hurt. Rae Sheldon is just someone in my class. Not even really a friend. I haven't really spoken to her before today."

Jane chose that moment to come through the door. Jane with the long straight white-blonde hair and determinedly unreadable expressions. Anne considered her roommate a close friend, in an odd sort of way. Completely different majors, they had no shared classes or friends. Jane came from staunchly Republican parents, hearty Midwesterners. Except for a love of music–certainly nothing unique–they had absolutely nothing in common. Since the university purported to pair up roommates according to common interests, Anne and Jane could never figure out how they'd ended up together their first year. Still, somehow it had worked, and they'd elected to continue rooming together as sophomores.

Anne was glad she'd finished changing–she had a feeling Jane would disapprove of finding her half-naked in front of Joey. Nothing explicit, nothing overt, just a look that she knew Jane would give, although her relationship with him had always been purely platonic. Jane was good with the looks.

Jane glanced at Joey and directed a "hey" to Anne.

"Hey yourself."

Jane stopped by Joey at the desk, frowned perceptibly at the salted finger in his mouth, and noticed the score to *Yeomen of the Guard* sitting on the desk beside him.

"Rehearsal?"

"Yeah, dinner first. You decided if you'll play in the orchestra?"

Jane held up her organic chemistry book. "Can't commit until after prelims." Anne nodded as she finished combing her hair.

"You see your message?" Jane asked. "Someone named Gallagher called. What kind of name is that for a girl?"

"Woman," Joey interjected and smiled at Anne.

"Whatever." Jane resolutely ignored him. "Anyway, she called long distance and wants you to call back. Keep track of the call for the phone bill, okay?"

Although Joey probably noticed the flush on Anne's cheek, and certainly understood the effect that Jane's news would have on her, he didn't comment. He really was her best friend, no doubt about it. Anne picked up her sweatshirt. "Okay, later. We gotta go."

" 'Kay, bye." Jane said over her shoulder as she walked into the separate bedroom area.

Anne pulled on her sweatshirt and grabbed her score. "Ready?"

Joey hopped down from the desktop. "So are you gonna tell me what you spent all that time talking about?"

Not so easy to describe. Life. Feminism. Sexual politics. But she wasn't going to talk to Joey about it. Not now, no way.

"Just stuff from class," she mumbled as she headed out the door with Joey scrambling behind her.

* * *

What had they talked about? As she walked back from rehearsal that night, she realized that she couldn't have answered that question even if she'd wanted to. The night air was cool and damp, the campus deserted, and Anne was finally left alone with her thoughts–Joey having gone with most of the cast to the Big Red. Now at last she was able to play over in her mind the events of that afternoon–or, more precisely, her reaction to them, because the truth was that she could not recall a single thing that had been said. Only sensations, images, the texture of it all.

It wasn't so much a discussion as a philosophical group encounter. Kaleidoscopic ideas jumping like static electricity among everyone. Four of them from class–Rosa, Jenna, Rae, and Anne, joined soon thereafter by Shirl–finishing each other's sentences over black coffee, Tab, and cigarettes. But for some reason the voice that now echoed in her ears, the face whose expressions she replayed in her mind over and over as she trudged downhill, were all Rae's. And that was the troubling part, the part she picked at in her mind like a loose scab, both painful and intriguing. She didn't like feeling this way, didn't like the sensation that something was a little bit off in her balanced, ordered world.

She had basically ignored her boyfriend Chris during the rehearsal, but, sweet guy that he was, he didn't seem to mind. Trying to memorize her lines, she'd explained to him–a ruse that didn't fool Joey, who knew that she had the entire Gilbert and Sullivan canon committed to memory. When Chris had approached her at the end of rehearsal to see if she was joining the cast at the Big Red, she begged off, inventing a lot of reading to do for her history class the next day. He'd smiled with understanding.

"But we're still on for Saturday, right?" he'd asked. "Music at the Gorge with Joey and Elaine?"

She couldn't remember having said yes when he'd asked the first time, but she'd nodded her head tonight in appeasement, as if agreeing to Saturday made up for blowing him off now.

When she got back to the dorm, Jane was just putting on a windbreaker, and looked up as Anne entered the room.

"Bagel," she said as she fumbled with the zipper.

"Okay." Anne dropped her score on the desk and followed Jane out the door.

It was one of their things–a roommate-bonding thing that they didn't share with anyone else. A long walk through campus to Collegetown, where Jane would buy a bagel and Anne a big cup of black coffee. If there were something important to discuss, this was the time for it. But usually they walked in silence, each content with being alone with her thoughts. Early on in their ritual last year, Jane had commented on the fact that the coffee never seemed to keep Anne awake. The truth was, nothing kept Anne awake. Between rehearsals, late-night study sessions, a full courseload, and several miles per week in the pool, she was nearly always running on empty and slept soundly as soon as her head hit the pillow.

They sat quietly for a while on a stoop outside a bicycle shop next door to the all-night Bagelry.

"Your friend called," Jane finally said.

"Who?"

"With the weird name."

"Rae?"

"No, Gallagher." Jane stared out onto the empty sidewalk, as usual. It was rare for Jane to look at the person she was addressing, just as it was rare for Jane to ask a probing question. Come to think of it, Jane rarely even asked a neutral question–if she needed a pen, instead of just asking if she could borrow one she'd usually walk up to Anne, hold up her empty pen and say "pen." Some people found her manner off-putting, but Anne liked it. She didn't mince words, and on those rare occasions when she had something to say, it was always worth hearing.

"She's coming to look at Cornell and wants to see you."

Anne digested this news in silence, grateful for Jane's offcast gaze, wondering briefly if Jane somehow knew the effect this tidbit would have on Anne. Was Jane just being polite, letting her experience it in private? No, Anne dismissed the thought, Jane couldn't know anything–hell, I don't even know what I think about it. One more thing to puzzle over. Great. As if sorting out my reaction to Rae today weren't enough.

"Who's Rae?" Jane asked, startling Anne so much that she spilled some coffee on her hand.

"Shit. Nobody. Someone in my class."

Jane continued to chew on a bite of bagel in silence, seemingly oblivious to Anne's scalded hand, but Anne knew better. She also knew that Jane would ask no more questions tonight, and gave quiet thanks for her quirky, deceptively wise roommate.

The Gorge was crowded on Saturday, but Joey had gotten there early and saved a table, so when Anne and Chris walked in around ten they had a spot right up front. Durango was just a local band, but popular with the college crowd, and the place was packed for the band's second set. Elaine got there a few minutes later, and draped her arms around Joey's shoulders as she greeted everyone. "I'm sorry I'm late," she said, "but I couldn't decide what to wear." God, what did Joey see in this bimbo?

Anne tried to be nice. "It's okay, we just got here too. The band's on break, so you haven't missed anything." Anne studiously avoided looking at Elaine caressing Joey, uncomfortable with their public display. Thank God Chris isn't into fawning all over me, she thought.

Elaine lit a cigarette, and Joey made a face. "Come on, baby," her voice was a high-pitched irritant, "it's a smoky bar and I'm drinking beer. I just have to have a ciggie." A ciggie? Give me a break, Anne thought.

"I'll go get an ashtray," Chris said, starting to rise from the table.

Anne beat him to the punch. "No, that's okay." She was on her feet in a flash. "I'm going to the bathroom anyway. I'll pick one up on my way back."

Now Elaine got up too. "Wait, I'll come with you. I wanna go before the band starts. Besides, you know what they say about girls going to the bathroom in pairs." She threw a theatrical wink toward Anne, who had to physically restrain herself from cringing. She shot Joey a "don't you dare open your mouth" look, and took off toward the back of the bar without a glance at Elaine.

The line was long, but fortunately Elaine was busy scoping out the crowd and wasn't interested in conversation. Her few comments about the people she spotted were barely audible over the blaring taped music any-way, so Anne was left in relative peace for a few moments—during which time her thoughts returned like clockwork to the incessant, relentless refrain of Thursday afternoon at the Dragon, interspersed occasionally with the conundrum of Gallagher. Anne still hadn't called her back.

"There's Rick Manger. Oh God, he's such a stud," Elaine squealed as she flicked her ashes on the floor.

"Who?" As if Anne gave a shit.

"Rick Manger, the bass player. Over there." Elaine used her chin to point toward the bar. "Hot, huh?"

Anne shrugged. "I guess," she said once she'd located the object of Elaine's lust. Neatly trimmed long brown hair, pleasant smiling face. A wholesome farmer-boy type, but his tight jeans and the rolled sleeves on his workshirt suggested a lifeguard's body underneath—and that was prob-ably all that Elaine saw.

Anne looked back toward Chris, who was chuckling at something Joey had said. She thought that Chris was hands-down better looking—thick, sun-bleached blond hair, strong square jaw, sensuous mouth, all put to-gether in a dreamy movie-star kind of way. She had certainly thought he was one of the most attractive men she'd ever seen when they'd started dating last year. He had a confident, easygoing manner that was endear-ing—he didn't work on impressing people, but it happened anyway. He was just an impressive kind of guy. And talented—that counted for a lot with Anne. But he didn't just rest on his good looks and talent, he worked hard to improve his craft—probably harder than any actor she knew, and she knew far too many actors. Anne respected him, even if she didn't really love him.

She also knew that some part of herself enjoyed the fact that they made such a seemingly perfect couple. Both blond, they looked like a matching set, and might even pass for brother and sister. She was comfortable with him, and his quiet, understated grace was a natural foil to her offbeat style. They got along so well that their relationship reminded her of some of her high-school friendships–easy, pressure-free and fun. So why didn't she love him? She had no idea.

Anne finished in the bathroom first, so she left Elaine to find her own way back to the table with the snide satisfaction that Elaine would be deprived of the chance to resurface her stupid joke about women visiting the bathroom in pairs. She picked up an ashtray from the bar and stopped dead in her tracks at the sudden sound of a husky, smoke-filled laugh that miraculously reached her through the din. Instantly recognizable. Don't look, just be cool. Deliberately turning away from the voice, Anne navigated back through the crowd to her table with her heart pounding in her ears so loudly that it drowned out the room. She was still holding the ashtray when Joey leaned over, took it out of her hand, and said in her ear, "Guess who's here?"

Chris was watching the band mounting the small stage, oblivious to her and Joey. "I know. And don't start, okay?"

"Did you say hi?"

"No, and I'm not going to. Let's just listen to the music, huh?" Yes, please, let the music start and let me crawl inside my head.

"Talking about me?" Elaine asked a little too cheerfully as she sat down. She draped her arms around Joey and pulled him away from Anne. "Come on, let me in on the secret."

"No secret," Joey said, pushing the ashtray in front of Elaine. "We just can't hear each other over the tape."

Anne poured herself a glass of beer, refilled Chris's glass, and sat back as the band was introduced. She liked Durango, although she'd only heard them a few times. Some pop, interspersed with some original tunes, the band could rock but also did some beautiful harmonies on their ballads. Anne guessed that they were former music majors who'd graduated several years ago from one of the area colleges. Probably in their late twenties, early thirties–old enough to know what they were doing and do it well. Anne wondered if they made enough to live on from their music, and decided that, good as they were, they must have had day jobs as well.

After the third number, a particularly loud rock song, Anne felt Chris's hand on her neck and reached back in response to put her hand on his knee. In the sudden quiet between numbers, she heard a low, unmistakable voice in her ear, "Aren't you going to introduce me to your friends?"

She looked up to see that it was Rae whose hand was on her neck, a slightly mischievous look on her face, iridescent green eyes flickering with amusement. She felt the blood immediately rise to her cheeks, and prayed that the poor light was masking the blush that she knew was blossoming there. In that speechless moment, Rae subtly increased the pressure on her neck, flashed that trademark crooked smile, and flicked her eyebrows in a "well?" that was both mocking and lovely.

Anne took her hand from Chris's knee and sat up straight.

"Hi," she said, perhaps a little too forcefully. Rae looked great–dressed in a sheer black blouse and black slacks, with a tiny gold necklace that was momentarily fascinating. Anne looked away. "Um, this is Joey, Elaine, Chris." She indicated each with a nod. "This is Rae. We're in a class together."

Chris stood. "You want to join us? We can pull up a chair."

"No, I'm at the bar, thanks," Rae said, returning her eyes to Anne in the middle of the sentence. Chris seemed not to notice the dismissal in it, but Joey did, and Anne could not decipher his look as Rae squatted down beside her chair. The band started a slow love song.

"I don't think I've ever seen you here before," Rae said. Her voice was soft, and she was moving her hand from behind Anne's neck to rest it on her bare arm. Anne tried to concentrate.

"I don't come that often." Anne forced herself to return Rae's bold gaze. "You?"

"Sometimes." Rae squeezed her arm slightly then–whether for emphasis or because she was losing her balance, Anne didn't know. "Listen, I've been thinking a lot about that day in the Dragon. I really had fun."

"Yeah, me too." Anne was all too conscious of Joey's obvious stare. She stole a quick glance at the rest of the table–Elaine was tapping the slow rhythm on Joey's shoulder, and Chris was in his own world.

"Come outside with me," Rae said. "I want a cigarette." It was almost an order, and Anne's baffled expression made Rae laugh. It was a delicious sound. "The smoke in here gets to me after a while. I only want *my* smoke in my lungs–not the leftovers from everyone else's. Probably a sign I should quit, but . . ." she shrugged and pushed her hair out of her face.

Anne turned to Chris to speak in his ear. "I'm going outside for a minute. Be right back."

"Want me to come?"

God, no. Anne shook her head. "I won't be long."

Rae's light hand on her arm turned into a clutch as she rose from her squat, and she continued her hold as they moved together toward the door. Anne forced herself to concentrate on putting one foot in front of the other, to ignore the feel of Rae's hand on her arm, and somehow she successfully made it to the door. Outside, the rain had stopped, and their ears rang in the sudden quiet. Anne was very conscious of the fact that, now that she was alone with this stranger, she had absolutely nothing to say.

Rae leaned against a car and lit a cigarette, offering one to Anne.

"No thanks," said Anne.

"Smart," Rae said while exhaling her first puff.

Anne shrugged. "I swim. It cuts down on my air." For some reason she felt the need to explain her lack of cool. Nothing new, Anne always felt uncool.

"A swimmer, huh? That's how you stay in such great shape."

Anne didn't know what to say to that, so she let it drop, and then felt awkward in the silence. Maybe she should have offered a witty rejoinder, but none had occurred to her and now it was too late.

The night was cool and still a bit damp, the air filled with a musky, natural scent of decomposing leaves and rich earth. A good, clean smell. Anne looked up at the night sky to avoid looking at Rae, whose eyes she felt studying her face. Why can't I just stare back at her? Take command of the situation and not let her make me so nervous? Because she's so beautiful? Although only medium height, Anne felt very tall beside Rae's petite form. She hadn't ever thought of Rae as short, but clearly she was.

Anne spent a minute silently quizzing herself on some of the constellations she'd learned about in Astronomy last year, and Rae broke the silence.

"Is Chris your boyfriend?"

"Yeah." Anne was still searching for the Pleiades, still too self-conscious to look at Rae. "We got together last spring."

"He's an actor." Rae said it as a statement, not a question.

"We were in a play together."

Rae took another puff and blew it out luxuriously. "I saw it."

She saw it? Anne looked at her, saw that the crooked smile had returned. She wasn't going to ask what Rae thought of her performance, and knew after a moment that Rae wasn't going to offer it. At least she'd gotten her eyes out of the sky and back onto the face that she wanted to admire. She smiled, and Rae's grin broadened. Here I am standing in the dark with this beautiful bisexual woman smiling at me. The implications–and possibilities–were more than a little terrifying.

"He seems nice."

Who?–oh. Anne caught herself before asking. Odd, "nice" was not usually the first thing people noticed about Chris, although it was true. People always remarked on his appearance first, and generally assumed that he was an asshole because of it–until they got to know him. Was Rae just particularly insightful, or immune to the charms of attractive men? And what would that mean?

"Is your boyfriend here?" Anne asked, hoping that she didn't sound too anxious to get off the topic of herself and Chris. She especially didn't want to talk about Chris.

"Yes." Rae was looking over toward the stand of trees lining the parking lot. She screwed up her lips slightly to bite the inside of her mouth, the resulting look on her face serious for a minute. Anne suddenly wondered if Rae could develop mouth cancer from chewing the skin inside her mouth while smoking a cigarette. Rae took one last puff and used her good foot to ground out the butt on the gravel. She then stretched, rubbed her hands over her cheeks, and stood for a moment with her hands clasped behind her neck.

"The moon in Florida looks different."

Huh? "What do you mean?"

"The half moon, or quarter moon, or whatever. It hangs sideways instead of up and down."

That was the most ridiculous thing Anne had ever heard, and she wondered if Rae could be kidding. Nope, she looked perfectly serious. Anne hated to contradict her–why?–but she just couldn't let something that absurd go by without a comment. It wasn't in her nature. She did, however, take a second to consider how to correct her graciously.

"That's not really possible," was the best she could come up with.

"Why not? It's what I saw. I was there last winter." Rae sounded almost petulant.

"Maybe you were mistaken. The phases of the moon don't work like that."

Rae was chewing the inside of her mouth again. "Well, they do in Florida."

"No, what I mean is, the moon looks pretty much the same from anyplace on Earth. We're a fixed point in space that the moon orbits, so. . . ."

"Anyway, that's how it looked to me." Rae paused before continuing softly. "How do you know so much about the moon?"

Maybe because I went to junior high school? This isn't rocket science. "I don't know." Anne hoped to spare Rae any embarrassment for having made such a foolish remark, but was secretly glad to see that she was fallible after all. "I guess I picked it up in Astronomy." A lie. "I took Carl Sagan's class last year." Well, that much was true.

Rae shook her head. "You're amazingly smart, you know that?"

Anne let that pass. She had always been told how smart she was, but didn't really believe it. Her friends always turned to her with their trivia questions, and Anne just chalked it up to the fact that she'd had an excellent education. After all, once you're taught something, you know it, and she'd been taught a lot about a lot of different things at Milburn Academy. She did appear to have a good memory, an enormous capacity to file away seemingly useless information, but she had always viewed it as a handy skill more than anything else. To her, real genius was the ability to process it all, to draw the lines between less obvious bits and pieces–a talent that Rae possessed in abundance.

"I was thinking," Rae went on. "We should get together some night, all of us, like the group at the Dragon. Maybe order a pizza."

Anne's pulse quickened noticeably. "That'd be fun."

"Solve the problems of the world." Rae cocked her head. "And drink some good wine." They looked at each other for a few seconds longer. As expressive as Rae's face was, it was cloaked just then. But still magnetic–Anne had to force herself to break the spell when she heard the band inside start a new number.

"I should go back in."

Rae reached out then and took her hand, interlacing her fingers with Anne's, the pressure gentle. They started toward the door in slow synchronized steps, Rae limping slightly, Anne acutely aware of the softness of the hand that held hers, thrilled by the subtle caress of Rae's thumb massaging down the length of her own. Rae did not let go as they walked through the door, and much as Anne did not want Joey to see their entrance, she also did not want to take back her hand. She escorted Rae to the bar and prepared to leave her there with a quick squeeze of her hand.

Just as she was about to turn away with a short goodbye, Rae suddenly pulled her in, kissed her quickly on the lips–just a peck, really–and whispered, "See you in class." The flicker of excitement that bolted through Anne was as much of a shock as the kiss itself. It all happened so fast that she wasn't certain she'd even heard the whisper over the blaring music, which itself was competing with a sudden hammering in her ears. She knew only that she'd never tasted anything as sweet, felt anything as velvet soft, as the feathery flash of Rae's lips.

Without saying goodbye, Anne turned and headed straight for the bathroom again. She had to be alone, had to calm her pulse and wash away the heat flaming in her face. The line was thankfully short, and soon she was locked away in a stall, head spinning, thoughts in a jumble, stomach in a knot. It wasn't until someone knocked on the stall that she realized how long she had been sitting there. She wiped herself and felt a guilty thrill at discovering that she needed a second wipe. Oh God. She left the bathroom feeling as if some profound change had taken place, had been thrust upon her, when she wasn't looking.

Rae wasn't at the bar when she emerged from the bathroom, and Anne deliberately kept her eyes directed to her table to avoid scanning the crowd to look for her. When she sat down, Chris gave her a quick kiss on the cheek and placed his arm over the back of her chair, and Joey gave her a curious smile. It was too loud to talk anyway, so she just nodded her hellos and poured herself another beer.

Chris really was a great guy, she thought, no games or ego-stuff, respectful of the space she increasingly, tacitly needed. She resolved to focus more on him, to give him more of the attention he deserved. Even though she had an early lane reserved at the pool tomorrow, she decided she would stay at his place tonight. Comfortable for the first time that evening, feeling safe in the knowledge that the next few hours would follow a predictable, easy course, she settled back against his arm and watched the band.

By the time they were in his car on the way to his dorm room later that evening, her lecture to Rae about the fixed position of the Earth had been proved wrong. The world had indeed shifted, brought on by the sight she'd witnessed as she'd left the Gorge with Chris, the glimpse of Rae laughing and getting into a car with Rick Manger.

Chapter Two

Ten three-quarter, ten top speed. The steady pounding of her heart set a comfortable pace for each stroke, although last night's smoke-laden atmosphere had definitely slowed her a bit–Anne knew her mile would come in somewhat over thirty minutes today. The beer probably hadn't helped either. She'd never increase her speed if she didn't start alternating sides to breathe on each third stroke, but her need for air was too great this morning. For now, she'd have to breathe on each right arm.

She lost her rhythm at the end of lap four and flubbed her racing turn, nearly colliding with the wall during her flip. Accelerating the pace, even though this was a three-quarter speed stretch, she soon regained her rhythm, and with it the hypnotic endorphin high that she'd grown to crave.

She recalled hearing one of Joey's druggie friends discussing heroin one night last year, explaining that the whole point of taking the drug was to recapture the euphoria of the first, mind-blowing high. Usually in vain, it seemed–you never got there again, and used more and more each time in the futile effort. She knew her workout high was like that in some ways. It took more and more effort just to get the endorphins to kick in, and it was never quite as satisfying as the rush she'd get after a prolonged absence from the pool. Her laps were more than just a fix, however–she did her best thinking in the pool. In the back of her mind she ticked off the laps like a metronome, while her fore-brain worked things over.

And the problem of the day was waiting for her as soon as she hit her stride. Her mind snapped to it with the sting of a rubber band, as if any attention she'd diverted to functioning in the world these past few days were merely a brief, insignificant distraction. Okay, approach it scientifically, methodically. How would Jane analyze the situation? What a laugh–Jane was the last person in the world likely to find herself in this situation.

It wasn't that she was horrified by the idea of being attracted to a woman. She didn't think she was homophobic. She just didn't know what it could mean, how it could play out in her life. And she had to admit, she was hung up on the label. Lesbian, bisexual, it made no difference–it was all frightening on a very basic level, and didn't mesh with her vision of herself. Always an outsider, for as long as could remember, really, she didn't mind the idea of being different, even in this way, but she was unnerved by the notion that she could be so markedly different from the person she'd always thought she was. At nineteen, she thought she knew herself pretty well, and didn't like to think that she could be so wrong.

Nine. Flip. Push-off.

She knew so many gay men, mostly musicians and actors. They seemed comfortable with themselves, happy even. But she didn't know very many lesbians. And the few she did know were nothing like her. Short hair, hiking boots, even manly. Butch, that was the word. Except for some of the lesbian feminists, but even they were uncharted territory, different in some way. As if their bedroom politics were just an extension of some political orientation.

Bedroom politics, now where did that come from? Had Rae used the phrase?

Does it really come down to the bedroom, anyway? Is it just about sexual partners? Or does it have to do with something more, some deeper feeling? Something like love? But then again, how do you even get to love without exploring the sex, or at least considering it? And if it's just a sexual attraction, without love, is it necessarily lesbian? She'd told Joey many times that it wasn't, that a simple schoolgirl crush did not make someone gay. But was a schoolgirl crush the same thing as a sexual attraction? If given the chance, would she have had a sexual relationship with Gallagher?

Eleven. Flip. Push-off.

Shit. She still had to return Gallagher's phone call. Shit, shit, shit. It couldn't be a worse time to see her, with all these confused feelings about

Rae occupying her every thought. Not that Gallagher would know that, or understand it. She had no idea what Gallagher thought about anything.

They hadn't seen each other since the summer, back in Philadelphia. That last cast party at the home of–whose house was it? Some cast member. Gallagher had worked on costumes, and Anne had played the lead mezzo roles in three of the four musicals that summer. Chris had come down from his parents' home in Vermont to see two of the shows, but had missed the last one. Anne and Gallagher both knew that meant they'd be going out together most nights after the performance, and they would attend the cast party together on closing night. They knew it without saying so, just because that was how it always was with them.

Gallagher was younger, in the class two years behind Anne at their private school, so their friendship was generally viewed as unconventional by their respective classmates. Anne had always been different from the other girls anyway–on friendly terms, invited to many of their parties, but always on the other side of some invisible line that divided the girls who really belonged from the girls who were merely allowed access. The division was subtle but very real, and Anne didn't really mind.

Not that she was aloof–she was just busy with a host of things that never included her classmates: swimming in the city league because her school had no pool, performing in shows with the city's light opera society. Most importantly, she was a scholarship kid, the product of hardworking middle-class parents who did not live in the school's elite neighborhood. Her sharp mind was a plus in the eyes of her college-bound classmates, so her consistent ranking at the top of the class kept her in the loop. But associating with girls from a younger class, no matter who, was tantamount to blasphemy at Milburn. No one ever said it, and certainly no one ever explained it to her, but hanging out with kids from younger classes simply wasn't done. Older girls, okay. In fact, most of her classmates attempted to cultivate friendships with the girls in the upper grades. But younger girls, never. Anne's forays into the junior classes were tolerated only because she was such an eccentric anyway. She liked to think that she was respected for doing her own thing, but she knew that deep down her differences, including this one, made her classmates slightly unsure about her, and that she had to conform in certain material respects or she'd be completely exiled.

She'd never really hung out with Gallagher at school, which partly explained why their friendship was tolerated. They'd met outside of school, at a party during Anne's junior year when Gallagher was a freshman. Gallagher's brother was in the same class with Anne's current boyfriend at the boys' school down the block from Milburn. After that first party, Anne and Gallagher had begun to run into each other fairly regularly at parties thrown by the boys, who seemed more flexible about the idea of inter-class socializing. Anne quickly found that she really enjoyed Gallagher, found something refreshing in her unique, dry sense of humor. Gallagher was very bright, very tall, and very beautiful. Dark tight curls framing a perfect heart-shaped face, dark brown eyes, pale skin that glowed red when she laughed, and a quiet, commanding presence that made her seem far older. In fact, it was precisely because of her manner that they were able to gain entry at a number of bars around town when Gallagher was only fifteen and Anne was only seventeen. And in 1974, God bless it, the drinking age was eighteen.

Sixteen. Flip. Push-off.

Maybe her feelings for Gallagher had always been unique, but she'd been clueless about it—Anne simply couldn't remember. All she knew was that ever since that night out together during her senior year at Milburn, she was aware of something different, something that had changed. They had decided that evening to go down to the seedier part of downtown to try to get into an R-rated movie, and had been shocked when the young man in the ticket window had actually asked Gallagher for ID. Barred from the movie and feeling reckless, they had decided to explore the city's demi-monde, and drove around looking for an unusual bar or nightclub. Anne had spotted the Rhino, a notorious gay hangout that she'd often heard her actor friends mention, and suggested they try it. Gallagher agreed at once.

"You know it's a gay bar, don't you?" Anne asked, keeping her eyes glued on her rearview mirror as she parked the car.

"Will there be any women there, do you think?"

Anne didn't know, and didn't know which answer Gallagher was hoping for, so she just shrugged and turned off the ignition. As they approached the entrance, they saw that the windows were painted opaque, so without any idea as to what they were in for, Anne feigned nonchalance and opened the door with Gallagher trailing right behind her.

It wasn't nearly as oppressive inside as the exterior would suggest. In fact, the place was almost festive. The lights were brighter than she'd expected, and the tasteful wood trim around the bar struck her as oddly juxtaposed with strands of tacky little Christmas lights draped across the ceiling and encircling the mirror over the bar. Anne was pleasantly surprised by the atmosphere–all the more so because she saw an equal number of women and men standing around the tall tables and dancing on the small disco floor at the rear. Gallagher put her arm around Anne at once, planting her hand securely on Anne's hip, and leaned in toward her. "You're my date tonight, okay?"

Anne laughed and looked up into Gallagher's serious face. The joke she was about to deliver died on her lips–she suddenly couldn't tell if Gallagher was kidding. She quickly scanned the tables.

"I doubt if they have pitchers. You want a regular drink?"

"I don't know, I've never ordered a real drink before. What are you having?"

Anne, feeling very sophisticated, ordered two gin and tonics from the picture-perfect bartender, very conscious of Gallagher's arm cemented around her waist. Whether she was holding her to fit in, or out of self-consciousness, or something else, Anne couldn't begin to guess. She only knew that, as she stood there feeling the warm strength of Gallagher's arm around her, she wanted it to stay there–content to stand quietly like that for as long as Gallagher wanted to hold her.

Twenty-one. Flip. Push-off.

When one of the high tables near the dance floor cleared, Gallagher pulled her close and leaned down to speak beside her ear. "Let's go sit." Without waiting for a response, she steered Anne toward the vacated table, the chairs so high that Anne had to climb onto hers. Gallagher situated herself millimeters from Anne's chair, and returned her arm to Anne's waist as soon as they were seated.

"I guess people think we're a couple, huh?" Gallagher was smiling as she said it, and Anne decided that that was exactly what Gallagher was hoping–that they'd be perceived as a couple so that no one would approach them. Still, Anne had never seen Gallagher act quite this way before. Flirtatious almost. It was a ridiculous thought, and Anne dismissed it. "I don't think people are thinking about us at all. They're too busy having a good time."

Gallagher picked up her drink and took a sip. "So am I," she smiled. "But I don't think I like gin and tonic."

"Me either," Anne laughed. "Next round's on you–you decide."

A slow song started just then, and they watched as the dance floor was transformed before their eyes–the strobe stopped, the lights dimmed, and wildly gyrating groups of people abandoned the floor to be replaced by couples who molded themselves into each other's arms. Anne was fascinated. She'd never seen two women dance together like this. She didn't want to stare, but couldn't help herself–there was something so erotically charged about it. She stole a glance at Gallagher out of the corner of her eye, and saw that she too was riveted. What the hell, let's play this to the hilt, she thought. She slipped her arm around Gallagher's waist and settled into her a bit, amazed at how well they fit together side by side. When the song ended all too soon, Gallagher stood and coyly announced that she'd bring back a surprise.

Anne watched her go, remarking to herself on Gallagher's loveliness even from the back. Her thoughts were interrupted by a shrill voice, "Anne darling, why I never!"

Bob Gundry, one of the tenors from the chorus last season, was suddenly on Gallagher's chair and hugging Anne with sweaty arms. "Girl, you look good!" He stood for a moment to show off his physique. "And what about me? Buff, huh? Been working out." He pulled out a cigarette and re-seated himself on Gallagher's stool, shaking his long brown locks across the back of his neck. "Not that any of these stud queens would notice. God, I don't know why I bother. Darling, d'you have a light?"

"No, sorry." How to get rid of him?

"So what's your girlfriend's name? She's hot, in a waspy whitebread sort of way. You two make a cute couple. Poster girls for the preppie fags."

Anne decided he must be speeding, and she needed to get him out of there before Gallagher came back. Bob was sweet, but he would attach himself to them for the evening and take a sadistic delight in teasing Gallagher. That was his specialty, finding a weakness–especially youth, innocence, or naiveté, all three of which Gallagher believed she possessed in abundance–and exploiting it with an acerbic tongue until the victim was utterly humiliated. "She's not my girlfriend, we're just friends. Listen, Bob, I was just . . ."

"She's not? Oh good, there's someone I want you to meet." He waved to a neighboring table. "Paula!" Anne looked in the direction of Bob's wave, and saw a woman sitting with a group of men, looking up in the middle of a sip from a bottle of Coors.

"Bob, I really don't want . . ."

"Too late, doll, she's on her way."

Indeed, the woman had risen already and was walking toward them, shyly pushing a few stray strands of her light-brown bangs out of her eyes. Her white oxford shirt was neatly pressed, and her form-fitting jeans showed off trim, athletic legs. Gold cuff links, matching gold earrings–the overall effect was one of studied casualness, and as Anne observed her fluid, easy gait, she decided that this Paula was actually rather nice looking.

Bob gave Paula a quick peck on the cheek as he stood and offered her his seat–Gallagher's seat. "Paula dear, this is Anne, a little preppie-babe just like you. But I've got to warn you, she's a young one, so watch your-self."

Paula was visibly embarrassed, and so was Anne. Bob flicked an ash. "Gotta run, girls. I see the man of my dreams has just come through the door and I have to introduce myself." He ran his hands through his hair dramatically, threw a Marilyn Monroe kiss at Anne, and took off toward the door. Anne looked down at her gin and tonic, the ice now nearly melted. Shit.

"Don't mind Bob, he's like that with everyone," Paula said. Her voice was warm. "He just loves to see how uncomfortable he can make people. And by the way, I'm Paula."

Anne lifted her head. "Hi. Nice to meet you."

Paula was not in prep school any more, that much was certain. She had to be in her twenties. Anne was suddenly feeling very exposed, as if the game that she had been playing was about to spin out of control. This woman was nobody's fool, and would quickly see Anne for what she was–a straight teenager who was playing grown-up.

"So what school did you go to?" asked Paula pleasantly.

"Um, Milburn Academy. Actually, I'm still there."

Paula smiled conspiratorially. "Too young to be in here, huh? Well, don't worry, I won't have you thrown out." She sipped her Coors. "I really admire that you're here at all." Anne looked up, puzzled. "That you know already that you're a lesbian."

Time to put an end to this right now and get the hell out of here. She cleared her throat. "Look, Paula, I'm not–"

"Can't leave you alone for a minute, can I?" Gallagher came up behind Anne and Paula, and not-too-subtly wedged herself between them to place two drinks on the table. She put her arm possessively around Anne's shoulder and smiled intriguingly. "Making friends?"

Anne looked up into Gallagher's face and saw there, or at least thought she saw, a mixture of emotions: amusement, curiosity, and tinge of some-thing else. Anne quickly put her arm around Gallagher's waist, happy to resume their charade and hoping that their posture would thwart Paula's attentions. Paula seemed nice, but Anne was simply not prepared to strike up a friendship with a twenty-something lesbian.

"Gallagher, this is Paula. She's a friend of a guy I knew from the light opera. Paula, this is Gallagher."

Gallagher gave Paula a perfunctory smile but didn't offer her hand, which was at the moment playing with the strawberry blonde hair behind Anne's left ear. Gallagher was really having fun with this game, Anne decided. Staying in character no matter what.

"Anne was just telling me that she's at Milburn. You too?" Paula moved her chair back slightly to give Gallagher more room at the table.

"Yes. You didn't go to Milburn, did you?" Anne knew that Gallagher was just making polite small talk–Gallagher knew damn well that Paula hadn't attended Milburn. There were only about a hundred students in the entire Upper Main, and everyone knew at least the faces of everyone else in the five or six grades preceding and following their own.

"No, I was at Bryndon. We beat you in hockey my senior year." So she was class of '72, Anne quickly calculated. Probably twenty or twenty-one.

"I'm on the tennis team," Gallagher offered, ever the gracious hostess. "We beat you this year." She smiled and picked up her drink. Anne followed suit, and was amazed that she actually liked the concoction that Gallagher had brought her. It tasted like grape soda.

"What is this?"

"Sloe gin fizz." Gallagher said it as if she'd been ordering them for years.

"Have you picked out a college yet?" Paula asked, seemingly determined to engage in conversation, and clearly not deterred by their fabricated intimacy. Maybe she just saw through it.

"Not yet," Gallagher began. "It's still–"

"Cornell," Anne interjected, keeping her eyes on Paula as she felt Gallagher's startled look. She hadn't told Gallagher yet about her decision.

"Good school. I'm at Penn."

"What are you studying?" Anne still didn't meet Gallagher's eyes.

"Nothing much. Girls, mostly." Paula's grin was huge. There was nothing really to say to that, so Anne reached for her drink and Gallagher did the same. The light repartee had suddenly taken on a hint of something else. Anne wanted to get them out of there, but they'd just started on their drinks and Gallagher seemed to be enjoying herself. She decided to escape to the dance floor.

"I feel like dancing," Anne said as she turned to Gallagher. "You up for it?"

The relief was evident in Gallagher's smile as she nodded and put her drink on the table, commenting to Paula that they'd be right back.

A fast Donna Summer number was half over when they fell into the familiar routine of dancing on the small crowded floor. They had danced together often. After all, it was a girls' school that they attended, and every school dance witnessed many girls unaccompanied by dates–or abandoning them–and dancing together in couples or in groups.

When the song ended and the floor lights dimmed for a slow song, neither made a move to return to the table. Anne looked at Gallagher, saw the playful smile, and stepped into Gallagher's outstretched arms as if it were the most natural thing in the world. In response to Gallagher's arms pulling her tight, Anne put her arms around Gallagher's neck and laid her head gently on Gallagher's shoulder. They fit together amazingly well.

"You're a natural," Anne said, hoping her tone was light.

"I'm glad you think so." Gallagher gently tightened her arms, and they swayed to the music easily. After a moment, Anne lifted her head and looked at Gallagher. "So do you think she's going to ask one of us for our phone number?"

Gallagher looked into Anne's eyes, her face an unreadable mask. The playfulness was gone, and Anne didn't know when it had disappeared. She suddenly felt uncomfortable, wondering if she'd crossed the line somehow, done something to alter the mood. She couldn't imagine what.

"Not if we convince her that we're a couple," Gallagher deadpanned.

Anne smiled, trying to coax one from Gallagher. "I don't think there's much doubt about that at this point."

"I think she's attracted to you," Gallagher said, still serious.

"Maybe it's you she's attracted to."

Gallagher ran her hands slowly across the small of Anne's back. "I'm not interested." She looked off across the dance floor then, but kept massaging Anne's back in slow, subtle strokes. "You know, I've never slow danced with another girl before."

Anne couldn't keep up with Gallagher's changing moods, and had no idea what reaction she'd provoke with any of the glib replies she considered. She decided the safest course was to keep her comments to a minimum. No subtext. "Well, I guess there's always a first for everything." Uh oh, was there subtext in that? Shit.

A few beats later, Gallagher broke the peace again. "You look really great tonight. No wonder she's interested in you."

Now where did that come from? Anne was determined to keep things light, the seriousness of Gallagher's tone seeping into some backwater of her consciousness that she was reluctant to explore. There was something frightening under the façade of their game, had been all evening, really, and with this slow dance it was threatening to surface. She had to keep a lid on it.

"Yes, I'll just add her to my collection of lesbian admirers."

She felt more than heard Gallagher's soft chuckle. "There are, you know."

"What?"

"There are a lot of girls with crushes on you."

Now this was a conversation that Anne definitely did not want to have. No way. She was shocked that Gallagher would come right out and say such a thing, and decided she must be little tipsy already.

It was the great unspoken taboo–especially at an all-girls school–and here Gallagher had done the unthinkable by voicing it, making it real, if only as a joke. Although her classmates kidded about lesbianism all the time, play-acted lesbian flirtations in an exaggerated, caricatured way, Anne understood implicitly that it was all in an effort to disguise any actual feelings along those lines. To bury a few very real attractions that nearly all of them had experienced at one time or another. The girls always danced together, held hands with their friends, sat on one another's laps, even engaged in pretend romances and break-ups–but all in jest, and never with anyone for whom they felt a twinge of genuine interest. They never, never acknowledged the real thing, but it was obvious to Anne that many of them felt it. The way some girls' eyes would follow the star of the basketball team as she walked down the hall, the way two girls would vie for the chance to sit beside the best soprano in the glee club. No, Gallagher's loaded comment was unprecedented, threatened to expose a carefully constructed fiction, and was better left untouched.

Anne loosened her arms from around Gallagher's neck and perched her hands gently on Gallagher's shoulders. At the same time, Gallagher took a small step backwards and brought her hands from behind Anne's back to rest on Anne's hips. Neither looked at the other as they silently danced out the rest of the song. Another slow dance started, and Anne was torn between a desire to step back into Gallagher's embrace and an urgency to leave. She hesitated a moment too long–Gallagher walked off the dance floor, leaving Anne to follow mutely. Whatever had happened–and Anne wasn't sure what, if anything, it was–it had opened a chasm, taken them to a precipice from which they both hastily, tacitly retreated. Whatever it had been, it was over.

They stayed on safe topics for the rest of the night as they talked about colleges with Paula, and by the time they saw each other again, the whole evening had been reconstructed in both their minds into a funny, exotic adventure that made for a lively tale. Neither acknowledged the careful editing of their story in the retelling, to each other or anyone else. For Anne, those poignant excised moments were relived on a regular basis, savored in the dark quiet of her room before she fell asleep at night, where she came to know without a doubt that her feelings for Gallagher were like none she'd ever felt for any boy, or any girl either. A crush, certainly, but maybe something more, and that was something she didn't want to examine too closely. The replay always ended the same way–with the unreadable look on Gallagher's face as she witnessed Paula handing to Anne a slip of paper with a phone number on it. Anne had thrown it away as soon as she'd gotten home, and they'd never discussed it.

Thirty-three. Flip. Push-off.

As poignant as her memories of Gallagher were, they were unsettling right now–threatening in their sudden reappearance just at the moment that Anne felt herself starting to experience some of the same terrifying feelings toward yet another woman. She really had convinced herself that all that was behind her. She and Gallagher had been kids, after all. Those schoolgirl feelings were over and done with. Besides, there had never been anything overtly sexual between them, never anything that either of them could precisely pinpoint.

Except, of course, that cast party a few months ago, at the end of the summer. The memory of it pounded her. How to explain away that night? Sure, they had both been a little drunk, but still–Anne had to admit that she had known exactly what she was doing, and what she had hoped would happen. There was no way to pretend that what she had been feeling had been anything other than naked sexual desire, and she was also pretty sure that Gallagher had been feeling the same thing too, although neither had ever admitted it. Gallagher may not remember, or may be filing it away in her mind as harmless fun, but looking back on it, Anne knew that, for her, it had been painfully serious.

It had been late in the party at the home of one of the cast members when Gallagher had grabbed Anne's hand to pull her along for a walk in the garden. Anne had been dragged off for private conversations with a variety of people all night, since every little nuance of her friends' existence that summer was cause for serious deliberation, and Anne had for some reason become a leading confidante. The feel of Gallagher's hand on her own as they'd approached the garden reminded Anne of their evening at the Rhino the year before. Gallagher was older now and, impossibly, had grown even more beautiful. She was going into her senior year at Milburn, a star of the tennis team and by all appearances the master of the world. Anne, meanwhile, had come back from her first year at college with several notable achievements of her own: a devastatingly handsome boyfriend who visited regularly, and leads in two of her college productions.

She and Gallagher had immediately resumed their inseparable ways–so much so that Chris had started complaining on one visit that he never saw Anne unless it was on a double date with Gallagher and Dennis.

Since that night at the Rhino, the ground rules had subtly changed: she and Gallagher studiously avoided ever touching upon any topic that could remotely rekindle the intimacy they'd played with that night, and, consciously or not, they'd made sure that they went out together accompanied by at least one other person. Except for the occasional car ride–including the one to this party, once Gallagher confessed that she'd started her drinking backstage during the show and was too drunk to drive–this walk in the garden marked the first time that they had actually been alone together for longer than Anne could remember.

"Let me wear your jacket," Anne said as Gallagher slid open the gate. "I got too much sun today, I think."

Gallagher stumbled briefly–was she really that drunk?–and took off her jacket. "Does it hurt?"

"No."

The jacket smelled of Gallagher, a mixture of conditioner and deodorant, and Anne loved it. Stop this, she thought. She's just a friend.

"It looks nice," Gallagher said as she comfortably slipped her arm around Anne's waist. Probably to keep her warm. It was working.

"The sleeves are too long," Anne replied. "God, you have long arms."

"No, I mean the sunburn. Your hair's lighter too."

"Yeah, it gets bleached like this every summer. It's kind of annoying–people think I dye my hair. By November it'll be back to its normal dirty-blonde blah."

"You can't get color like that out of a bottle. I love it. And it goes with your eyes–what are they, blue?"

"Blue. Gray. I don't know."

"Mood eyes." They laughed. They'd bought mood rings a few years ago, and Anne still had hers in a drawer somewhere. God, I hope she can't read the mood in my eyes right now. "Your hair and eyes–you look like a commercial for California." Gallagher used her free hand to pull on her own tight curls that were falling on her shoulders. "Not like this rat's nest."

"I like your hair. The little bit of red catches the sun. It's nice." Anne's fondness for Gallagher's hair could get her in trouble, so she stopped there.

"So when do you go back to Cornell?" Gallagher slowed their pace deep inside the garden.

"Next week. My dad's driving me up."

"Oh."

"He thinks we need a family vacation, so we're actually leaving on Tuesday to spend a few days somewhere on the Finger Lakes before I have to be back on campus on Saturday."

Gallagher withdrew her arm and went to look at an inscription on a plaque beside one of the shrubs. Who puts a plaque in their garden?

"So I guess this is goodbye."

"Guess so. I'll probably come down around Christmas."

"Not before?"

Anne folded one of the sleeves into a cuff. "Not if I get cast in a fall show. I'd probably have rehearsal over Thanksgiving."

Gallagher turned to look at her from a few steps away. "You'll get cast." She smiled. "You always do."

That wasn't really true, but Anne didn't correct her. She smiled at the compliment, and Gallagher smiled back, locking her eyes onto Anne's. "It's been a great summer. I'm really gonna miss you." Gallagher's voice sounded odd as she stepped forward and pulled Anne into an embrace.

"Me too," was all that Anne could think to say. It was just a goodbye hug, nothing more–but Gallagher didn't let go when Anne expected her to, didn't let go at all, and the longer she held onto Anne standing there in the garden, the more Anne's ears began to pound and heart to race. All that Anne could think was that she was finally here, finally back in the arms she'd dreamed about for over a year. She realized that she must be more drunk than she'd thought because instead of stepping back, she found herself melting into the body that held her, surrendering herself to the sensations of strong arms, clean smell, beating pulse. She felt the subtle stretch of Gallagher's hands across her back, as if Gallagher were trying to cover as much of her as possible.

She didn't care how it looked, didn't care that they were starting to tread dangerously close to something they'd religiously, wordlessly circumnavigated for so long. It just felt so good, so right, and she was leaving town in a few days anyway. She took her arms from around Gallagher's back to move them up her arms and drape them around Gallagher's neck in a posture all too reminiscent of their forgotten slow dance. This time, however, she didn't make a joke out of it, and she didn't lower her eyes, either. She looked frankly, directly into Gallagher's eyes as her fingers explored the soft curly hair that fell on Gallagher's neck. Gallagher looked back just as boldly, seeming to dare Anne to immerse herself in those fluid brown eyes, and tightened her hold. Anne met the challenge, matched the gravity of Gallagher's penetrating gaze inch for inch, and gently, slowly began to move her body against Gallagher's in candid eroticism, feeling Gallagher's breasts rolling against her own chest. She drank in every feature of Gallagher's face, and did not realize she had begun to subtly grind her hips into Gallagher's until she saw Gallagher suddenly close her eyes with an exhale that seemed to catch in her throat, almost a moan.

Aware that they were long past the point of joking it away, and not caring–indeed, craving more and more of the unearthly sensations that were so far beyond anything she'd ever experienced–Anne nuzzled her face into Gallagher's neck and decided it was okay if the world stopped right there. She felt Gallagher kiss her then, a slow, gentle kiss on her forehead, and she was powerless to stop herself from kissing the neck she nuzzled in return. And, oh, God what a neck–she'd never known skin could be so sensuous. Gallagher pulled away just then, and Anne felt a clutch of fear that she'd gone too far, but was quickly reassured when she saw the look on Gallagher's face: flushed, heavy-lidded, with a small smile playing on lips that, amazingly, seemed to be preparing to kiss her. Anne tilted her head in a slight angle toward Gallagher's lips and locked her eyes on Gallagher's, ready to receive the kiss she knew was coming with an anticipation that had been building for far too long.

A man's voice shattered the magic. "Hey, you back here?" They froze, deer caught in the headlights, the kiss that Anne still wanted so desperately hanging unconsummated between them, now impossible. They stepped apart quickly, and looked away from each other. Anne rocked on her feet for a moment, unsure if it was the beer or the insistent throbbing between her legs.

"Hey, guys, where you been?" Sam called out as he approached with his date in tow. "Gallagher. Dennis just got here, he's looking for you."

Anne looked at Gallagher, whose eyes were icemelt.

"He wasn't supposed to come tonight," Gallagher said dully, her voice matching the shrouded look in her eyes. "I told him I wanted to be with my friends."

"He's getting a beer in the kitchen, I think," offered Sam's date, whose name Anne could not recall.

"A beer sounds pretty good," Anne said, forcing some brightness into her voice. "I think I'll get one myself." She turned to leave, still a bit unsteady but determined to compose herself and escape. She stopped and turned back to Gallagher, who had remained rooted to the spot. "Coming?"

Gallagher smiled sadly, suddenly looking far older than her years. "Almost," she mumbled as she took off after Anne.

Anne left town two days later without finding another moment alone with Gallagher, that night having become just one more evening on a

growing list of encounters that they would pretend had never happened–buried, and maybe forgotten.

Fifty-two. Flip. Push-off.

The problem with doing her laps at a time like this was that everything
came tumbling back to her, everything that she'd just as soon relegate to
the back burner. It all came right to the forefront, but there were still no answers. She had no idea what she felt about Gallagher at this point, no idea
what to expect, no idea what Gallagher felt or expected, and no idea where
Rae fit into any of it.

Fifty-three. Done. Thirty-two minutes. Shit.

Chapter Three

Joey plopped his tray down on the table across from Anne in the dining hall, and stared at her intently until she couldn't avoid it any longer.

"You shouldn't be in here barefoot," she said.

"I'm getting my feet used to the cold so I won't get frostbite when I go rock climbing." Anne watched as he mixed a glass of orange juice into his milk.

"That's ridiculous," she said. "And that looks disgusting." She returned her attention to the unrecognizable mess on her plate.

Joey took a few bites of something resembling mashed potatoes, and drank his orange juice-milk combo in two gulps. "So?"

Anne sighed. "So?"

"Don't tell me you're not going to talk about it. Come on, I've left you alone all day. Now spill it."

"Forget it." Anne ignored his stare. "Look, Joey, I don't know what you want me to say. There's no big thing here, and I don't know why you have to go apeshit just because I'm making friends with somebody from class."

"Oh, that is such bullshit and you know it," he laughed. "Do you hear yourself?" It was amazing how Joey could talk and smile at the same time. He pulled a few hairs in his beard. "You've got to admit that you don't go around kissing your other friends."

Anne kept her voice low. "I didn't kiss her, she kissed me. And it was just a friendship thing, like a kiss on the cheek."

"Only it was on the lips."

Anne looked away. "Well, yeah." She saw Jane heading their way. Great. Anne shot Joey a look but he didn't seem ready to give up.

"And it lasted longer, too," he said.

"What did?" Jane asked as she put her tray beside Joey and sat down. Time to nip this in the bud. Best defense is a good offense.

"Joey was just trying to educate me on how women relate to each other," Anne explained to her roommate.

"That should be interesting," Jane said drily. "By the way, I left you a message on your desk. She called again."

Joey's eyes lit up. "Who, Rae?"

Jane gave Anne a puzzled look. "Why do I keep hearing that name?"

"Gallagher," Anne said, immediately realizing her mistake when she saw Joey's head snap to her. Anne picked up her tray in an effort to exit before Joey said something stupid. "I'm going back to the room. I haven't been there all day."

Jane opened her chemistry book, ignoring them both, as Joey got to his feet, a huge grin beaming on his face. "I'll come with you," he said.

"Lucky me," Anne sighed.

Getting rid of Joey proved to be far easier than reaching Gallagher, who wasn't home that night, or on the next three nights after that. Her mother sounded thrilled to hear Anne's voice on the phone each time she called, and informed her that Gallagher was out with Dennis. By the end of the week, Anne had given up.

"Papers should be no longer than ten typed pages, double-spaced—I don't want to read any dissertations here." Shirl ran her hand through her short brown hair. "Okay, what else—oh, Rae has graciously invited us all to her apartment for a feminist soiree this Thursday at . . ." she looked at Rae seated at the end of the conference table.

"Seven."

"Seven. We'll order in, so bring cash. Is there anybody who can't make it?"

No one raised a hand.

"Okay, in that case, Thursday's class is cancelled. Don't tell the dean."

"One more thing," Rae chimed in, her voice like melted butter. "If no one minds, I'd like to see if we can make it just women—no boyfriends. Is that okay?"

"How about girlfriends?" Rosa asked, drawing a few snickers.

Jenna piped up. "Sounds feminist to me."

"Don't bet on it," said Rosa.

Jenna approached Anne as everyone stood to leave, a 1930s cap rakishly angled atop her mop of Harpo Marx curls. "So, Anne, you're coming to the Dragon now, aren't you?"

"Actually, I can't today." She wished she could, wished she could steal a few moments with Rae. She'd gone to the Dragon with them after both classes last week, but never had a chance for a private word with Rae. Not that she had any idea what she'd say anyway. She looked across the room at Rae busily talking to Rosa, and felt Jenna tugging on her sleeve.

"Oh, come on, one cup of coffee, we'll shoot it directly into your veins."

"No, really," Anne shook her head. "I have to go to the library. I'm so far behind in everything." She really was. Much as she'd love to blow off yet another afternoon in Rae's company, she was losing too much time in rehearsals, and feared she'd never get caught up without putting in considerable effort now.

Reluctantly, she picked up her backpack, and suddenly felt Rae behind her. "Going to the library, Anne?"

Anne turned around and looked at her blankly for a moment. Did she have ESP, or just exceptional hearing? "Yeah, I've got a lot to catch up on."

"I'll tag along," Rae said. "If that's all right with you?"

Anne's heart skipped a beat or two—my God, alone at the library with Rae. She'd never be able to concentrate, never get any work done, but who cared?

"Sure," she said lightly, and smiled as Rae grabbed her arm to walk toward the door. Jenna and Rosa followed, mumbling about boring overachievers.

Out in the quad, Rae lit a cigarette and blew the smoke away from Anne. "The smoke doesn't bother you, I hope."

"No, it's okay."

They walked in silence for a minute, Rae hobbled slightly by her sore foot and flicking her ashes in front of them. She seemed deep in thought, and Anne pushed aside the thousands of questions she had, realizing she had no way to articulate them. Chief among them concerned Rae's relationship with

Rick Manger, but she sensed that Rae wouldn't want to talk about it. Unable to come up with anything suitable to say, she kept quiet and enjoyed the walk.

"So you think you'll be able to tear yourself away from Chris on Thursday night?"

Anne laughed. "You have no idea how easy it is to tear myself away."

Rae gave her a sidelong glance. "I think I've got a pretty good idea." They paused as she stubbed out her cigarette on the path that ran between two statues on opposite sides of the quad, and continued their walk in silence.

She'd been right—she got absolutely nothing done at the library, although they stayed there into the early evening. Locked away in a private study carrel, they had immediately gotten into a discussion about women writers, and somehow segued into talking about the writing assignment for Shirl's class. Rae's mind worked at an unbelievable pace, picking up on the thread of an idea voiced by Anne, and bouncing it in a dozen different directions at the speed of light. Her green eyes seared, blazing with each new thought, her smile quick and engaging, and Anne was completely mesmerized by the whole encounter.

Somehow, and afterwards Anne could not say precisely how, they'd cooked up an idea to write their paper for Shirl together. They would ask Shirl's permission on Thursday at the get-together, but they were pretty confident she'd allow it. After all, they were planning to produce twenty pages of work. As they saw it, the topic they'd hit on was just too big for a mere ten pages, and they were both interested in exploring it.

As they left the library, Anne heard the clock tower chime seven o'clock, and realized she'd missed dinner. She'd have to hurry or she'd lose her lane at the pool. With Rae limping at her side, they started down the steps, and halfway down ran into Chris, who was laden with several enormous tomes. He smiled as he leaned down to give Anne a quick kiss. "Hey."

"Hey," Anne responded, looking into his eyes for some sign of discomfort, and finding none there. "You remember my friend Rae?"

Chris gave Rae a friendly smile. "Sure, from the Gorge. How are you?"

Rae nodded as she lit a cigarette, somehow managing an ironic smile at the same time. Chris turned back to Anne.

"Heading back to the dorm?"

"No, I've got a lane reserved. In fact, I'm gonna be late."

He shook his head. "Jock," he said as he turned to continue up the stairs. "I'll call you later."

Anne waved and turned back to Rae, who was studying the cigarette in her hand. Rae flipped her hair off her shoulder and took hold of Anne's arm.

"So I guess I have the pool to thank for these strong arms," Rae said. Her limp was bad today.

"I guess." Great, Anne thought, that was a clever thing to say. Why did being with Rae always make her want to be charming, and make it impossible to be?

"That's also why you always smell so clean, I'll bet. The chlorine. You must have chlorine in your blood by now." Was Rae making fun of her?

"Eighty percent chlorine, twenty percent caffeine," said Anne.

"I could do with some caffeine right now." The invitation was clear in Rae's mischievous look. They were heading across the quad in the general direction of the Dragon, which also happened to be on the way to the pool and the parking lot where Rae's car was parked.

"I wish I could," Anne said, meaning it, but she wasn't going to start blowing off her workouts–not now, when the chaos of her life demanded them more than ever. She decided to change the subject as they passed through the center of the quad.

"You know the legend about these two statues?" Anne asked.

Rae flicked an ash, seemingly lost in her own thoughts for the moment. "No," she finally answered.

"It's really sexist, but what do you expect? They say that if a virgin coed crosses this path at midnight on the night of a full moon, the two statues will get up, walk toward each other, shake hands in the center of the quad, and return to their podiums. Supposedly it's never happened before because there are no virgins at Cornell."

Rae snorted. "Your friend Joey tell you that?"

Anne felt a surge of protectiveness for Joey. "No, I don't remember who–it's just one of those stupid Cornell legends." She paused for a beat. "And Joey's not sexist."

"You know what I think?" Rae had that look in her eye, her mind was ticking away. "I think they re-wrote the story." She paused. "I think the real story is that the statues get up and shake hands if *two* women are on the path at midnight." She paused again, looking at Anne. "Two women who are lovers." She shrugged and gave Anne's arm a little tug. "But men re-write history all the time." It was just the kind of provocative thing she'd come to expect from Rae, and Anne felt her face flush for a moment.

They stopped outside the Dragon, where Rae deliberated about whether to go in. She stubbed out her cigarette and looked up at Anne. She really is short, Anne thought.

"Sure I can't convince you to join me?" Rae's crooked smile curled her lip seductively to one side.

"No." Anne shook her head. "I really have to get in the pool."

"Tell you what." Rae stepped toward her and took hold of Anne's jacket to pull it tight over her chest, in an almost maternal way. Almost, but not quite. She looked up into Anne's eyes, cocked an eyebrow, and Anne found it hard to breathe. "How about I meet you here at midnight on the next full moon? We can conduct a little experiment." She stared into Anne's eyes for another few seconds, and the smile playing on those moist cherry lips was tantalizing, almost mocking. Anne smiled in return, painfully certain that everything she was feeling was written all over her face. Rae let her go and backed away a step. "Bye." She turned and limped into the Dragon.

Anne rang the buzzer a second time and shifted the bottle of wine to her other hand. She was over an hour late, and wondered for a horrified moment whether the party could already be over. First she'd had a hard time getting rid of Joey, who had thoroughly enjoyed watching Anne decide what to wear and begged her to tell him where she was going. In the middle of ordering him out of her room, the phone rang and Jane informed her it was Gallagher on the line–news that animated Joey all the more and confirmed his resolve to stay. To top it off, she'd gotten lost looking for the apartment after she'd gotten off the bus that brought her downtown.

Rosa opened the door and Anne could tell immediately that she was half crocked. "We're in the middle of a fight about *Orlando*. Communists on one side, fascists on the other." Rosa led the way up the narrow staircase to Rae's second-floor apartment, and since Anne had no idea what she was talking about, she kept her mouth shut.

As she entered the living room, she was assaulted by a heavy fog of to-bacco and pot. She saw Shirl holding court off to one side, surrounded by a group of students and joined by Rosa, who promptly took up the debate where she'd left off. Another group was seated cross-legged on the floor, pass-ing a joint and laughing hysterically about something. In the overstuffed chair across the room sat Jenna, with Rae in her lap, their heads together as they talked earnestly about something. Empty bottles of wine littered the floor, to-gether with two boxes of half-eaten pizza.

Feeling awkward and very aware of the fact that she was the only person not stoned or drunk, Anne went into the kitchen to open her bottle of wine. She had just started to figure out how to work Rae's corkscrew when Shirl came up behind her. "Annie!" Shirl was the only person who ever called her that. Well, Shirl and sometimes Gallagher, but she didn't want to think about that right now. "I'd begun to wonder if you'd make it."

Anne fiddled with the corkscrew as she delivered an edited version of why she was late. Shirl took the bottle from her hands and expertly uncorked it. "Comes with practice. Like most things." A friendly wink–what was that about? Did Shirl know something? What was there to know? "Get a glass."

As Shirl poured Anne's wine, Anne thought about how to ask her about the paper, and then decided to just plunge right in. "Listen Shirl, I don't know if Rae's mentioned it to you yet, but we were wondering if–"

"Rae told me." The smile disappeared from Shirl's face, and Anne's heart sank.

"Oh?"

Shirl sighed, handed Anne's glass to her and ran her hand through her short hair. "Look, I don't know what to say. I know you'll do good work. And as your teacher I'm not going to tell you that you can't do it together. It's just that, I'm telling you this as a friend, I'm not sure it's such a good idea."

Huh? Anne could only look at her. Whatever reaction she'd expected from Shirl, this wasn't it. Shirl seemed to sense her confusion. "I'm not being very clear, am I?"

"No." To say the least.

"Okay." She took a breath and started again. "I don't have a problem with the idea of a joint work. That's fine. I'll just give you both the same grade. I just don't think that it's in your best interests to do it with Rae."

Now she was really confused. Anne had always thought that Shirl really liked Rae. They'd become friends right at the start of the semester, seemed to have become rather close, in fact. Anne had the impression that they'd gotten together outside of class fairly regularly, and Shirl must have observed that Anne and Rae were now spending a bit of time together too. It just didn't make sense.

"Here's our late bird," announced Jenna as she walked into the kitchen and put her arm around Anne. Rae trailed behind.

Shirl lifted her glass as if in toast. "Just think about it," she said as she turned and passed Rae on her way back into the living room.

"Just think about what?" asked Rae, leaning against the sink.

"The paper." Anne wished Jenna would take her arm away.

"Oh, yes, did she tell you? It's okay." Rae took out a cigarette and offered one to Jenna.

"Aren't you going to offer one to Anne?" Jenna asked, tightening her arm around Anne.

"She doesn't smoke."

"Sometimes I do," said Anne. Now what had made her say that? She was suddenly aware of trying to pretend that she was someone she wasn't, and was certain that Rae saw right through it. She took a cigarette, lit it, and made sure that she didn't inhale. She remembered all too well the hilarity of watching Gallagher gag on her first puff one night at a bar, and knew that she could get away with this lunacy only if she kept the smoke out of her lungs. Rae and Jenna didn't notice–or were too polite to comment on–the thick cloud of uninhaled smoke that she blew out after each puff.

Someone had put a Cris Williamson record on the stereo, and several of the stoned women on the floor were singing along to the chorus of a song called "Waterfall." Anne had never heard it before, and listened with half an ear as she tried in vain to follow the heavy discussion that Jenna and Rae had resumed beside her. Something about Hegel. Or was is Schlegel? Fortified after finishing her first glass of wine, she poured herself a second and, carrying the bottle with her, left Rae and Jenna to their German Idealists and wandered into the living room.

As if she could glean some insight into the soul of its owner, she took in the room as a whole–worn but comfortable-looking sofa, posters of something called the Michigan Womyn's Music Festival on the walls, interspersed with wall hangings that looked like hook rugs. Closed door off to the right, unadorned. Probably her bedroom. Anne took another sip of wine and sat on the sofa beside Shirl, who was explaining something terribly important but incomprehensible to the disciples encircling her. Anne nursed her wine and tuned out, forcing herself not to think about the scenes that had undoubtedly been played out behind that blank closed door.

Long after her wine bottle was empty–and Anne had no idea if she alone had consumed the contents–Shirl turned to her and offered her a ride back to campus. Was it that late already? She'd participated in several of the conversations around her, but had spent most of the party in her own head, and had no sense of the passage of time. Anne shook her head, unwilling to be the first to leave. "I'll stay a bit, thanks. I don't have an early class." Shirl looked at her a minute, as if deciding whether to say something, but then got up. "Suit yourself."

Seemingly on cue, the stoned group on the floor stumbled to their feet en masse and started making noises about wanting a ride from Shirl. Jenna and Rae, who had returned to their cozy spot in the stuffed chair, rose as well, and started saying goodbye to everyone. Anne stood and was relieved to discover that she was fairly sober. Someone must have helped her with the wine. She went into the kitchen to deposit her bottle on the countertop, anxious to get away from the group for a minute. Except for when she'd first arrived, Rae hadn't spoken to her all night, and Anne couldn't help but feel a little excluded. Rae was clearly tied up with Jenna tonight. Oh, well, it was a predictable ending to a night that had begun with that baffling conversation with Gallagher, a phone call that she'd obsessed about nonstop throughout the entire party. I should just go, she thought as she pulled on her shoulder for a minute, trying to stretch out the sore muscle she'd hurt in the pool that day. Resolved to get out of there right away, before she made a fool of herself, she turned and was startled to find Rae standing quietly behind her, blocking the doorway.

"I'd like it if you'd stay and help me clean up a while. If you want." Rae's smile wiped clear the entire evening, and with it all of Anne's doubts.

"Sure," Anne smiled.

Jenna was winding a scarf around her neck as she nudged her way past Rae into the kitchen. She reached out to pull on Anne's sleeve. "I'm in the dorm next to yours–you'll walk me home, won't you?" With the floppy dark hat she pulled on, she looked more than ever like Harpo Marx. Anne resisted the urge to pull her arm away, and wondered how Jenna knew where she lived.

"No," she said, hating herself momentarily for the satisfaction she felt in watching the Cheshire cat grin dissipate from Jenna's face. "I'm going to stay for a little while."

"We have to talk about the paper we're doing," Rae said, and Anne wondered where Rae had come up with that. She was unexpectedly thrilled by the guilty notion that Rae might be lying, conspiring to be alone with her–at least that's how it appeared. Then again, maybe it was the truth–maybe that's exactly what Rae intended.

Jenna looked at both of them for an instant before slapping a smile across her face. "Well, have fun!" she said with perhaps a little too much cheer.

Jenna was the last one out the door after all the goodbyes, and once Rae saw everyone downstairs and closed the door, Anne emerged from the kitchen and turned her attention to the pizza boxes on the floor.

"I just realized I never ate tonight," she said, feeling a little foolish.

"Help yourself–you want me to heat that up in the oven? It'll just take a few minutes."

"No, I like cold pizza."

"How about some more wine to go with it? I've got another bottle in here somewhere," Rae said as she hobbled into the kitchen.

What the hell. "Sure."

They settled on the couch and Rae joined her in finishing the pizza. "I never paid you," Anne said, swallowing the last bite.

Rae lit a cigarette. "Oh, don't worry about it." She offered the pack to Anne, who accepted. What the hell again. Rae chuckled. "You know the old joke, 'Do you smoke after sex?' 'I don't know, I never looked'?"

Anne laughed, and for a few moments they puffed and sipped their wine in silence. "So do you want to talk about the paper?" Please say no.

Rae curled the end of her cigarette against the side of the ashtray on her lap, so that the ash fell off and the burning tip turned into a conical point. It was incredibly sexy. "Not particularly," she said slowly.

Anne flexed her sore shoulder and pulled on it.

"Something wrong with your arm?"

"No, not really. I hurt my shoulder in the pool today. It's nothing."

Rae gave her a quizzical look. "I thought swimming was supposed to be non-impact, you don't get hurt."

"Yeah," Anne smiled, "that's the idea. But I screwed up a turn and ran into the wall."

"How'd you do that?"

She wasn't about to admit where her thoughts had been at the time. "My mind was wandering."

Rae stubbed out her cigarette and put her glass and ashtray on the floor. "Come here," she said softly, climbing behind Anne on the sofa and straddling her from the back. "Let me see what I can do."

And then Rae's hands were on her. Strong, much stronger than Anne would have guessed, kneading the muscles in her shoulder in a pleasant, steady rhythm that was immediately mocked by Anne's suddenly racing pulse. Anne tensed and relaxed all at the same time–her body ready to melt under the magical fingers that were so certain in their enterprise, her stomach clenching at the fact that this was Rae doing this to her. Rae whose face invaded every dream these days, Rae whose sexy voice echoed in her mind late at night, Rae whose lips she imagined each time Chris pressed himself against her.

"Mmm, you're really tense," Rae purred as her fingers crept upwards and started their seductive dance along Anne's neck. Anne felt a now-familiar wetness start between her legs, emanating from the low, dull throbbing centered at the core of her being. She had a moment of panic, the treacherous thought returning to her that she was reading the situation all wrong, that this was all just some kind of feminist sisterhood thing. Rae had a boyfriend, and knew that Anne did too. And what about the fact that Rae had ignored her all night, spent the entire party cuddled up with Jenna? On the other hand, it was Anne she'd asked to stay, not Jenna. And it was Anne she was molding with her incredible hands at this very moment. She simply had to be doing this deliberately. She must know what she's doing to me–how could she not know?

For all the tension she was feeling in her nether regions, Anne was aware that up above, where Rae's hands were working their wonder, she was more relaxed than she'd been in weeks. She leaned back into Rae and wondered if she could die from this, the hollow thrum of pounding between her legs intensifying, swelling. She shuddered perceptibly at the warm breath she felt against her ear when Rae leaned in and whispered, "I think you should stay the night."

Without waiting for an answer, Rae swung her leg around to Anne's side and gracefully hoisted herself off the sofa, apparently knowing without being told that Anne was powerless to say no. She walked into the bedroom, and while Anne tried to decide if she was supposed to follow, Rae returned to stand in the doorway holding a tee shirt in her hand. "I think you can fit into this." Anne rose to catch it as Rae tossed the shirt to her. "You want to use the bathroom first?"

Puzzled, Anne left for the bathroom beside the kitchen, wondering why she was putting on a shirt that she fully expected to take off again in a short while. She felt completely unprepared for whatever awaited her back in the living room, the elaborate seduction nothing like what she'd fantasized, nothing like anything she'd ever experienced with men. Chris had always been very clear about their lovemaking–there was never any question about when he wanted to have sex. Really, the only question with Chris was always whether *she* was interested.

This was Rae's show, that much was clear–Anne had no clue as to what was expected of her, no clue as to what she would do if she somehow found the courage to do anything other than simply respond to Rae's caress. She inhaled deeply into the cotton shirt as she pulled it on, looking for Rae's scent, and decided to just accept the fact that Rae was calling the shots–she would follow, wherever it went.

When Anne emerged from the bathroom clad in the long but tight tee shirt, she discovered that the sofa had been pulled out into a bed. Rae wasn't there, and Anne felt self-conscious about sitting on the bed alone. Nor did she want to sit in the chair–how stupid would that look? She opted to go into the kitchen and pour herself another glass of wine. By the time she returned to the living room, Rae was standing in front of the stereo, her own small tee-shirt showing off perfect olive-tanned legs. Anne stood beside the bed a moment, feeling her pulse quicken from the view of Rae's remarkably broad shoulders and firm thighs, and watched as Rae put a Dan Fogelberg record on the stereo. She was reminded of Rick Manger in that moment, and felt a boulder lodge in the pit of her stomach.

Rae turned and smiled at her. "My bed's just a single," she said. "I'll sleep out here with you, if that's okay."

Okay? Isn't that the point? Anne wondered if she'd had too much wine after all, if she'd horribly misconstrued everything. Rae casually climbed onto the bed and sat at the head, lounging back against the pillows propped there. Anne figured that was her cue, so she climbed in beside Rae, still holding her wineglass. Rae took it from her, took a sip and handed it back to Anne.

"So what kept you tonight?" Rae asked, shifting her position to look at Anne. God, she was gorgeous.

"Oh, a bunch of things. And I got a call from someone I really had to take."

"Chris?"

Now why would she think that? "No, this woman I know. A friend."

Rae arched an eyebrow. It was charming. "Really?"

"Yeah." What to say about Gallagher? Even if she wanted to talk about her, which she really didn't at the moment, she wouldn't know where to begin. "It's complicated. Anyway, that took some time. And then I got lost looking for your place."

Rae pushed her hair away from her face and played with a few strands. Her exposed neck was long and smooth, alluring even without the tiny gold necklace. "What's her name?"

Anne looked down and swished the wine in her glass. "Gallagher."

"Are you lovers?"

Anne's head snapped up and she found Rae looking directly in her eyes, a playful smile curling her incredible mouth. Where would she come up with that idea?

"What? No, I'm not . . . I mean, no. She's not my lover."

Rae laughed. "Doth the lady protest too much?"

Anne felt herself blush, and cursed herself for it. She was way out of her depth here, and she knew it. And Rae seemed to be enjoying it all far too much. Anne was sure she was laughing at her. Time to come clean.

"I've never been with a woman. That way." There, take that. She looked Rae in the eye and dared her to laugh. But Rae just smiled.

"Well, it's something every woman should experience at least once, I think. It's . . . well," Rae plucked the word out of the air, "mindblowing." She reached for Anne's wineglass again. "But there's something there with this Gallagher, isn't there? Some undercurrent?"

Anne exhaled slowly. *The only undercurrent I'm interested in right now is the one I was feeling when your hands were on me a little while ago, and I'd like to get back to exploring it if you don't mind.* "I don't really know what there is with Gallagher. I knew her in high school and we sort of, I don't know, we had some stuff between us, I guess. But we never talked about it and now it's just sort of awkward."

"But she called you. Did you talk through your feelings?"

What feelings? I'm only sure about my feelings for you, at least I think I'm sure, and I don't want to talk about anyone else. Anne shook her head. "She's coming for a visit, looking at colleges. I guess I'm going to have to see her."

Rae seemed to be enjoying her role as lesbian spiritual advisor. "You don't want to?"

"I don't know." That was the truth. She didn't know what she wanted when it came to Gallagher. Some part of her was excited at the idea of seeing her again, but she was afraid, too–afraid that their last encounter had irreparably damaged their friendship, which she cherished, and at the same time afraid that maybe it hadn't and that they'd find themselves drawn even further into the sexual torment that had twisted Anne into knots. Worst of all, they could end up going on as if nothing at all had ever happened between them. Anne felt an incredible sadness at the thought. "Part of me wants to, I guess."

Rae chuckled softly. "I bet I can guess which part." Anne felt her blush deepen, and shrugged.

They sat quietly listening to the record, Anne's thoughts pulled in a thousand directions–all of which converged on the fear and excitement she was feeling right now, and imagining what the next few minutes might bring. Rae got up after a few moments and turned out the lights, so that the room was illuminated only by the streetlights streaming through the window, and a soft yellow glow from the stereo. "Let me hold you," Rae whispered when she climbed back into the bed.

Anne allowed herself to be pulled down into Rae's arms, her head resting on Rae's shoulder. When Rae began to softly stroke her hair Anne felt a surge of heat rekindled between her legs, and luxuriated in the sensation. Finally. She put her arm across Rae and held her quietly, drowning in the feel of those satin arms around her, smelling Rae's smoky wine breath beside her face. She lay there listening to the last song on the side play out, conscious of wanting to capture and preserve every second of this experience, to imprint it indelibly in her memory. The needle's rhythmic scratch against the record label interrupted her reverie just as she was beginning to wonder whether she was expected to make the first move. Rae made no move to turn off the stereo, and Anne felt a leaden heaviness settle in her chest as she shifted slightly and realized that Rae was asleep.

Joey was sitting cross-legged and barefoot on the wall outside the dorm, a shit-eating grin plastered on his face, when Rae drove up to drop her off the next morning. There being no ashtray in the car, Rae flicked her ashes onto the floor mat before putting the car in park. Anne just wanted out of there, wanted to get the whole sordid night behind her, and felt trapped when Rae turned off the engine. They'd barely mumbled two words to each other since they'd awakened that morning with splitting headaches. Anne's own unique mix of sexual frustration, acid stomach, cigarette mouth, and self-consciousness had combined to form a firm resolve in her mind not to entertain any more fanciful imaginings about Rae's reckless flirtations. She was straight, or at least uninterested in Anne, and Anne was not going to let herself be played with any more.

"Well, thanks for the lift. It really wasn't necessary," Anne said as she reached for the door handle.

"I needed the air, needed to clear my head. And, Anne?" Rae reached out and pulled her arm, turning her back gently. "I'm really glad you stayed over. I wish . . ." she paused, filling the silence by chewing the inside of her cheek as she tossed her cigarette out the open window. She continued softly, "I wish I hadn't fallen asleep. I was just so tired." She looked into Anne's eyes, trying to coax a smile. It didn't work. She moved her hand up Anne's arm and around the back of her head, and Anne found herself being pulled toward Rae's up-turned face–pulled against her will, which was quickly evaporating.

Fully turning in the driver seat, Rae snaked her other hand around Anne and up her arm, where it came to rest on Anne's burning cheek. Rae held Anne's face mere inches from her own, and gazed deeply into her eyes, smiling softly. "Okay?"

Anne's resolve melted at the sound of that smoky voice suddenly thick with a universe of possibilities. How does she do this to me, even when I'm pissed off at her? Anne searched the green eyes and found no answer. What she found was an unmistakable invitation, and Anne held her breath as the liquid green beacons pulled her closer, closer, and the earth stood still for the eternity it took for Rae's lips to bridge the gap and press into her own. Rae's mouth was somehow even softer than she'd remembered it, and Anne could not pull herself away, could do nothing but savor and match every delicious move of Rae's moist, succulent lips. When she felt the tip of Rae's tongue gently dart against her, she eagerly welcomed it and, enfolding Rae's lithe form in her arms, let her spirit soar as their intertwined tongues began their own searching, erotic dance. She couldn't breathe and didn't care–she wanted nothing, nothing in the world except this velvet mouth, this exquisite tongue that was thrusting her insistently, urgently to the edge of climax. She had never in her life been so electrified by a simple kiss.

Rae pulled away first and looked at her, the arousal plain on her face. Anne didn't trust her voice, and gulped for air that felt thick in her lungs. Rae pushed back her hair, which had become tangled somewhere along the way, and let out a small laugh. "Well, I think I need a cigarette," she said. She lit up and said on a smoke-filled exhale, "I knew that would happen if I kissed you."

Anne tried to get her breathing under control. "What?"

Rae smiled seductively, a look that gored Anne on the spot. "That I'd regret having fallen asleep last night."

The blast of heat that erupted between Anne's legs nearly made her shudder. She was past caring about whether her desire was too obvious.

"In that case," Anne said slowly, letting her eyes devour Rae's face, "I guess I regret it too."

Anne shook her head when Rae offered her the pack–she didn't want anything but to take back up where they'd just left off. Anne looked out the window instead, and saw that Joey was gone. She considered telling Rae to turn the car around and take them back to her apartment. But she knew she wouldn't–it would be forced now, mechanical. The moment was already cooling. She knew that she should just get out of the car and be patient. The greater delayed, the greater delighted, Shirl had once said in class. But she just couldn't make herself move yet.

Rae put an end to it for her. "Well, I guess you'd better go before we start something that could get us arrested."

Anne nodded. "Yeah, I guess so." She opened the door.

"We still have to talk about the paper, you know. Maybe we can get together on Sunday?"

Anne had rehearsal at night, but she could give Rae the afternoon if she got a lot of work done on Saturday. Hell, she'd give Rae anything at this point.

"In the afternoon," Anne said as she stepped out. She watched Rae start the car and noticed that there was no key, just an empty ignition slot that Rae turned. "Hey, what's with your starter?"

Rae flicked an ash on the floor and put the car in drive. "Who'd steal this piece of shit?"

Anne heard the bells of the Clock Tower up on the Arts Quad ringing out the alma mater as she approached the vaulted doorway of the dorm. Jane was coming down the stairs as she was headed up, and Anne felt a guilty wave of relief at the realization that she'd have a little time to herself before having to leave for class. Maybe enough time to masturbate–lose herself in a replay of that kiss and ease some of the throbbing in her groin. That certainly shouldn't take long.

"Joey's in the room waiting for you," Jane said as they passed on the steps.

Shit.

Chapter Four

The Big Red had set aside the cast's usual long table in the back after rehearsal on Sunday night. A Collegetown haunt for as long as any of the old-timers could remember, the decor was functional '50s kitsch, with formica tables, bright lights, and red drapes that made the interior look more like a small-town Chinese restaurant than a bar. It was run by an elderly couple who had owned it for decades and had a particular fondness for Gilbert and Sullivan. They bent over backwards to accommodate the comic opera club that bought endless pitchers of beer and platters of french fries. In return, the group graced the house at least once a night with a rousing chorus from their repertory.

Anne was seated between Joey and Chris, caught in the middle of their argument about the current age of Frederick in the *Pirates of Penzance*. She sipped her beer and tried to focus on the conversation across the table, which seemed to involve some recent translation of *The Marriage of Figaro*—whether the Beaumarchais or the Mozart, she couldn't tell. She also didn't care. She had a lot of homework waiting for her back at the dorm, and was beginning to think that she'd never get it all done.

The paper for Shirl was coming along well though. As frustrating as it had been today when she'd found Jenna at Rae's apartment—thereby foreclosing any chance that they'd do anything other than work all afternoon—Anne had to admit that the hours at Rae's had been productive. They would probably finish the paper that week. But then what? What would be her excuse to see Rae anywhere but in class? She had to know where this was going—whatever "this" was, if there even was a "this" at all. But Rae was maddeningly elliptical. In fact, she'd let it drop today that she'd spent last night with Rick.

And then there was Chris. She knew she couldn't just continue sleeping with him and pretending that her attention wasn't directed elsewhere. Then again, exactly where was her attention directed? To a phantom, at this point. Not even that. Joey had been emphatic—she had to tell Chris. Af-

ter he'd listened to the whole story the other day–she could never keep
something this important from Joey for long–he'd insisted it was really un-
fair to Chris to keep him in the dark. But the sex with Chris was good–he
was a wonderful lover–and she genuinely did like him. People have stayed
in marriages based on far less, she'd argued. "But you're not married,"
Joey had countered. "That's the whole point–you can walk away when it's
not right for you anymore."

She knew he was right, but she wasn't ready to break up with Chris. It
wasn't just the relationship she'd miss–although it was by far the most comfortable one she'd ever had, and made her social life very easy. No, she'd
also miss having Chris around. And, underlying it all, she knew that she
just wasn't ready to acknowledge what her feelings for Rae might mean
about her. She wasn't ready to come out as a bisexual, or whatever she
was. She didn't want to have to make such a fundamental decision about
herself now, with so little information, and felt certain that's exactly what
she'd be doing if she took so bold a step as to break up with Chris, whether
or not she told him the reason. And if she told him what was going on with
her, she knew it would change things between them so much that it might
as well be a breakup.

If there had been no Rae, she told herself, I wouldn't even be considering it. So maybe it's just an aberration, a glitch that has everything to do
with Rae and nothing really to do with me. As soon as Rae is out of my
life–her heart skipped a beat at that one–I'll be back to my old, boring, totally normal life.

Joey hadn't bought it. What about your high school crushes, he'd
asked. She reminded him that, other than Gallagher–which defied any
easy definition anyway–there had only been one or two, fleeting and insignificant. Certainly nothing like the attention she saw many of her classmates lavish on some of the girls at school. And remember too that she'd
fallen in love with a man in her last year of high school, at least she was
pretty sure it was love. Even if she didn't feel that way for Chris, she had
been crazy about Bill–how gay could she be?

But what about Gallagher, he'd responded–thank God she'd never told him the details about that cast party. Don't you see you're never going to really know where you're at in this until you stop hiding behind a boy-friend? She didn't like that–didn't like the suggestion that she would use Chris in such a way. She mostly didn't like the possibility that it might be true.

She joined in on a loud but slightly off-key chorus of "Hail Poetry" in or-der to avoid turning her attention to Chris, who seemed to have concluded his debate with Joey. By the time the applause from the Big Red's few non-chorus patrons had died down, Chris was ready to leave and offered a ride to her and Joey. He held her hand as they walked to the car a few steps in front of Joey, and asked if she wanted to see a movie the following weekend. Early in their relationship Anne had laid down the law–other than occasional evenings at the Big Red after rehearsal, she wouldn't go out on weeknights. They were both far too busy with rehearsals and schoolwork to have it any other way.

Anne cringed at the thought of a date, and immediately hated herself for it. It would be nice to get off campus and see something–maybe the new Jane Fonda movie about Lillian Hellman–but she wanted to keep herself free in case Rae wanted to get together. And besides, tech week would be starting in another week, at which point she'd be seeing him every night at rehearsals until the show opened.

"Let's just see how the week goes," she said. "I'm totally buried–I shouldn't even have come out tonight. And once the tech starts, I'll be in serious trouble if I don't get some of this reading done."

Chris was quiet a minute and then let go of her hand.

"Listen, honey, is anything wrong?"

Shit, not this. "No, why?"

"I don't know, you just seem kind of distant or something."

Fortunately, Joey was out of earshot behind them. Anne took back his hand and tried to sound reassuring. "No, I just have a lot of work. I guess I'm distracted." She felt like hell. He was too nice to do this to him.

"Well, if you want to talk about it, I'm here, okay?" The concerned look in his eyes was just too much. She was a disgusting excuse for a human being and deserved to die.

"Yeah, I know. And I appreciate it. Thanks." Shit.

Winter descended that week in its typical Ithaca light-switch fashion, the dreary overcast days of the preceding month replaced in a matter of hours by a clear sharp sky and temperatures hovering around freezing. Windbreakers and sweatshirts around campus were replaced with parkas–everyone knew the snow would be coming soon, and would stay with them until at least April. There was an undercurrent of excitement in it–the first snow was always fun.

For Anne, the change in weather simply meant having to take particular care after her laps to dry her now too-long hair. She'd spent most of last winter with a relentless head cold, and the words of her grandmother, so blithely ignored during her adolescence, had echoed in her head with every sneeze: Don't go out in the cold with a wet head! As a child, she had always been far too busy, in way too much of a hurry to bother with such basic details as drying her hair. Just as she would always wait until she was in bladder-agony before interrupting her outside fun to go inside to the bathroom. It still happened sometimes that she'd wait to relieve herself until the pain was unbearable–whatever she was involved in was always somehow more important. She'd read somewhere that it was good practice for childbirth. Or maybe it was supposed to stave off the onset of old-age incontinence–she couldn't remember which.

She skipped two history lectures that week to finish her portion of the paper for Shirl, and had felt for some reason personally insulted when Rae missed the seminar on Tuesday. Rae had left a message with Jane while Anne was in the library on Wednesday night, saying that they could get together after Thursday's class to put the paper together and finalize it. She also needed to use Anne's portable typewriter.

Meanwhile, Anne still hadn't given Chris an answer about Saturday, and he hadn't asked. He was preparing for an audition and, thankfully, seemed as distracted as Anne. In the back of her mind she admitted to herself that she was holding out until she knew if there were any chance to see Rae on Saturday, and hoped that she'd know before she saw Chris at rehearsal on Thursday night. Things were getting very complicated, and she didn't like the feeling of juggling the people in her life. Not that Rae was really in her life, of course, and that too was disturbing.

She walked downhill with Rae after class on Thursday accompanied by the midday music of the bells chiming from the Clock Tower. Someone actually got gym credit every semester for climbing all those stairs and playing the bells, which were apparently enormous and could certainly be heard all over the campus. Although occasionally you'd hear a commercial jingle or the theme from a TV show, the standard repertory consisted of traditional Cornell songs, concluding with an especially lovely arrangement of the alma mater. None of it registered with Anne today, however–she was too focused on Rae chattering about the paper to take note of anything else.

When they walked into her room, Anne was surprised, and a little disappointed, to find Jane at her desk. Jane had classes on Thursday in the Ag Quad, on the other side of campus, and usually didn't appear back in the dorm until dinnertime.

"Hey, don't you have class?"

Jane didn't look up. No surprise there. "Just a review session. I'm better off studying on my own. Prelim tomorrow."

"This is Rae." Anne hoped she sounded cordial. "My roommate, Jane."

Jane nodded in Rae's direction and returned to her book. Rae barely acknowledged Jane as she scanned Anne's record collection.

"We've got a paper to work on. I hope we won't be bothering you." She hoped they would.

Jane continued to underline a passage in her book. "Go ahead. I'm fine."

Parking themselves at Anne's desk where the typewriter was already set up, they got down to work and produced a fairly coherent draft within a matter of hours. As she worked on incorporating Rae's handwritten scribblings, Anne made extensive suggestions on grammar and syntax, and Rae seemed only too happy to oblige. "It's 'as,' not 'like.' Remember–'Winston tastes good like a cigarette should'? The whole point was that they used the wrong word." Rae didn't seem to understand most of the points on which Anne tried to instruct her, and Anne just chalked it up to the fact that Rae's mind operated on a wholly different plane.

Being the faster typist–her mother had insisted she take a typing class one summer, observing that if a woman could type she'd never be at a loss for a job–Anne did the typing as well as the editing, while Rae paced back and forth behind her, spilling forth a stream of consciousness that was totally brilliant but devoid of any structure whatsoever. As Anne saw it, Rae supplied the genius, and Anne gave it form.

Jane completely ignored them until she heard Rae pull out a cigarette. How could she hear that? Before Rae even opened the matchbook, Jane looked up and said in her brooking-no-argument tone, "I'd rather you didn't smoke in here." Rae smiled sweetly in her direction and said, "Okay, no problem" before walking out of the room to smoke in the hall. After Rae closed the door, Anne heard Jane's wry "shouldn't smoke in the hall either"–although it was mumbled, she knew Jane intended for her to hear it.

As she neared the end of the typing, Anne was aware of her time with Rae today running out. She didn't want it to end, not without the chance to spend a few moments alone with her, not without finding out whether they could see each other on Saturday, or anytime.

"What are you doing for dinner? You want to grab a bite to eat after this is finished?" Anne hoped her tone was sufficiently casual.

"I'm sorry, I can't. I'm seeing Jenna later. Maybe another time."

Anne knew she shouldn't push it, but couldn't help herself. "Well, how about this weekend? Maybe Saturday?"

"Oh, I'd love to. But I'm seeing Rick."

So that was that. Anne nodded and returned to the paper. What else did she expect? This was stupid, she was acting like a love-struck teenager—which, technically, she was. Enough, she resolved as she typed the last sentence. She can call me if she wants to see me, and if she doesn't then I'll know this whole thing is bullshit and that's fine. She wasn't going to put her life—or Chris—on hold any longer.

She handed the stack of typed pages to Rae, who handed them right back to her. "Could you get it copied before we turn it in? I'm running late so I can't do it now, and I'll probably lose it if I hold onto it longer than a day." She asked with such a charming smile, Anne couldn't refuse.

"Sure, no problem."

Rae was already gathering her things. "Great. Thanks for everything. I think it's a terrific paper."

The phone rang then, and Jane answered it as Rae headed for the door, her limp barely noticeable anymore.

"It's for you," said Jane as she laid down the receiver and returned to her desk.

Anne had wanted at least to walk Rae to her car up on campus, but before she could get to the phone and get rid of the caller, Rae was out the door. "Take your call," Rae said, "I've got to run. See you in class next week."

Tech week was the most grueling time for everyone involved in a production. It was unavoidable, because the cast and crew, rehearsing and building sets up to that point in various spaces around campus, never had access to the theatre until that final week. A mountain of details—blocking adjustments, hanging and focusing of lights, set modifications, timing of costume changes—all had to wait until the production moved into the theatre. As a result, by the time opening night arrived everyone would be exhausted—not exactly ideal for performing at one's best.

Anne was stuck at rehearsal until well past midnight every night that week, and had to forego the pool and several classes in order to even remotely keep up. One class she made a point of attending was Shirl's, but Rae skipped class on Tuesday and left early on Thursday without a word to Anne or anyone else. Anne was almost relieved to lose herself in rehearsal.

As the week progressed, she found that she was feeling better about her relationship with Chris, too. He was in a great mood every night–his big audition had gone well and he'd gotten the part–and they'd had a nice time together on Saturday. It had been a little awkward for her at the movie, which Anne hadn't realized was going to depict such a powerful bond between the two women. The references to Hellman's *The Children's Hour* were not lost on Anne, or Chris either, but they didn't discuss it afterward, and the rest of the night had been fun and relaxed.

Jane joined the orchestra and started attending rehearsals in the middle of the week. It was good to have her there–she was a fine musician, but more importantly, her mere presence was calming for Anne. Jane was not the kind of person Anne was used to seeing in a hectic theatre environment, and her stoic facial expressions from the pit during the many hilarious mishaps onstage were a real treat. Somehow, it all came together, though. It always did. When Friday night finally arrived, the cast, crew, and orchestra felt as though they'd gone through a ritual hazing and emerged as a cohesive clockwork unit, primed for the opening. Everyone felt a slight edge about the weather–a heavy snowfall could have a serious impact on attendance–but the snow had held off all week, and although the skies continued to look ominous, nothing definite was forecast for the weekend.

Anne got to the theatre early on opening night. Her call was for six, but she always liked to walk the stage in solitude for a little while before the crew arrived. She loved dark theatres–the smell of paint and glue, tiny motes of sawdust visible in the air under a harsh whitewash of worklights, her footsteps muted on the padded floorboards. It was a peaceful, pregnant time–the stage dormant, ready; the empty house a patient, waiting receptacle.

Yeomen of the Guard was her favorite Gilbert and Sullivan operetta, partly because it was so different from the rest of their work. Despite the usual patter songs and witty plot twists, it was essentially a dark, brooding piece. And operetta scholars always debated the ending, in which the lead baritone, the jester Jack Point, falls senseless onstage as the woman he loves is married to another man. The romantics insist that he dies of a broken heart; the cynics are equally convinced that the character is just clowning around. Gilbert's stage directions provide no help, so it's up to the director to decide how it will be staged. Anne didn't know which way she leaned–she had seen and performed it both ways–but conceded that, if handled properly, staging the ending as a death scene could be quite moving.

The last time Anne had performed this show had been as a chorus member, two summers ago. Gallagher's first season with the summer rep back in Philly. No, she didn't want to think about Gallagher now. She had to focus. She'd successfully buried the thought of Gallagher's impending visit for over a week, but now–she must be tired, her resistance low. She started some breathing exercises. Her heart rate slowed, but the thoughts of Gallagher did not retreat. Not entirely.

Gallagher would be here in ten days–just after the show closed. Although Anne wouldn't have the excuse of rehearsal, she could still claim in all truth that she was severely behind in her studies and couldn't give Gallagher much time. Why did she feel the need to avoid her? That was a hard one–she'd devoted several sessions in the pool to sorting it out, and had reached no real conclusion. She knew it was partly due to her confusing feelings about Rae, although the whole Rae issue seemed at the moment fairly nonexistent. No, she figured it had much more to do with a reluctance to have her intuition confirmed–to have Gallagher either expressly or implicitly convey that the attraction that Anne had felt all this time, that Anne had begun to believe that Gallagher had felt too, was nothing more than a product of Anne's sick imagination. All the flirtations, all the moments of seeming intimacy, all the signs and subtle indications were in fact just gossamer, fantasy layered upon wishful thinking. Why else had they never spoken about that night in the garden? Why else would Gallagher have been so uncommunicative, almost aloof, when she'd called to say she was coming? And Anne knew that as soon as it was laid out in the open, as soon as Gallagher's true feelings for her were revealed to be nothing more than friendship, something would change between them. She would lose some secret, fragile tether to this person she adored.

She made her way back to her dressing room as the stage crew started their light check and, after changing and getting into makeup, she headed downstairs to the warmup room to begin vocalizing. She ran into Joey on the way, and he wished her luck–not saying so, of course. It was considered bad luck to say "good luck" before a show. Most of the cast also refrained from the traditional "break a leg" too, preferring the savvy sound of "merde a puissance treize." Anne didn't bother herself with any of the superstitions, and offered only something neutral like "go get 'em" to anyone she saw.

At eight o'clock, Anne was in the Green Room with the rest of the large cast, listening to some final words of encouragement from the director. The house was full, so they would hold the curtain for ten minutes. Seated beside Chris on one of the sofas, she sipped her tea with lemon and silently ran lines in her head. The tea was supposed to soothe her vocal chords, weary from incessant rehearsal and the handful of cigarettes she'd smoked that week. She didn't know why she'd done it, knew they would clog her throat and screw up her tone and air, but there was something comforting in it. And it was a connection to Rae. Weird as that sounded, she knew that was part of the comfort. Joey had lectured her, and Chris had just smiled with a shake of his head. So far, Jane hadn't seen her smoking, so at least she was spared any disapproval from that quarter.

As soon as the director finished, the room erupted in a cacophony of laughter, vocalizations, and shouts about last-minute costume emergencies. Forty-five sets of opening night nerves set on edge. Anne held Chris's hand and cleared her throat for the millionth time, a nervous habit that made her feel as if her throat were open and relaxed, even though she knew it actually strained her vocal chords a bit. The stage manager appeared in the door–"Five minutes to places!"–and Anne rose to take her place onstage. Part of the uniqueness of this show in the Gilbert and Sullivan canon was that the curtain rose not on a lively chorus, but on a lone character onstage singing a soft ballad. Anne's character.

Chris gave her hand an encouraging squeeze and took the cup of tea from her. "You're going to be great tonight." He knew not to kiss her–it could smudge the makeup. And anyway, they had a long kiss during the first act finale. She smiled and brushed back his beautiful bangs.

"You too. Knock 'em dead."

Everyone took their places in the wings and Anne strode onto the dark stage alone, shielded from the audience by the thick red velvet curtain that would rise in just a moment. She listened to the final strains of the overture and waited for the intro to her song that would accompany the rising curtain. She couldn't hear Jane's violin, but knew she was there, sawing away as the overture approached its crescendo. Slow breath, in, out. Steady. There's nothing but the breath. Nothing. It was hypnotic, really, the blank place she manufactured for herself in her mind during those final precious seconds before facing an audience. A place of centered, grounded calm. In, out. She was ready.

"Three curtain calls! D'you believe it?!" Chris was ecstatic–the show had been spectacular and the audience was still cheering as the cast poured through the wings after the final bow. Anne was laden with flowers from Chris and several others–she didn't even know whom–and made her way past a crowd of well-wishers in the hall to get to the dressing room she shared with the other two female leads. They had already deposited their bouquets on the cramped makeup counter beside the mirror, so Anne left hers on one of the chairs. She had to change for the opening-night party.

She was too tired to go, really, but she knew it would be a short night and she was expected to make an appearance. When she heard a knock, she turned and found Joey bustling through the door before she could even say "Come in."

"Why do you always walk in on me changing?"

"I knocked." He was impossible. He only got away with this shit because he looked like Jesus. "You've got a visitor. In the Green Room." There was something about his know-it-all smile that made her antenna twitch.

"Who?"

He paused to torment her with the suspense. "Rae Sheldon."

A flood of conflicting emotions swept her, among them annoyance at Joey for bringing the news, annoyance at Rae for just showing up unannounced like this, elation for the same reason, curiosity–what the hell did she want after avoiding me for an entire week? And how did she like the show?–all jumbled together in an incoherent stew. Well, she wasn't going to hurry. She'd finish changing in her own good time–make her wait.

Anne put on her party dress in record time, and didn't bother to remove the stage makeup–in fact, after a quick glance at the mirror, she touched it up a bit and wasted five extra seconds brushing her hair to a golden sheen. Satisfied, she emerged from the dressing room with Joey on her heels, a shit-eating grin plastered on his face.

"Don't follow me, Joey. I mean it."

It seemed that the friends and family of the entire cast were all crowded into the Green Room, and Anne paused in the doorway before she spotted her. There, seated alone on the sofa in the corner, casually smoking a cigarette under the "No Smoking" sign and looking off into space with utter detachment. Amidst the chaos of congratulations, she was surrounded by the ebullience, but not a part of it. She looked up at Anne just then, and smiled, and Anne forgot all about being annoyed. She didn't feel the jostling of people around her, didn't hear any of the compliments shouted at her as she made her way step by step to the island of calm in the corner, guided by a pair of green eyes that never left her.

Rae stood to greet her, and Anne panicked for a second that she would kiss her right there. But then she didn't care, actually hoped she would. She didn't.

"Hi," Rae said. She took a puff and blew it out to the side of Anne's face. Her ash was way too long–it would tumble onto the floor any minute. "It was a great show."

But what about me? What about my performance? "I'm glad you liked it. It's great to see you." Someone bumped into Anne from behind, but she didn't notice. "I've missed you."

"Did you get my flowers?"

What? Anne hadn't even bothered to look at the cards, and now was dying to go back into her dressing room to see what Rae had written her. That's stupid, here's Rae standing right in front of me–God, is there any way she could look more beautiful?

"Well. . . ." Just be honest. "I got some, but I actually haven't looked to see who they're from yet." Rae smiled, seemed to accept that. "It's been pretty crazy."

Rae's ash dropped on the floor, unremarked by either of them.

"I hadn't realized you were the star of the show," Rae said. "You never mentioned it."

That was true. For some reason, her theatre life seemed very far removed from everything else. Or was it her Rae-life that was removed? And why was she being so easygoing about it, as if they hadn't just spent an entire week acting like strangers? What was she even doing here?

"I guess it slipped my mind." Maybe because I can't think of anything but you when I'm with you. "I'm just glad you came."

"You know," Rae said, stepping closer and letting her eyes stray to the plunging neckline on Anne's dress. Anne hoped the pancake makeup would hide the blush she knew was burning on her face. "You looked very hot up there. It's hard to believe Chris ended up with that other woman."

Huh? Oh, the character. Anne's character is dumped at the end by the leading man, who's in love with the soprano. "Yeah, well, the mezzo never gets the guy at the end, you know." Why were they talking about this nonsense when there were so many other things she wanted to say to Rae?

"Maybe she gets the woman, instead," Rae said, her smile broadening. She was making a joke. It wasn't funny.

"I should find you an ashtray before someone yells at us," said Anne. Rae's ash shouldn't have been her problem, but that thought never entered her mind. Anne leaned down to retrieve an empty paper cup from the floor. It had lipstick on it, obviously discarded by one of the female cast members sometime during the show. It might even have been Anne's. Rae noticed the lipstick too.

"Was that yours?" Rae said as she flicked an ash into the cup.

Anne shrugged. "Could be."

"I guess this is about as close as I'll get to your lips tonight, huh?" she said quietly–not that anyone else could have heard it anyway–and Anne felt the now-familiar drumbeat begin in her heart and move instantly to her groin. She decided she'd had enough. Enough of the flirting and innuendo. She was fed up with the constant arousal–Rae was playing with her, and it was time to take charge of the game. She took a stab at it.

"Well, I guess that depends," Anne said. See, I can be as intriguing as you.

Rae cocked an eyebrow, surprised for once. "You don't have somewhere to go right now? Some cast party or something?" Rae started fingering the tiny gold necklace around her neck. Absentmindedly, maybe, but its effect on Anne was powerful.

"Well, I do, but . . . I can get out of it. If I need to." She'd have to think fast–Chris was expecting her to go with him. Was probably looking for her right now.

Rae laughed softly, conspiratorially. "I think you need to." She pushed her hair behind her back, exposing a satin shoulder under her peasant blouse and a more perfect view of that lovely long neck. Her smile was so inviting, Anne couldn't possibly turn down this chance. "Of course, I wouldn't want you to miss out on anything."

Anne laughed at that, couldn't help herself, and felt emboldened. "There's only one thing I'm worried about missing out on right this second."

Rae took her hand then and moved in for the kill. Anne held her breath, drowning in the heat of Rae's eyes and certain that she was about to feel the devastating press of those lips. But instead, Rae put her mouth right next to Anne's ear and whispered with a warm breath, "Let's go, before you make me come right here." And the effect on Anne was immediate, a pounding surge that raged through her core and melted her legs. In a daze, Rae dragging her by the hand through the packed room, Anne followed blindly, barely able to walk with the blossoming agony between her legs, massaging herself in her own juices with each step she took. They made it as far as the hall—where they ran smack into Chris, who was holding Anne's coat.

"Hey, sweetie, ready to go? Hi, Rae. Are you coming?"

Rae laughed and Anne swept her mind for something to say in answer to Chris's puzzled expression.

"Actually . . ."

"I know I shouldn't be telling you this," he continued, "but some of the guys have planned a little skit in your honor."

"What?" That one came in from left field.

"It's just this thing. Remember how you flubbed the lyrics in the second act during the first tech? Well, it's sort of based on that. Anyway, it's really funny, you'll see. But we shouldn't get there too late. So, you ready?"

Guilt started to creep into her desire, competing for attention with the warm pulse of Rae's interlaced fingers subtly stroking her hand.

Rae spoke up, her voice amazingly natural. "We'll meet up with you in a minute. Anne's just coming with me to my car to get something." Anne took her heavy coat from Chris and let Rae pull her out the side door into the parking lot. Did I miss something? Now we're going to the party?

They walked in silence to Rae's car, which was parked at the far end of the lot, dark and isolated. Opening the passenger door–it was never locked–Rae slid in and made room beside her. Anne looked around to assure herself that they were completely alone before climbing in and enclosing them in the musty, ash-strewn interior. She turned to look at Rae, mere inches away.

"I take it we're not going to your place," Anne said, hoping that her disappointment didn't show too much.

"Do you mind terribly?"

Me? What about you? You were the one who was almost coming. "Don't you?"

Rae took Anne's face in her hands and looked into her eyes. The crooked smile was back. "God, yes," she sighed. "But you can't disappoint all those people." She ran her fingers through Anne's hair, and continued in the sexy deep tone that Anne could feel in her chest. "And when I finally get you alone, I want you all to myself."

Anne felt the heat rush into her cheeks and her hammering clit all at the same time. It was too much. Whether fortified by desire or just past the point of caring, she leaned into Rae and kissed her then and there, tenderly at first, but with a rising urgency as her blood raced. And Rae returned her kiss in equal measure, her tongue soon darting against Anne's lips, enfolding Anne's tongue, threatening to swallow her in a tide of groaning need. Rae's hands were suddenly on her breasts, oh God, fingering her straining nipples beneath the sheer fabric, while Rae's tongue ignited her with each frenzied thrust.

She pulled Rae against her, desperate to feel every inch of her small, writhing body. She slipped her hand under Rae's blouse and gently toyed with one of the incredible bra-less breasts she found waiting there–firm, round, beckoning for attention. She'd never in her life felt anything like it, and couldn't quite believe that it was actually happening–that she was really sitting here fondling a woman's breasts. And loving it. Drowning in the softness, the silken smoothness that was almost more than she could bear. Rae's nipples swelled to a point under her fingertips, rock-hard little pebbles puckering to be sucked. And oh, how Anne wanted to, could practically feel them between her lips as she pinched them tenderly and moaned against Rae's ravenous tongue. Her clit was thundering, she would come any second, as Rae's hand slowly began to move toward her hem and the bellowing, groaning center underneath. She had never felt excitement like this, an awesome yearning beast on the edge of volcanic eruption. Rae massaged her nipples into a frenzy, and she could not take it, could not withstand the powerful tide a moment longer.

Rae pulled away just then and nailed her with a razor look. Anne's head cleared a bit, just a tiny bit, but enough to know that one more kiss would send her spread-eagled on the seat, begging to be fucked, and she'd never make it to the party that Rae had now committed her to. She took Rae's hand from her breasts, slowly, and held it in her lap as she tried to catch her breath and temper the searing heat that engulfed her.

She looked at Rae, somehow resisting the overwhelming temptation to lose herself in that cherry mouth again. The look on Rae's face nearly did her in, the lust pouring off her as she moved her hair out of her eyes and returned Anne's gaze with naked desire. Anne wondered for an instant if the puddle she felt in her panties would seep through, stain her dress, leave a mark on the seat. She tore her eyes away from Rae to look out the window, where she spotted Chris across the parking lot, leaning against his car. "Shit."

"I'm sliding all over the seat here." Rae's voice was husky. "You've made me so fucking wet."

Enough, no more teasing. If they weren't going to do it—and Anne knew she couldn't, not here, not like this—then they had to just knock it off. "I've got to go."

"I know." Rae squeezed her hands. "To be continued?"

Anne swiveled the rearview mirror to check her appearance. Lipstick smeared hopelessly, but otherwise okay. She used her hands to wipe the red smears from her mouth, and only after she was satisfied did she look back at Rae. "I'll tell you what. No more cars. The next time I kiss you, I expect to be near a bed. And I'm not stopping until morning."

Rae leaned over and whispered in her ear, "I can't wait." She kissed Anne gently on the cheek. "And by the way, you can tell Chris he can thank me later."

Anne opened the door. "What do you mean?"

"I have a feeling you're going to fuck his brains out tonight."

"All set?" Chris asked as she approached the car slowly. She was acutely aware of her excitement squishing between her legs with each step, and that she'd better pull it together, right away. Opening night was nothing compared to the performance she'd have to give now.

"Yeah." He opened the door for her and she slid into the seat. "Rae's not coming, though," she said.

"Okay. Well, did you get what you needed?"

What was he talking about? "Huh?"

"In Rae's car."

"Oh, that. No, she didn't have it after all."

As they pulled out, she saw Rae's car still parked off in the far corner of the lot with only a glowing orange dot visible in the darkness. She realized she'd forgotten about the flowers she'd left in her dressing room–they'd be dead by morning.

Chapter Five

"You have to help me with this study," Joey said. He had totally taken over her side of the room, covering every available surface with pages that each contained a drawing of some geometric shape.

"I'm not going to help you cheat, Joey. Sorry."

"It's not really cheating. It's just exaggerating. Come on."

"Look, I took this course last year, and you can't bluff your way through it. Sagan's not an idiot."

"But I would have done a real study if there were time. I was in rehearsal so much I just couldn't get it done."

The study was supposed to gauge the incidence of telepathy. He'd devised the test himself—he would look at a picture of a geometric shape and try using his mind to transmit the image to her from across the room. What any of this had to do with astronomy was a mystery—but then, Anne's term paper about Atlantis last year hadn't had anything to do with astronomy either. This prof was cool.

"I'll tabulate the results and apply them across the board to all my other test subjects, plus or minus a little bit."

"But all your other test subjects are just made up. I'm the only one taking this stupid test."

"Well, yes, but the science is sound." In Joey's twisted universe, this actually made some sense. He would never consider fabricating the whole thing. Instead, he would conduct one test, fudging some of the results, and it would be justified in his mind somehow by the fact that he had actually gone through the exercise of conducting the study on one person.

"Joey, it's Thursday already, and the show opened last Friday. You've had all week to do this."

"I know. But I've been busy."

"Busy rock climbing."

"Look, are you going to help me or not?"

"You know," she said, "I've got a few things going on too." He gave her that puppy-dog look that killed her every time. At least he had his long hair tied back in a ponytail today. With his face showing, even with the scrawny beard, he wasn't all that bad looking. Funny, it was hard to think of Joey as a guy. "Okay, half an hour, that's it. Hit me with your dirty pictures."

He plopped himself cross-legged on the floor and started assembling the pages into a pile on his lap. "Isn't Gallagher coming this weekend?" he asked. "Will she see the show?" He shuffled the papers.

"No, not 'til Monday. But who knows, if there's a blizzard. Isn't it supposed to snow?"

"It's been about to snow all week. Don't count on it." He rearranged some more pages. What could be so complicated about a bunch of pages with diagrams? "You gonna tell her about Rae?"

Anne sighed. "Shit, I don't know."

"Don't you think you should?"

Not really. "It's none of her business. And anyway, I don't see how the subject could even come up. Where do you want me?"

"Over by the door, and turn your back."

Anne took a desk chair and placed it facing the door. "You know, I hate to disappoint you, but I have absolutely no psychic ability. Just a warning."

"That's okay. I've read some studies–I know what the percentages should be. And I ran a model in the computer lab last night, see?" He held up a stack of beige cards punched with little holes.

"Yeah, like I'm supposed to have any idea what that means." God, this is a waste of time. She sat in the chair, facing the door. "Okay, shoot."

He paused for a moment, and then said, "How about this one?"

Anne concentrated on trying to make her mind a blank. It was no use–images of Rae kept popping up. Rae's breasts in her hands, Rae kissing her, Rae's hands on her. . . .

"Anything?"

"Nope."

"Try harder."

Jesus. Rae had been right about that night with Chris–she'd practically attacked him as soon as they were back in his room after the party. She had been an animal, which had surprised him somewhat. He'd been more than willing to comply–several times–but for her, it hadn't come anywhere near the incendiary experience in Rae's car. His touch just didn't do it, and she knew her intense arousal that night had only been due to the visions of Rae replaying in her mind. Even so, it was a poor substitute. She'd felt like a heroin addict, striving in vain to recapture the exhilaration of her Rae high.

"Circle," she said.

She heard Joey shuffling the papers behind her. "Next?"

She'd definitely used Chris, there was no other way to see it. She'd used him to get off, like a human dildo. He seemed unaware of it, and certainly didn't mind, but the whole thing left her feeling dirty and hating herself. Worst of all, now he probably figured that they were in some kind of steamy sex phase. That was the last thing she wanted with him.

"So?" asked Joey behind her.

"Circle."

"This is a new one."

"I know. Circle again."

"You're not concentrating."

"Look, Joey, you're welcome to get someone else to do this."

Jane opened the door at that moment and stopped at the sight of Anne seated in her chair a foot away. "I'm not even going to ask what you guys are doing."

"Hey," said Anne as she got up and turned to Joey. "You know, Jane's probably a much better test subject than I am. Why don't you use her?"

Jane walked past her and headed for her desk, ignoring Joey in the middle of the floor between the beds. "I've got work to do."

"Sit back down," Joey instructed Anne, "we've already started."

"Look, Jane's the scientist, not me."

"Come on," he insisted. "Focus."

She sat in the chair again and tried to wipe her mind clean as she heard Jane dumping some books on the desk. They would have a quick brush-up rehearsal tonight, just to get everything refreshed before performances resumed tomorrow. It would be nice to immerse herself in the show again for this final weekend–it had been a long week.

"Triangle."

Paper shuffling again. She had seen Rae in class that day, and on Tuesday as well, but they had made no plans to get together. Anne had scoured her face for any sign of . . . she didn't know what. Something. Some acknowledgment of the intense connection they'd forged in the car. But Rae had been the picture of cool. Not aloof, really–just her usual friendly, slightly provocative self. There had been no special intimacy directed toward Anne, and she was of two minds about that–on the one hand a little disappointed, but on the other a little thrilled by the notion that they were harboring this secret together, protecting it from prying eyes, safeguarding it to relish and explore in private. If they ever got around to it.

She still had the card that had come with Rae's bouquet. The flowers had been beyond hope by the time she'd gotten to the theatre on Saturday, but at least she had retrieved the card, and had carried it in her pocket all week, a talisman to continually finger and reread: "The future is yours," it read. She had no idea what that meant. A future in the theatre? A future with Rae? Was she being prophetic, or making a promise? For someone so articulate, Rae could be awfully oblique.

"Well?"

"Nothing yet."

Rae hadn't joined them for coffee after class this week, which partly explained why they hadn't had a chance to talk alone. Nor had they sat together during either class. Shirl had handed back their papers today, so when the seminar ended she and Rae had gotten together for a few minutes to pore over Shirl's glowing comments and congratulate each other on their joint A. Rae had taken her hand as they stood beside the conference table, and didn't let go when Jenna had walked up to them. Rae and

Jenna had plans to go shopping in Collegetown, but before they left, Rae had turned to Anne, given her a quick kiss on her mouth, and said she'd be seeing her soon. Much as she'd wanted to, Anne just couldn't make herself ask when. It would look too desperate, too pathetic to try to pin her down. She returned the pressure of Rae's hand and satisfied herself with the knowledge that they shared this incredible secret, along with the hope that they would eventually act on it.

"Come on."

"Joey, maybe you're just a poor transmitter."

"I'm getting a headache, I'm thinking so hard."

"I'm getting a headache from both of you," Jane offered from her side of the room. "How long is this gonna take?"

"Not long. Anne, just do it."

Shit. "Okay, just shut up and let me think." Great, I'm supposed to make my mind a complete blank while I've been walking around in a constant state of arousal for the past six days. I'm sopping wet twenty-four hours a day–could I get a yeast infection from that? At least it doesn't show. Shit, if I were a guy I'd have a hard-on every minute. How do guys deal with that? I should remember to ask Joey later.

"Circle."

She heard Joey's exasperated sigh as he pulled out the next diagram.

"How 'bout this one?"

With rehearsal tonight, the show Friday through Sunday, and then Gallagher's three-day visit starting Monday, there was no way she'd be able to see Rae before the middle of next week. Funny how the no-weeknight-dating rule was automatically suspended when it came to Rae. Maybe they could go to a movie. Who was she kidding–all she wanted was an uninterrupted night in Rae's apartment. She'd pin her down after class on Tuesday. She had no choice–her groin couldn't take much more of this.

"Triangle."

"That's it. You're hopeless."

"Are we finished?" Anne asked as she rose and turned around.

"You are. I swear, you've got circles and triangles on the brain."

"Sorry, but I told you I'm not psychic."

"No, you're psychotic."

Jane popped her head up and graced them with one of her rare, beautiful smiles. "I could have told you that."

Chris knocked on her dressing room door as she was changing after Sunday night's show. She knew it was him by the little "shave-and-a-haircut" rhythm that he always used–he could be pretty annoying sometimes–and she knew that, unlike Joey, he would wait for her to open the door. He was too considerate to just barge in.

She wasn't looking forward to the closing night party tonight, dreaded it actually, because of the decision she'd made over the past few days. She was going to break up with him tonight. It hadn't even been the persuasiveness of Joey's arguments, which she conceded were good. It was just that she felt like a lying sack of shit whenever she was with him. Maybe it looked like she was ending things for his sake, but she knew the truth was that she was doing it for herself, to stop feeling so guilty. And he had no idea it was coming.

"Hey, you look great," he said as soon as she opened the door. She cringed and hoped it wasn't obvious.

"Thanks. You were terrific tonight. I think it was our best show." She gathered her personal possessions from the cluttered dressing table and stowed them in her pack and bag. Tonight's party was casual–just jeans and sweatshirts–and she was grateful. She hated dressing up. But then, she hated everything tonight. At least the show had been good.

"Is Rae coming with us?"

"What?" A cold wave suddenly swept her and was gone. She swallowed and kept her eyes glued to the straps on her backpack. "Why?"

"Well, she's in the Green Room. I thought you knew."

Oh, shit. "I'll be right back." She grabbed her parka off the back of the door and flung her backpack across her shoulder, leaving Chris to cart her makeup case and bag of odds and ends out to the car. She tore a beeline through the throng amassed in the backstage area, straight for the Green Room. There she was, as Anne knew she would be, in a world of her own, seated in the same spot on the far sofa. Anne worked to get her breath under control as she nudged her way through the crowd. She wasn't sure what she was feeling right then, but was certain that it was shaded with a touch of anger, and didn't care if Rae saw it.

"What are you doing here?" Anne asked with a trace of irritation as she approached Rae.

Rae's look was searing–a mixture of alarm and defensiveness. "Hello to you too."

Anne flipped back her hair and folded her arms across her chest, ready for battle. "I didn't expect to see you tonight."

"So I gather." Rae smiled then, totally disarming. "Should I leave?"

No. Yes.

"I have some more flowers for you. A little closing night gift."

Anne didn't see any flowers. But her resistance was waning. Shit, why does she have this effect on me? Anne's Main Line schooling reared its ugly head, forcing her to be polite.

"That's very nice of you. Thanks." What else was she supposed to say?

Rae started in on the dance right then–the eyes locked on Anne's, the cigarette slowly pulled out of the pack and lit, the crooked smile after the first puff. She knew exactly what she was doing.

"I don't actually have them with me. We'll have to go get them."

No way. Not again. "Rae, I'm really not up for any more car scenes."

Rae took a step closer. "You know, I think that's the first time I've ever heard you use my name." Her eyes were unimaginable pools of green. "I like it."

Anne shook her head. "I mean it."

"And the flowers aren't in my car." She took another step closer, her body practically touching Anne, who felt the pull between them as if it were a living thing, with mass and a will of its own. It sucked her own will right out of her.

"They're in my apartment." She took Anne's hand and started stroking her fingers. "I was hoping you'd come there with me. Tonight."

And wasn't that exactly where Anne knew this was headed as soon as she'd learned that Rae was here? She was being forced into a choice, deliberately—Rae must know that she would have plans on closing night. She must be getting some kind of satisfaction out of forcing a choice on Anne like this. It was a power play, plain and simple. And they both knew that Rae had all the power.

It was easy to convince herself that she was making the right decision as she headed out to the parking lot to lay some feeble excuse on Chris. In a way, the decision had already been made days ago, when she'd decided to break up with him—that was the only reason she was planning to attend the party anyway. Tonight or later in the week, it would make no difference. And, little did he know, he'd have a much better time tonight if she wasn't there.

"You're sure you're okay?" he asked with genuine concern that felt like a blow to her gut. He was holding her stuff for her, such a gentleman, ready to load it into Rae's back seat when she drove up. She had to keep a check on her anger at him, at his insipid, aggravating niceness. Why couldn't he just be a prick and make it easy for her?

"I'm fine. She just really needs to talk. There's some shit going on." Rae's ashtray on wheels pulled up, and Anne opened the door. "I'll be fine. Have fun at the party."

Rae took her hand as soon as Chris shut the door, and lifted it to her lips to kiss Anne's fingers before they had even pulled out of the lot. Anne shifted uncomfortably in her seat, the low dull hum of her relentless arousal immediately igniting the flashpan between her legs into a full-scale, agonizing fire. When she felt Rae's lips curl over one of her fingers and start to suck on it, Anne could barely contain herself.

"Rae. . . ."

"There, you did it again." Rae let go of her hand to grasp Anne's thigh. "I love hearing you say my name." She pulled on her leg a little. "Come closer."

"I can't. I can't move or I'll be all over you."

"Really."

"Yes, really. Let me have a cigarette." Rae laughed softly and handed her the pack.

They rode the dark streets in silence, Anne trying to quiet the unbearable roar between her legs, wondering if she would know what to do when the time came. She'd read one or two lesbian novels, had a vague idea of how it was done, but the details had been very sketchy and Anne was certain there was a lot that she'd have to improvise. Rae had done this before—she'd know what to do. She might even be disappointed in being with such a novice. What was she getting herself into?

The car stopped in front of Rae's apartment, and they sat there in the dark for a minute finishing their cigarettes. Something felt off. Maybe it was just Anne. At least her lust had abated a little for the moment—replaced by a growing sense of insecurity.

"You haven't asked me how I liked the show," Rae said, looking at the empty street in front of her apartment building. All the windows were dark.

"You saw it again tonight?" It hadn't even occurred to Anne. "I figured you just showed up at the end."

Rae turned to her. "I can't get enough of watching you up there. But," she smiled, "I have to admit, it was a little hard to concentrate on the show." She scooted across the seat a few inches toward Anne, but did not reach out for her. "All I could think about was what I wanted to do to you." She said it quietly, almost like a confession. Her lips were screwed up slightly as she momentarily chewed the inside of her mouth. So kissable.

"I'm glad I didn't know you were out there, because that's all I would have been thinking about too." That's all I've been thinking about for weeks.

Rae reached out to slide her hand along Anne's thigh, pausing for a brief pulsating moment at the damp crotch, and moved it possessively up and around her waist. Anne stared into that lovely face, willing at last to let Rae see the vulnerability, the desire that was building of its own accord, accelerating, reflected in each other's eyes as it bounced between them like a strobe between two mirrors.

Anne reached over to touch her face then, that flawless olive skin, those delicious ripe lips that acted as a beacon to her wailing clit. Rae caught one finger between her teeth and gave it a gentle bite, and Anne couldn't help but let a tiny moan escape as the flood of awesome want inundated her again. She nearly cried from the pleasure, the gaping need.

"Come upstairs with me," Rae said, her voice deliriously deep. "Right now."

She didn't have to ask twice. Intoxicated, Anne left her gear on the back seat and followed Rae into the apartment building.

In the weeks that followed, Anne could never precisely remember how they'd gotten from the stairwell to the bed. It was all a blur, images jumbled together in no particular order: Rae's mouth engulfing her own, Rae's shirt being lifted over her head by one of them, she couldn't remember who, Anne's jeans and parka discarded in the middle of the living room floor. She had a clear recollection of Rae pulling her into the bedroom, almost frantic in her insistence that they not waste time opening the sofa bed. And when Rae rolled on top of her after what seemed an eternity of teasing, nipping and sucking at her swollen starved breasts, and finally slid her fingers into the aching maw that was screaming for her touch, Anne could savor it for only a second before she bellowed from the primal, shattering force that rocked her. And she knew in that instant that she was in the only place she could ever be, that she had been destined from the start to find her center, her home, right here in the arms of a woman.

It was sometime near dawn that, finally sated for the moment, they fell into a light sleep, entangled in each other and utterly exhausted. When Anne awoke an hour later to the touch of Rae's tongue lapping at her nipple, she felt her sore vagina give way to renewed desire, and marveled at her body's instantaneous response. Rae had her own special key for this ignition. When Anne stirred, Rae lifted her head from the breast she was devouring, and the crooked smile coaxed Anne's juices to flow even more.

"I didn't want to wake you. But I couldn't help it."

Anne closed her eyes and stretched. "I'm glad you did." Her smile was playful as she boldly spread her legs. "Why don't you see for yourself?"

"Ooh, baby, how do you get so wet?" Rae purred as she dipped her fingers into the running sap and stroked her to perfection. "After last night, you're still going to let me have more?"

Oh God yes. Anne could only nod.

"I guess that's one of the benefits of being with an athlete." The cocky mischief on her face faded as she lifted her fingers to her mouth and licked them. Her voice was tentative. "I want to taste you."

Anne's heart flipped into overdrive. That was one thing–one of the very few things–that they hadn't gotten around to last night. Maybe it was just a vestige of some reserve they felt, the last line they hadn't felt compelled to cross yet. Or maybe it was just that they'd never gotten that far because the orgasms had been tumbling forth so rapidly, with such intense frequency, that they simply hadn't had the chance, or need, to explore each other any further. Whatever the reason, Anne was ready now, beyond ready, and she squirmed with anticipation as she watched Rae lower herself between her legs and felt for the first time the unearthly sensation of that warm velvet tongue slipping between the dark folds of her dripping, yearning cunt. She rode Rae's tongue like an expert, molded herself to it and let it take her into another universe, where she shed all inhibitions and soon let loose with a torrent of flailing and moaning like never before.

And the incredible taste of Rae–she couldn't wait for the waves to subside before she plunged herself down there–it had been worth the wait.

How could she have gone so long without this? She was a parched desert wanderer who happened upon an oasis of unspeakable delight, and she worked her tongue slowly, lovingly into every crevice with insatiable thirst to devour the last ounce of Rae's splendid nectar. Rae bucked against her, but she held fast to her course, licking and sucking on the clit that throbbed under her teasing probe, and the howl that finally erupted from the other end of the mattress was as guttural as her own had been. Afterwards, she rested her head on Rae's twitching thigh, and breathed deeply of the heavy musk, enveloped in a stupefied peace.

The need for food finally drove them up for air a few hours later. Anne had skipped dinner last night, and it was nearly lunchtime now. She was ravenous. Clad in a sweatshirt and underpants, she watched Rae making toast, sexy even in a baggy oversized robe. As she sipped the coffee that Rae placed in front of her, she reflected on the fact that in less than a day her existence had been reduced to the elemental: sex and food. She could live on just this.

The sky she viewed through the small kitchen window was a brilliant blue, and the morning light–was it still morning?–seemed particularly bright. In fact, too bright.

"Hey, you know what?" she said as she went to the window, knowing what she'd see. "It snowed last night!"

"You're kidding–I didn't even notice." Rae joined her by the sink and slipped her arm around Anne's waist as they peered through the curtains at the magnificence of the season's first snow blanketing the town. Rae had to stand on tiptoe to see through the window to the ground. It was adorable.

"I'm declaring a snow day," Anne announced. "Classes are cancelled." It felt like Christmas, and she'd already opened her gift. It occurred to her that Jane would wonder where she'd been, since she never stayed out all night when she had classes the next day. She'd think of something later. Rae put their toast on a paper towel and brought it to the table. It was in the middle of Anne's first bite that Rae dropped the bombshell.

"You know, I'm leaving for England in a few weeks. After exams."

Anne tried to swallow mid-chew, and nearly gagged. Her mouth was suddenly dry. "Um, no, I didn't know." How could she have not told me something like this? "How long?"

Rae stirred her coffee and didn't, wouldn't, look up. "The spring semester."

What was she saying? Back up, things were moving too quickly. Anne started to feel the first tendrils of nausea creep into her belly. The coffee was acid, she was going to be sick. Breathe. But Rae was still talking.

"I know this is kind of sudden, it's probably crazy, but . . ." she looked up into Anne's deathmask, a cautious hopefulness in her eyes, "I was thinking that maybe you could come with me."

Rae drove her up to the dorm around three. Anne had been serious about the snow day–she couldn't possibly sit in class today, and even though she would probably have benefited from a mile in the pool, she had figured that last night's workout more than made up for it. Instead, they had lingered at the apartment and discussed the impossible idea of Anne going to London. And somehow, the more they talked about it, the less crazy it seemed. It would take a monumental effort on Anne's part, completing a thousand forms and cajoling various administrators into accepting her application so late, but after several hours of brainstorming and Rae's infectious enthusiasm, it began to look as if it might actually, amazingly, be possible. Anne could participate in the theatre program that was jointly sponsored by Cornell and an affiliated British university. They'd leave after the Christmas holidays, and celebrate New Year's in London. Anne could talk them all into it, she knew she could–her parents, her dean, her department head, and all the rest. It really might work.

As exhausted as she was, she was nevertheless exhilarated when Rae pulled up beside the entrance. Her emotions were in tatters, but the feelings were all good–excitement, anticipation, and always, incessantly, the background drone of arousal from being anywhere near Rae. She was a Skinner rat in Rae's car, unable to sit inside it without immediately feeling the flicker of desire. Would she *ever* get enough?

She turned to Rae to say goodbye. "I'll *see* you in class. I can talk to Shirl about a letter of recommendation then."

"I'm coming with you. You need help carrying all this crap, and you're not even wearing boots."

"Yeah, well," Anne smiled, "for some reason I didn't make it home last night."

Rae opened the door. "Besides, we might have the room to ourselves for a little while."

Hmm, that could pose a problem. Jane's schedule was unpredictable these days, and the last thing Anne wanted was to have Jane walk in on them. As they collected Anne's bags from the back seat, Anne heard the chimes of the Clock Tower pealing forth with an old Beatles tune, and smiled to herself at the pun it inspired: I'll get *bi* with a little help from my friends. They made their way along the path that had been cleared in front of the dorm, Rae in front.

"Hey," Anne commented, "you know, your foot looks like it's much better. Your limp is completely gone."

"I still feel it sometimes, but yeah, the pain's mostly gone."

They trudged up the three flights, and Anne wondered if Rae was as sore as she. Who was the athlete here, anyway? When they walked into the room, Anne saw with both relief and a touch of anxiety that Jane wasn't around. She would have a hard time stopping anything that Rae might start. They dumped their coats and Anne's backstage paraphernalia on Anne's bed, and Anne excused herself to escape to the bathroom down the hall, where she had a few precious moments to herself to think. And to try to get her mind off the desire to get back into bed with Rae.

Anne checked her face in the bathroom mirror. So this is what a lesbian looks like. Because that's what she was—there was no doubt at this point, no halfway, no fence-sitting. She had vaulted bisexuality entirely and landed squarely, undeniably, on the other side of the great sexuality divide. She knew she'd never really made love before last night, never really had the experience of giving herself over wholeheartedly to the sensuous pleasure of pleasing someone else. Never before wanted to. Can the world really make sense, really become crystal clear, in just one night? She washed her face and hands, not trusting that the residue of their passion had really been cleaned away in Rae's shower, especially since Rae had joined her in it halfway through.

When she got back to her room, the scene that met her there didn't register at first. There was Rae seated on the bed surrounded by their coats and Anne's stuff, smoking a cigarette. But there was an extra bag sitting in the middle of the throw rug between the beds. And as she proceeded through the outer room, she heard a voice talking to Rae, a voice that rooted her to the floor.

Gallagher.

Chapter Six

"Wait up!" Joey sprinted through the snow to catch up with Anne as she slowly made her way uphill on the icy path. He never took the easy way. At least he was wearing shoes.

Anne turned and, seeing that he'd reach her in a minute, continued her precarious trek. If they'd just throw salt on the paths after plowing them, it wouldn't be so bad. Obviously the university thought that broken legs were preferable to snowy shoes.

"Since when do you get up before noon?"

"I'm going to my botany lecture this morning," he said. Anne didn't even know he was taking botany. "I have to ask you something."

"Walk me up the hill then, I'm in a hurry. I have to go by Shirl's office to get her to write me a recommendation."

"You're really going through with it?" She'd given him an abbreviated version of her night with Rae and her England plan when he'd called yesterday.

"Of course I am. It's a great opportunity."

"Oh, get off it. That's not why you're going and you know it."

"Thanks for the support."

"Listen, do you think Jane would go out with me?"

Whoa–that one stopped her. She looked at him incredulously, but he seemed to be serious. "You're joking."

"No, really, would she?"

It was an absurd idea. Jane didn't date, for one thing. She was thoroughly involved with her schoolwork, and that was it. But above all, a free spirit like Joey would probably be the last man on the planet she'd consider. It was just too weird to imagine.

"I have no idea. She's never mentioned you one way or the other." The truth is, she pretends you don't exist. But Anne didn't want to hurt his feelings, and tried to think of a way to discourage him gently.

"I'm going to the barber after class."

Okay, two earth-shattering events in the span of five minutes was more than her brain could take this morning. "I don't believe it."

"Yep, shaving the beard, haircut, the works."

"Don't do it because of Jane."

"Thanks a lot–I'm doing it 'cause I feel like it. Time for a change, now that the show's over and I can change my look. The seventies are ending, you know."

"Not for another two years. And I don't think the seventies will ever end for you."

"Just find out about Jane, will you? Drop a few hints or something."

"No way. I'm not getting in the middle of it."

"You're already in the middle."

"What about Elaine?"

"I broke up with her."

Make that three earth-shattering events. "When?"

"Over the weekend. It just wasn't happening for us. She doesn't even like music."

"Yeah, well, sorry."

"Don't be. Hey, Gallagher ever show up? I forgot to ask yesterday."

Boy, did she. "Yes."

"So where is she?" He was very much out of breath by now. What about all that rock climbing? Despite the cigarettes, Anne's wind seemed to be holding up.

"Asleep, I guess. Jane's bringing her by the Dragon later."

"She's been here since yesterday?" Anne nodded, and he gave her one of his world renowned snorts. "This should be good."

"Well, you're just going to have to wait." They had arrived at the Theatre Arts building. "I gotta go."

"I'll come by later. Don't forget about Jane."

* * *

Shirl was not enthusiastic, and Anne immediately regretted having asked her. But who else could she have asked? Shirl knew her work best, and liked her.

"Of course I'm happy to write you a letter–you'll walk on water by the time I'm through. But are you sure this is really something you should do? Taking a whole semester away from performing? You're really on a roll in the department."

"I don't see the problem. I need the classroom credits anyway, so why not do them in London where I'll be exposed to so much more theatre? It's perfect."

Shirl sighed and lit her pipe. The aroma was nice, not sickly sweet or cloying like the tobacco smoked by so many of her male profs. And the image of Shirl drawing on it seemed fitting in her tiny book-lined office. She had an enormous number of books–piled high on her desk, and in the floor-to-ceiling shelves that lined all four walls, interrupted only by the door and one small curtained window. Very Victorian.

"Look, you can tell me to butt out, but isn't this really about Rae?"

The look on Shirl's face was cautious, but showed genuine concern. Anne couldn't imagine what she was so worried about. Maybe she just didn't understand the situation.

"Well, yes, it's about Rae to some extent. She's going anyway, and she gave me the idea to go too. But I'm going for me, because I think the program would be really interesting."

"And so you can be with Rae." What was she pushing for? Did she really need to hear Anne say it? Okay.

"Well, yeah. Rae and I are lovers. Of course I want to be with her." It was the first time Anne had said it, and it came out more easily than she'd expected. She felt warmed just hearing herself say the words.

Shirl tapped a metal doohickey into her pipe and lit the bowl again. She didn't look at Anne until she was ready.

"Annie, I'm going to say something that I hope you won't hate me for, even though I know you probably will. Please see that it's coming from a good place." Anne's stomach clenched again. What was with her stomach these days? Maybe she had an ulcer. Too much black coffee and Tab. "I like Rae, don't get me wrong. She's smart. And beautiful. But believe me when I tell you that she's always going to look out for herself first, and she gets what she wants no matter what. I just want you to ask yourself how well you really know her."

Anne started to get pissed off. She was tired of people telling her about Rae when she knew her probably better than any of them. "I think I know her pretty well."

"I think you know aspects of her pretty well. Probably very well. But not all of her—only the parts she's shown you. And I'm sure those parts are charming. She's a very charming woman. But Annie, stop to think for a minute about all that you don't know about her. Are you really willing to make such a drastic move without really knowing what you're getting into? Do you even know if she's gay?"

That was a stupid question. "I didn't even know that *I* was gay until a few days ago. And I don't see what labels have to do with it anyway."

Shirl puffed a few more aromatic wafts into the stuffy office air, and eventually laid her pipe in an ashtray. "Okay, look, it's your decision. I care about you, Annie, and I don't want you to get hurt."

Why did people keep saying that? Anne got up to go. "Thanks, but I'll be fine." She still needed that letter. "So can I come by after class for the letter?"

Shirl sighed. "Sure."

"Oh," Anne paused at the door, "I'm bringing someone to class this afternoon. She's looking at Cornell. Is that okay?"

The shower at the pool had a nice strong pressure for once, and Anne stood under the full blast as she tried to cool off. Today's mile had been a real struggle—she was gasping by the halfway mark, and never really hit her stride. All those damn cigarettes. Shit, she'd have to cut back. And find a pool in London. They must have public pools or gyms or something.

She turned back the hot water knob, hoping the cooler spray would get her body temperature down a notch. It felt wonderful, and immediately took her back to the shower at Rae's yesterday–not that yesterday had left her thoughts for a single second anyway. She had some time before she had to meet Gallagher at the Dragon, so she stood there enjoying the feel of her tired muscles under the blast for a while. At least she'd already picked up the paperwork for the trip, having stopped at the Administrative building on the way to the pool. Fortunately, the lines were much shorter in the early morning. Now she just needed about a hundred signatures on various forms.

For right now, though, she needed to collect her thoughts. Yesterday had been just too weird, and she needed a game plan going into today.

Rae hadn't stayed long yesterday, and had behaved herself for the most part as the three of them had engaged in some stilted conversation about the university. Rae had taken the lead, had actually displayed an uncharacteristic interest in Gallagher, and had been downright engaging in asking her about herself and the colleges she was considering. Shirl was right–she could be so damn charming. Irresistible. Anne had occupied herself with putting away her backstage accoutrements, and generally trying to disappear. Then Joey had called, and with Rae and Gallagher steeped in a conversation about Cornell's various colleges, Anne had quickly and quietly told Joey the reason she'd missed the cast party. When Rae had stood and announced that she had to get home, Anne had hoped to steal a moment alone with her by walking her to the car, but Rae had gently insisted that she stay with her guest.

"I'll see you in class tomorrow," she'd said beside Anne at the door. Then she'd kissed Anne full on the mouth, just long enough to fall somewhere between a friendly peck and something more. It had been expertly executed–anyone observing it wouldn't be sure exactly what they'd seen, which was probably the point. And Anne didn't know if Gallagher had witnessed it at all, since when Anne closed the door and turned to face her, Gallagher appeared intent on opening her suitcase.

They'd busied themselves for the rest of the afternoon with gossip from Milburn and the new Bee Gees album. Who would have guessed that old group would have changed their sound so completely and come out with the soundtrack for a movie? Gallagher saw it as a passing fad, but Anne found something original in it, and wondered if this disco sound would be around for a while. When Jane had showed up at around six, the three of them had trudged through the snow to the dining hall, and Gallagher didn't appear to hear Jane's query about where Anne had been all night. Anne had quickly changed the subject after commenting that she'd stayed with a friend.

Anne had been pleased and somewhat relieved to see Jane and Gallagher get along so well. It made sense. They were both exceptionally bright, and the few chinks in their reserve were naturally compatible–they were quirky in similar ways, and shared a wry sense of humor that quickly set up Anne as their foil. They took singular pleasure in making jokes at Anne's expense, fell into the roles almost immediately. Most of all, Jane's presence took the heat off Anne, helped her steer clear of any potential land mines in the conversation. Not all threesomes worked–in fact, when it came to Anne and Gallagher's relationship, there had never been a third person who could comfortably step in–but, thankfully, Jane was just unusual enough to fill out the triangle perfectly.

Anne's exhaustion had finally caught up with her soon after dinner, while Gallagher and Jane had talked about the pre-med program–she'd fallen asleep on top of her bed without even changing out of her clothes. She'd awakened sometime after midnight to find the room dark and quiet, with Gallagher in a sleeping bag on the floor. How long had they sat up talking?

The Dragon was buzzing with caffeine- and smoke-induced hyperactivity when Anne walked in shortly before eleven. Hair still a little damp, she had run the risk of a cold in an effort to get there early enough for a cigarette before Jane arrived. She saw Jenna parked at a corner table, wrapped in a scarf and beret that created a Toulouse-Lautrec effect. Anne helped herself to the self-serve coffee urn, deposited a quarter in the basket beside it, and joined Jenna with a silent prayer that she not be too outrageous when Gallagher showed up.

"I was just reading a review of your show. I had no idea you were such a star," Jenna said as she folded the newspaper and reached out to clasp Anne's hand. "You should have announced the show during class. We all would have come."

Anne pulled back her hand to dig in her backpack for the cigarettes she'd bought that morning. Vantage cigarettes. "Yeah, I didn't think to. Anyway, Rae came." She took a special delight in pointing that out.

"Oh, I'm sure. Rae's such a star fucker."

Now what did that mean? Before Anne could ask, she saw Jane and Gallagher walk in. Shit, have to wait for a cigarette until after Jane leaves.

The introductions were quick, and Anne almost burst out laughing at the predatory once-over that Jenna gave Jane. She hoped Jane hadn't noticed, but knew that was unlikely. There were very few things that Jane didn't notice. Same for Gallagher.

"That woman called this morning," Jane said to Anne. Jane had recently, inexplicably, taken to referring to Rae in this way, no doubt as a token of her disdain. Anne didn't question it–she could have predicted that Jane would dislike Rae, if she'd ever given it a thought. And so what if she did? There was no rule that all of her friends had to like one another. "She woke us up, as a matter of fact."

"Sorry about that," Anne said. "She want anything in particular?"

Jane zipped her parka. "I didn't ask. See you later. Bye Gallagher." Ignoring Jenna, Jane turned and headed out to class.

Gallagher pulled up a chair as Jane left, and Jenna beamed a knowing smile that made Anne's skin crawl. "Rae, I presume?" Jenna asked innocently. Fortunately, she appeared to be leaving too, so Anne was spared the need to kill her.

"I guess," said Anne.

Jenna stood to button her heavy coat. She was one of the few people around campus who didn't don a parka in the cold weather. "Well, I saw her last night, and she said she'd be in class today. She'll have to skip Thursday, though. She's going out of town with Rick for a long weekend."

Anne burned her mouth on the hot coffee that she was sipping, and barely heard Jenna's goodbye. Rae hadn't mentioned anything about a weekend with Rick.

"She seems nice." Gallagher-speak for "I think your friend is weird."

"Want some coffee?" Anne didn't know where to let her eyes rest–not on Gallagher, not on Jenna's retreating back–so she kept them on her apparently fascinating coffee cup and used her tongue to feel around the inside of her scalded mouth. Gallagher went to help herself at the coffee urn, and by the time she returned to the table, Anne was capable of social interaction again–having talked herself into the belief that everything was fine because of course Rae still had to deal with Rick. After all, Anne herself still had to deal with Chris, and why should Rae's relationship be any different? Funny, they'd never gotten around to talking about how they were going to gracefully extricate themselves from their boyfriends. No matter–there were lots of details they'd have to sort through, and they had all the time in the world to do so, now that they were together.

Once Gallagher resumed her seat, Anne had already lit up and offered her the pack. Gallagher seemed to have learned how to inhale in the past few months, and Anne wondered how that had happened–Dennis didn't smoke. Nor did any of Gallagher's other friends, so far as Anne knew. But then, Anne didn't really know Gallagher's friends anymore, and felt a little sad at the realization.

"You and Rae seem awfully close," Gallagher said naturally. Leave it to Gallagher.

"Yeah, we are." And Anne decided then and there that she wasn't going to tell her, not now, maybe never. It was still too new, too precious, to expose to the clear light of day and Gallagher's penetrating gaze.

"Ready for the nickel tour?" Anne asked, forcing some energy into her voice, and Gallagher smiled beautifully. She was so lovely, how could Anne have forgotten?

"Sure."

Sipping their coffee along the way, they hit the major attractions–the quads for the different schools, the administrative buildings, the women's gym, the various libraries–and ended at the main student center, Willard Straight Hall, which served as the social nerve center for the entire campus. Outside the main door stood the Stump–the remains of an old tree that had graced the landing for decades. As Anne explained to Gallagher, although the tree itself had been cut down years ago when it had become diseased, the university had decided to leave the tree stump to mark its demise. Over the years, the Stump had become a central fixture–a podium for speakers at demonstrations, a natural billboard that was regularly painted, decorated and leafleted to advertise various campus events. Today it was painted yellow.

The gorgeous old Willard Straight housed all of the student organizations, as well as a dining hall and a dozen quiet, book-lined reading rooms. Anne confessed that she was learning as much as Gallagher on their walk–she had never explored many of these campus nooks and crannies before. They climbed to the top floor of the old building and roamed through one of its tiny attic hallways, where several of the student groups had offices.

Suddenly, Anne heard a familiar voice call to her through one of the open doorways. She turned to see Brian, a chorus member from the show, seated behind a desk in a cramped little office. Anne didn't know Brian well, but she'd always liked him.

"Hey, Brian," she said, walking into the office. "You survive the cast party?"

"Yeah. Where were you?"

"With a friend." She looked around the tiny gabled office. Quaint. "Hey, what's this office?"

"Cornell Gay Lib. It's my office hours–we take turns." He walked around the desk and held out his hand to Gallagher. "Hi, I'm Brian."

Brian was gay? Anne looked around the room as Gallagher introduced herself to Brian–so much for Anne's Main Line education–and smiled at the sign on the tiny closet door: Can I come out yet?

"I'm sorry I missed your show," Gallagher was saying. "I just got in yesterday."

"Well, it was Anne's show more than anyone else's. I was only in the chorus."

Anne was startled when she felt Gallagher's arm encircle her and give her a quick squeeze around the shoulders. But it felt nice. "I'm sure she was great," Gallagher said. "She always had the lead in our shows back home, too." She left her arm around Anne's shoulder. It still felt nice. "I wish I could have seen it."

Anne broke away to look at some of the flyers on the desk, and then quickly stepped back when she realized what she was reading–flyers about Gay Lib meetings and peer counseling services. Deciding she'd have to come back another time, she turned to Gallagher. "We should probably go if we want to eat lunch before my next class."

Gallagher stepped beside her and lifted one of the flyers from the desk. It advertised a mixer that was taking place the next night. Gallagher smiled at Anne, mischief playing on her face, and turned to Brian. "Well, it was nice meeting you. Maybe we'll see you tomorrow at the mixer."

Anne left Brian's quizzical look unanswered as she followed Gallagher out the door. Once they were sufficiently down the hall, she decided to speak up. "You know, he probably thinks we were making fun of him. With that crack about seeing him tomorrow."

Gallagher laughed and put her arm back around Anne's shoulder. "Oh, come on. How do you know I wasn't serious?"

"Yeah, right."

* * *

They didn't go to the mixer on Wednesday night, although they walked by it as they headed into Collegetown for a round of bar-hopping before Gallagher's return to Philadelphia on Thursday. It was bitterly cold and, bundled in their heavy winter wear, they made their way slowly through the empty campus. When they got to the student center, Gallagher stopped and looked in through the giant arched doors.

"Sure you don't want to stop in? Just one dance?"

Anne was sure that Gallagher was just teasing, but she wasn't in the mood–and didn't feel like explaining why. Rosa and her girlfriend Rebecca walked up just then. Great. Now we'll never get out of here.

"Hey you guys, coming in?" Rosa called out.

"No," Anne jumped in before Gallagher could respond. "We're on our way to Collegetown. You remember my friend Gallagher?"

"Yeah, from class yesterday. Hi–how'd you like it?"

"It was cool," Gallagher said. "The teacher's amazing."

Rosa treated them to her famous belly laugh. "Shirl's a pisser. Listen, we're stopping at the women's coffeehouse on the second floor–a women's band is playing. It's so great to see someone playing a guitar without pretending it's a penis." She winked at Gallagher, who didn't seem to know what to make of Rosa. Few people did. "Sure you won't come for a little while?"

"No, we're going to get drunk."

Rebecca pulled on Rosa's arm. "Come on, honey. It's cold."

"Okay," said Rosa. "Well, see you later."

Gallagher was quiet as they walked over the huge bridge that spanned the gorge separating Collegetown from the rest of the campus. Outside the first bar they came to, they heard the blaring jukebox and shouting patrons all the way into the street, and Gallagher suggested they find somewhere more quiet. They ended up in a dingy townie bar on the other end of Collegetown, far off the beaten student track. It was dark and had only two other patrons, plus the bartender who needed a shave and shampoo. It was perfect–just the kind of place they'd loved to explore back home.

Gallagher bought the first pitcher and steered them to a table in the back. She waited until they were seated before plunging right in.

"You seem to have a lot of gay friends," she said. Typical Gallagher, no pulled punches. Anne wasn't drunk enough for this conversation, however, not yet. She'd sensed that Gallagher was angling for something along these lines ever since yesterday's class, when the discussion had touched on the homoeroticism of certain modern playwrights–and especially since the end of the class, when Rae had pulled her aside to tell her about going away with Rick and kissed her quickly before taking off with Jenna. Well, Anne wasn't entirely sure she was ready to explain it to Gallagher. And she had a feeling that Gallagher knew anyway, was just looking for confirmation.

"Well, I have a lot of friends in the theatre. You know how it is."

Gallagher chewed on that for a minute and nursed her beer. "Is Rae in the theatre too?"

"No, I'm not sure what her major is. Psych, I think."

"She's older, isn't she?"

"Some. She's a junior." Three years older than Gallagher. What will Gallagher be like in three years? Will I still know her?

One of the guys near the front fed the jukebox, and a minute later some country-western song wailed through the bar. This was probably the only jukebox in Ithaca that had country-western music. Gallagher finished her beer and poured herself another, and Anne hurried through her first glass in order to keep up. It was good, and Anne enjoyed the beginning of a buzz. She pulled out her Vantages and offered the pack to Gallagher, who lit up with her. Some of the tension dissipated–it was beginning to feel like old times, and here she was with one of her favorite people on Earth. So why was she unable to think of anything but the silk of Rae's arms?

Anne tried to focus on here and now. "You certainly got the hang of inhaling."

"So did you." Gallagher raised her glass in a toast.

"Remember that first night you tried it–where were we, some dive by the water?" Anne's eyes lit up with remembrance. "Wait a minute, wasn't that the night. . . ."

"Oh, please, don't remind me!"

"Yes, yes! The night you said you were afraid of having an orgasm!"

"I can't believe I said that!" Gallagher was getting giddy, somewhere between embarrassed laughter and just plain laughter. God, she was beautiful when she blushed.

"I hope you've gotten used to more than inhaling since that night!" said Anne.

They laughed some more and refilled their glasses again–must be awfully small glasses–and settled in for some reminiscences. When Anne came back with the second pitcher, the cigarette pack was half empty and they were loose, connected once again in that unique space that they always seemed to create, where everything was funny and okay. It was great to be alive. Anne lit up again. "God, I love the filters on these. Hard little nuggets. You really know you've got something between your lips."

Gallagher smiled as she took the cigarette from between Anne's lips put it between her own. "Hmm, sounds very inviting."

"You know, this was supposed to be a tour of Collegetown hot spots. We're never gonna make it out of here if we finish this pitcher."

Gallagher gave her back the cigarette. "I don't know, this seems like a pretty hot spot to me." She took a sip of beer, clinked her glass to Anne's, and they laughed some more at nothing in particular. It was only then that Gallagher's tone changed, turned to a deeper, more serious chord. "I have to ask you something."

The light seemed to change as well, or maybe it was just a trick of the eye, because Anne could feel the weight of Gallagher steeling herself for something. Gallagher looked at her, cheeks bright red even in this dim light. "I saw her kiss you."

Anne paused to take a sip before responding. "That's not a question."

"I know," said Gallagher. "Give me a minute." She took a shallow breath, refocusing on her beer glass, and Anne's heart raced in the interim. It had been such a fun night. Oh, well.

"Is there something between you and Rae?"

So there it was. Come clean or play word games—what do you mean by "something between us"? Deny it or tell all? Maybe just tell part of it? Anne's mind raced through the possibilities as she stared at her own glass, knowing with dread certainty that her next words could change everything.

"Do you remember that night in the garden?" Anne eventually asked. "Last summer?"

Gallagher looked up, clearly not having expected that. Her "yes" was barely audible.

"I mean, do you ever think about it?" Gallagher nodded and took another sip. "Well," said Anne, "when you do, what do you think about it?"

"I don't know." Gallagher's eyes did a quick circuit of the bar and returned to Anne's. "What do you think about it?"

Anne shrugged and took another sip of beer before looking Gallagher directly in the eye. Go for it. "I think about what might have happened if Sam hadn't come along." There, it was out. Wasn't as hard as she'd imagined it, wasn't hard at all. Just words. Ball's in your court, Gallagher. What are you going to do with it?

Gallagher looked in her beer again, but Anne could have told her the answers weren't in there. "We were both pretty drunk," Gallagher said softly.

So that's how you're going to play it. Should have guessed. But you asked for it, so here it is. "I wasn't that drunk, Gallagher." She stared across the table until Gallagher met her eyes, the beer making it easy to pretend that she felt bolder than she actually was. "And I wasn't drunk at all when I spent the night with Rae."

Gallagher nodded slowly, seemed to be absorbing it, and Anne waited her out, let it register. If there was any chance that they could continue being friends, continue with any part of this relationship intact, then Gallagher had to accept this new information without reservation.

"Do you think you're gay, then?" she finally asked.

Anne smiled. Gallagher was trying to be polite, trying to tread gently. It was going to be all right.

"Yeah, I think I probably am. You okay with that?"

"Sure, I'm okay with that. We're just different, that's all. We don't have to make the same choices to stay friends."

Well, it's more than that, and you know it. I thought I was in love with you for a while there. And thought that maybe you were a little in love with me too. But you're not ready to hear about that, and I'm not drunk enough to say it. Not by a long shot.

Gallagher looked up brightly, her cheeks flaming and the devil in her eye. "So you gonna tell me about it, or what?"

Anne gave her a highly edited version, and they closed the bar.

"Joey? Did I wake you?"

"Anne? Jesus, where are you?"

"Athens. Listen, I have to ask you a favor."

"It's three o'clock in the morning! I'm going back to sleep."

Anne heard a "who is it" on the other end of the line. "Is that Jane?"

"Yeah, she says call back later. I'm hanging up."

"No, wait! It's important."

"Are you okay?" She heard Jane's "is she okay" in the background too, and the tears welled up again. She had known it would hit her hard, as soon as she heard their voices. A man approached her phone booth and said something that could only be lascivious. She should have learned how to say "fuck off" in Greek–in some ways it was more essential than "where's the bathroom."

"Joey, I'm coming back. I need somewhere to stay for the summer."

"What do you mean? You're supposed to be there through August." She heard him filling in Jane, and took the time to try to collect herself. She'd never get it out if she broke down now.

"Stop talking to Jane—you can tell her later. And . . ." she fought to get her voice under control, used the anger that ignited at the sight of yet another man approaching her, used it to help focus herself and get through this phone call. The next one would be even harder.

"Anne, what's wrong?"

She took a breath—God, this heat was murder—and mastered the turmoil enough to begin again. "I'm coming back now. Today. I'll be in Ithaca next week." After a stop in Philadelphia to eat some humble pie with her family and try to find a way of putting her life back together. "Can you put me up?"

"Where's Rae?" he asked. His voice was so gentle, so full of concern, that she began to break down despite the massive effort. Even the sight of the disgusting teenager licking his lips at her from across the street didn't help.

"I don't know. Probably Rome. She's with some guy she met. So can you put me up?"

"Yeah, sure, no problem." He didn't even check with Jane. "Do you need money?"

That was a laugh—Joey never had more than a few dollars to his name. The outrageousness of his offer brightened her considerably.

"No, I'm okay. The travel agent she was sleeping with in Milan got us cheap tickets back to America. So that's one good thing that came out of it. I just picked up mine at the Athens office." Her anger was good, better than tears.

"She's hooked up with a travel agent?"

"Not anymore. I don't know who this new guy is." And I don't want to know. Don't want to see him or her, or anything having to do with her. Not ever.

"What the hell is going on?" He seemed fully awake now. Anne sniffed back the tears and wiped some of the ever-present sweat from her neck. No wonder this place stinks of rotting garbage and unwashed bodies.

"Where do you want me to start? The flight over? She sat on my lap most of the way and told me all about the night she spent with some woman she met right before Christmas. How about the week in February she spent sleeping with an actor from the Royal Shakespeare Company? I was sick in bed with pneumonia and she didn't even know, didn't bother to come back to the flat all week." She was on a roll now, bulldozing through the hurt, on a binge of rage that served as her first real respite from despair in weeks. "I don't want to hear any I-told-you-so's. I just have to get out."

She saw the teenager from across the street start sauntering toward her with a leer on his face and the unmistakable outline of a hard-on in his shorts, and she lost it–let loose at him with a torrent of invective in French, German, and English, her eyes bulging with such ferocity that he cut her a wide swath and passed her by with all due speed. Probably thinks I'm crazy. Which I am. I really am.

"Jesus, what was that?"

"Nothing." The outburst left her depleted, though. Numb. "Listen, I have to make another call. I'll see you in a week?"

"We'll be in the middle of exams here. We're not moving into the apartment until the end of the month." Oh yeah. Exams. Things real people did in the real world. "Jane says you can stay in her room until we move."

"Okay, thanks." She choked up again briefly, but swallowed through it. "I love you guys."

She waited until she was at the airport several hours later before making her next call. What was it, Saturday? Eight a.m. in Philadelphia. She'd be there.

"Gallagher? It's Anne."

"What? Where are you?"

"Athens. At the airport. I'm. . . ." This was proving to be harder, but she had to get through it. At least it was air conditioned in here. "I'm getting on a plane back to the States. Can you pick me up at the airport?"

"You . . . sure, I mean–what's happened?"

"I didn't know who else to call. I can't talk to my parents about it. They won't–they don't know about Rae. I'll have to think of something before I get there."

"I'm glad you called. Of course I'll come." Her voice got softer. "But Annie, are you all right? Talk to me."

She sobbed then, didn't mean to, had tried so hard to hold it together, but the tenderness in Gallagher's voice, the way she said her name, all of it, just reached into her soul and pulled out all the stops. Gallagher let her cry it out, her patience infinite.

As the weeping subsided into intermittent, snuffling hiccups, Anne let out a small laugh, her shredded emotions laid bare. "I'll be better as soon as I get out of this fucking country." Fucking-cunt-Rae.

"You're alone?"

Anne blew her nose on a napkin she found in her pocket. From that taverna on Mykonos, where she'd hung out for the last three days, from four to seven every day, waiting for Rae to walk off each boat that docked. Where she'd turned down the advances of that delightful Australian woman as she sat sipping Retsina and swatting flies, waiting for Rae. Until last night, that is, after she'd gotten Rae's fucking telegram saying she'd be fucking late–no shit, she was already three fucking days late–and was enjoying a marvelous time fucking someone named Luigi. Anne had certainly turned that news into an Australian holiday. She'd taken it out on that woman–the sex raw, intense, totally devoid of anything remotely human but still unbelievably hot. Anne had left her this morning with a kiss and a note to give Rae if she ever showed up. It was a small island.

"Yeah, Rae's gone. Or I'm gone. I'm not sure which."

"Since when?"

She laughed a little. "Since forever, probably. But the last time I saw Rae was in London, about a month ago."

"You mean you've been travelling all this time by yourself?"

In a manner of speaking. But it's funny how not-alone you can be when you hitchhike through Europe. She'd only spent a few days, or even hours, with the various people she'd met along the way, but for the short period they were together these people had been the closest things she had to friends. They knew where she was at any given moment–not even her parents knew exactly where she was, only that she was somewhere in Europe, presumably with Rae, what a laugh–and she had relied on these people, and they on her, to translate directions, find cheap food, deal with the border guards in Yugoslavia. They were certainly more dependable than Rae, these strangers. She sometimes didn't even know their names.

"Rae decided to stay in London and fly to Greece. To meet up with me after I got here."

"Why?"

"Probably had something to do with one of the men she was screwing. Anyway, she didn't show up. At least not yet."

"But isn't she going to?"

"I won't be here if she does. It's over. I'm done." She felt surprisingly good saying it. Empowered, even. That in itself was amazing, given that Rae had been on a steadfast and largely successful mission to suck every ounce of power from her over the past few months. At least it was a start.

"I'm so sorry, Annie."

The sobs threatened to convulse her again. If only she wouldn't call me that, I could handle this call. She breathed deeply and forced it all back down. Maybe she hadn't completely lost everything from her days of performing.

"I know. Listen, they're calling my flight. I'm supposed to land around five your time."

"Okay, I'll be there. I'm supposed to see Dennis tonight, but I'll get out of it."

"You don't have to do that."

"I want to. I want to be with you. Really. And look, you can stay with us if you don't want to see your parents yet. My mother likes you."

"I'll think about it. Thanks. And Gallagher?"

"Yeah?"

"This may sound crazy, but can we go to a hair salon after I land? The first thing I want to do is get my hair cut."

THE NINETIES

Chapter Seven

"I'm sorry, gentlemen, but that's simply not good enough." Anne Henderson's voice cut through the mumblings of the assembled suits, carefully modulated and deadly. It was one of her best assets, well cultivated from years of theatre training, and she used it sparingly, with devastating results. "You've got until 3:00 tomorrow. After that, we file suit." She picked up her satchel. "This discussion is over."

Not waiting for the response that she knew would follow, the display of ego that would rise up to challenge her temerity at being the first to draw the line, she turned her back on the conference table and strode out the door. She had already warned her client that she would probably make a quick exit, so he was prepared and followed on cue. The truth was, she could have stayed and haggled for the remainder of the time allotted for this meeting, but it was pointless–she knew she'd have to issue the ultimatum in the end. Besides, she wanted to get to the pool before the firm cocktail party that evening.

Sue greeted her with a stack of pink message slips as soon as she rounded the corner and headed toward her office. They provided a nice excuse to get rid of her client–he might be the CEO of a multi-billion dollar manufacturing company, but she didn't have time to dally with him just now. Sue saw him out after alerting Anne to the message on top. It was from Walter Driscoll, the managing partner of the firm. Shit.

"I'd like to know what the hell you said in there," he shouted over the speakerphone. Walter never used the receiver–with Anne or anyone else–and she hated it. She also knew it was unnecessary–his hands were free to pick up the phone, but he simply chose not to. It was just one of his little power games.

"I just gave them the lay of the land and outlined their options for them," she said pleasantly. "With a few veiled threats."

"Not so veiled. I just got off the phone with Crocker. He's demanding we give him someone more reasonable to deal with."

Anne laughed. "Be my guest."

"Not on your life. The more they don't want you, the more I do. They'll cave with an hour to spare. Nice work."

She heard the phone go dead before she could acknowledge the compliment, which was about as generous as Walter got. And it meant a lot–especially since she was up for partner this year. If this thing really came off, she would probably get the nod. She leafed through the remaining messages–nothing, nothing, stupid, shit, and nothing–and decided to deal with it all tomorrow. Sue buzzed her with two more calls, and Anne instructed that they be transferred to the associates working under her on the cases. She had to get out of here.

Parker came by as she was gathering her things. The only other openly gay lawyer at the firm–although they had their suspicions about several others–he was tall and gorgeous and ensnared everyone he met in his charismatic web. He reminded her a lot of her old boyfriend Chris–whatever had happened to Chris? Parker had made partner two years ago, and was the loudest member of her cheering section.

"You're stopping by tonight, aren't you? I can't face it alone."

"Yeah, yeah. God, I hate these things."

"Come on, where's your team spirit?"

"Give me a break," she said. "We pay these kids a fortune for doing practically nothing during eight weeks in the summer, just to try to convince them to let us pay them a fortune for being associates next year, and on top of it all we have to wine and dine them."

"It's the way the game works. We just want to put a friendly face on the firm. Let them think we're not all work and no play."

"Bait and switch," she huffed. "Anyway, I've got to get out of here. If I don't make it to the gym soon I'll be waiting forever for a lane." She threw her gym bag over her shoulder. "If anyone's looking for me, tell them I died."

Parker followed her down the hall. "By the way, I hear you sewed up that Rattinger negotiation pretty tight. They didn't know what hit them."

Anne checked her watch. "That was less than an hour ago. Does anything happen around here that you don't know about?"

He straightened his tie, which was already perfect. "Not if I can help it. I have a reputation to maintain, after all."

The reception was in a trendy yuppie bar on the East Side. Manhattan was full of them, dark doors in the middle of the block that were easily overlooked if not for the incongruous red rope set up on the sidewalk, seeming to rope off nothing, yet guarded by a husky bouncer who was always dressed in black. Whoever picked these places, Anne was sure it wasn't any of the attorneys–no one she knew had the time or inclination to scout out these obscure haunts.

Anne slid through the bodies crowded in the stairwell–on top of it all, the place was underground, and she had to negotiate the stairs in high heels. Smart. She made her way to the bar.

"Any non-alcoholic beer?"

"Sorry," the bartender said, looking as bored as Anne felt.

"Let me have a Diet Coke."

Parker found her as she scanned the assembly with half an eye–her other half was on her watch as she wondered how long she was expected to stay. She was still annoyed that she had arrived at the pool too late to get a lane. Maybe she could cut out of here early and squeeze in some laps.

"There you are," he said as he nudged in beside her. "I need another drink. None of the boys are even cute this year. What are you having?"

"Diet Coke."

"Boring." He turned to the bartender and flashed him the million-dollar smile. How did he get his teeth that white? "Vodka tonic. With lime." He turned back to Anne and said in a stage whisper, "He's my type."

"If it has a pulse, it's your type."

"Any girls catch your eye?"

Anne killed him with a look. "Not funny. I don't shit where I eat." He snorted and took the drink that the bartender scooted over to him. "Besides," she continued, "I'm old enough to be their mother."

"Not exactly. Anyway, you've got to live a little. You don't drink, you don't smoke, you don't screw around. We've got to find you some vices."

Anne shook her head. She really did like Parker, and he was a godsend at a party like this, even if he did always make it a personal crusade to corrupt her. "I used up my quota a long time ago. You do the indulging for me. I'll watch."

"That's all you ever do, Anne. You stand by and watch."

"You're full of shit."

"Really. You go up to the edge, but never really cross the line, like you're on the verge of living without really doing it."

"My, aren't we philosophical tonight."

"You can joke, but I mean it. If only you lived your life the way you fight in court, now that would be living."

Anne sighed. "I've had enough therapy for one night. I'm going to find some normal people to talk to."

He leaned back against the bar and eyed the bartender off to the side. "You do that, dear. Let me know if you find any."

She was supposed to meet her "little sister" somewhere in this throng. The whole sibling system was a little too cutesy for her taste. It reminded her of her Milburn days, when the freshmen had each been assigned a senior in the Upper Main to act as the "big sister," responsible for showing them the ropes and serving as a sort of mentor. In the same spirit of one big happy family, idiotic as that was, Farnsworth Crowley assigned each summer associate to a senior attorney for the summer. And, ever conscious of the potential for sexual harassment issues to arise even in the most innocent of circumstances, the pairing of siblings didn't cross gender lines–even in the cases of Parker and Anne, despite the obvious incongruity. Go figure.

Dee-Dee Hart, the director of recruiting, found Anne by the fruit bowl. Anne had often thought that she was probably destined for this cruise-director of a job when her parents had heartlessly given her the name Dee-Dee. Her only function was to organize parties to make the firm look good. Right now, she had a clipboard in hand and a look of utter exasperation on her face.

"There you are, Anne. Okay, I have you assigned to . . ." she checked her list. Gee, what a fun party for her. "Emily Simmons. She's already picked up her name tag, so you should be able to find her. Short, brunette, blue suit." How original.

"Okay, I'll find her."

"And wait a minute. Alice Gray is on trial in Denver, so if you don't mind, I'd like to assign her little sister to you. Temporarily, of course. Just until Alice gets back."

"Does that mean I have to do two lunches this week? Can I just combine them?"

Dee-Dee gave her an iron look. This cruise director could morph into Cruella DeVil on a dime. "Forget it," she said as she consulted her clipboard again. "Name's Elizabeth Rachel Evans."

"She has three names?" Give me a break.

"So it seems. Take each of the summers to a separate lunch, minimum hour and a half each. We need to give them the personal touch." She was off before Anne could laugh in her face.

Anne turned back to the fruit bowl–where did they find such delicious strawberries this early in the summer?–and was accosted by three junior associates who sometimes worked for her. Darryl was already three sheets to the wind.

"Fearless leader," he said, "word is you slayed the Rattinger dragon today single-handed."

"Don't believe everything you hear," Anne responded. "Hey, any of you seen some summers named Emily Simmons and Elizabeth Evans?"

Amanda picked out a peach from the fruit bowl. "Who'd you piss off to get tagged with two little sisters?" She bit the peach, made a sour face, and put it back in the bowl.

Anne removed the peach and handed it back to her with a smile. "Tell me about it. And don't leave your leftovers for the guests to munch on, huh? We're pretending we're civilized tonight."

Amanda appeared more than a little mortified and slunk back behind Darryl, who laughed.

"Hey, listen," Darryl said, "I got a call from Don Moore over at Morex." He sounded very pleased with himself that Don would have placed a call to him. No doubt Sue had just transferred the call from Anne's line after she'd left for the gym. "He's got to talk to you first thing in the morning."

"What's he want?" asked Anne. Probably just to shoot the breeze. They'd known each other for years, ever since he and her old college buddy Joey had formed that computerized music company back in the mid-eighties. The company had grown astronomically over the last ten years, and even though Joey was long since out of it, Anne and the firm had continued to handle all of their legal work, which by now was no small feather in Anne's cap. But more important than being a major client, Don was a friend—one of the few clients whom Anne genuinely liked.

"He wouldn't say. Says he needs to speak directly to you. But he sounded kind of anxious." Darryl put on his most ass-kissing smile. "You know, if there's anything I can do to help, I'd really love to work on more Morex stuff."

So that was it. Darryl was the consummate political law firm associate—ingratiating himself with the people who handled the most interesting matters, attaching himself wherever possible to the heroes of the day, all in an effort to move up through the ranks and catch the eye of the power brokers who could make or break his career. He was reputed to be ruthless with the associates working under him—pushing the menial or difficult work onto their backs while he left the office by six every night, taking credit for their good work and holding up the delegation excuse when the shit hit the fan. He had an uncanny sense of when to duck and when to stand up to take credit, and it fooled a lot of people.

But not Anne. She'd seen many associates fall by the wayside over the years for employing precisely the same tactics. Several of the partners at Farnsworth Crowley had undoubtedly gotten their start in the same way, but they were the ones who most quickly recognized the barracudas for what they were, and were the first to cut them down.

By contrast, Anne's success had been almost accidental–she had never really thought she'd have a long-term future at such a large firm, and so she had developed relationships with clients and partners over the years based solely on the ridiculous premise of doing good work and being a decent person. She was hard on the juniors, it was true, but she was harder on herself and everyone knew it. She'd routinely stay long after most of her subordinates had gone home for the night–checking their work, improving it, making it right. Being a perfectionist was a significant drawback for her social life, but a real plus in her work. Associates strove to please her–and learned a lot in the process. And she never hoarded the glory, recognizing that there was always plenty to go around. Besides, loyalty runs both ways, and associates who received their share of the credit were always eager to do more work for her, and do it well. The result was that partners valued her work product, and many clients insisted that she run their cases.

Darryl was bright-eyed and nearly salivating at the prospect of hooking himself up to a new Morex case. She'd only staffed him on one small research matter a few months ago, and he obviously felt that he'd earned the right to take on more responsibility with this client.

"Let's just see what he wants," said Anne, "and we'll go through the appropriate channels if we need to put together a team for anything." Parker was the assignment partner responsible for doling out the work of the younger associates. She could hide behind him, and planned to if necessary. Anne hoped her dismissal of Darryl wasn't too obvious–and given his inebriated state, it didn't appear to be.

Amanda poked her head around Darryl's shoulder and asked, "Who were those summers you were looking for? Someone named Simmons is standing over there." She cocked her head in the direction of the hors d'oeuvre table a few feet away.

Anne located the woman. "Gotta run, gang. Duty calls."

She heard Darryl's mumbled "duty's the only thing that calls her" as she scooted through a few groups and came up beside the young woman, who looked about twelve.

"Emily Simmons?" asked Anne. The woman nearly jumped out of her skin. She was dressed and coifed in the standard lawyer fashion–short brown hair professionally styled, unremarkable navy blue business suit–but it was all just a little off. The suit didn't quite fit, her lipstick extended just a tad over the lipline. She automatically stuck out her hand for a handshake, her arm extended in a straight line from her shoulder as if it were a lance, and Anne tried to keep a friendly smile on her face. This was such bullshit.

"I'm Anne Henderson, your big sister. Sorry I couldn't find you sooner in all this crowd."

"Very pleased to meet you." Oh, brother. "Are you an attorney?"

No, we pair up the summers with the guys in the mailroom. "Yes, in litigation. Are you interested in litigation?"

"Not really." Great. "I don't really know anything about it."

"Well," said Anne patiently, "that's sort of the idea of the summer program. You can rotate through lots of different practice groups and get the feel for what everyone does." Emily stared at her blankly. Maybe Anne was speaking Martian by mistake. "To see what you'd like to do. See what fits."

The music started up, loud. Why do they always think that loud music makes a party? As if we came here to dance. The two of them stood side by side for a moment, Anne secretly relieved that the music had put on hold any more awkward conversation for now. The room was far too crowded, and Anne wondered why they couldn't hold one of these functions in a more accommodating space–maybe with lights bright enough to see people, music low enough to talk, and sufficient floor space to let people move around comfortably. A tall blonde woman walked by just then, and Anne couldn't help but notice her. She appeared older than the rest of the summers, and was absolutely stunning. She wasn't one of the attorneys at the firm, that was certain. Intrigued, Anne considered looking for Dee-Dee to ask about her, when she remembered that she was obligated to baby-sit Emily for the evening.

Anne turned to the twelve-year-old by her side and suggested they head over to the buffet table for some of the food on which the firm had spent thousands of dollars. Anne didn't touch anything but the salad–she still hoped to make it to the pool later tonight–and noted that Emily did the same. They set up shop standing by one of the pillars near the bar, and Anne delivered some of her routine recruiting patter between bites of arugula. She was running out of steam when Parker walked up to them with another Diet Coke for her. Relieved, she considered marrying him.

"Anne dear," he said, "I've got someone here I want you to meet." As he stepped aside to let someone join their circle, Anne looked up to behold the face of the tall blonde she'd noticed earlier, and froze on the spot. Her face was even more beautiful up close, and Anne found it difficult to breathe for a second. "Anne, this is Elizabeth Rachel Evans." He gave Anne a quick wink that could have been an eye twitch if Anne didn't know him better. "Elizabeth, this is one of our star litigators, Anne Henderson. I believe you're temporarily paired up until Alice Gray gets back in town." Oh my God.

"It's just Rachel," the woman said. "I don't use my first name."

Well, that was something. Anne held out her hand and felt a firm, confident handshake as she stared into the blank face before her. Although utterly devoid of expression, Rachel Evans's face was somehow mesmerizing–fine chiseled cheekbones, square jaw, and unusual, almost violet eyes. The overall effect was breathtaking and, worst of all, she was a dyke. Anne was sure of it.

It was more than just the handshake, and more than the short layered haircut that was just this side of stylish. It was something in her no-non-sense manner, the boldness of her frank stare, that set off all the buzzers on Anne's lesbo-meter. Anne sized her up in two seconds flat and closed the door–this was definitely someone worth getting to know, if she'd met her anywhere else. As it was, she was someone to avoid at all costs.

"You're a litigator?" Rachel asked Anne. Of course she had a wonderful voice, too–low and resonant. Controlled. Get away from her fast.

"Yes," said Anne. "And this is Emily Simmons, my little sister for the summer." No time like the present to start drawing some lines. "Have you two met?"

Rachel gave Emily the same flat-walled stare and nodded. "Yes, hello again." She returned her attention to Anne, who felt its weight acutely. "I'm very interested in litigation. I'm looking forward to rotating through your department." Of course.

Parker saved her again, God bless him. "I hate to break up the soiree, but Anne, we'll want you to say a few words about the Oronco trial." He flashed Rachel a captivating smile to which she appeared immune. "We like to parade out the superstars at these events. You understand." With a promise to return her shortly, he marshaled Anne onto the dance floor where a microphone had been set up. The three or four people who had been awkwardly dancing moved to the side when the music faded, and Parker couldn't resist taking a jab at Anne as Dee-Dee called for everyone's attention.

"Guess you lucked out, honey," he whispered. "She's incredible."

"Don't start."

Dee-Dee called him to the mike, and Parker delivered some welcoming remarks before introducing Anne. She didn't appreciate the cheering cat calls she heard from Darryl amidst the polite applause as she stepped up and quickly organized her thoughts. It was short and sweet, just a few highlights from the trial she'd won last year against a major pharmaceutical supplier that had stolen some trade secrets from her client. Parker shared the mike and filled in some of the more colorful details, including a lively recital on how Anne had cross-examined the opposition's expert with such devastating precision that he'd eventually ended up doing a 180-degree turnaround and conceding his client's liability. The summers probably didn't understand half of it, but the laughter and applause from the attorneys signaled that whatever it was she'd done, it had been quite a feat.

Exiting the spotlight as quickly as possible when Walter Driscoll started his little speech, she headed for the bar to refill her Diet Coke, and wondered if she would be too wired to sleep tonight if she made it to the pool by nine. As the bartender slid her glass to her, she sensed someone standing behind her. She knew who it was even before turning around.

"Sounds like an interesting case," Rachel said. Her face was still a mask, her eyes still unwavering as they bored holes into Anne, but then she suddenly smiled, just a slow small one, and her face was completely transformed into something alive, animated. Engaging, even. Get out of here.

"It was," was all Anne could think to say. She didn't want to talk to this woman.

"Fun, too?"

That was odd, coming from a summer associate. Anne knew that she was unusual among her colleagues in considering her work to be fun. Trial work was generally regarded as the icing on the cake, the most enjoyable aspect of a litigator's life, but few people would call it fun. And she never expected some wet-behind-the-ears law student to see the thrill in it. She returned Rachel's look and felt the ice begin to melt just a bit. Maybe they could be friends after all.

"Yeah, it was a lot of fun."

Rachel kept her eyes glued to Anne's–didn't she recognize the line beyond which a glance in the eye became an uncomfortable stare?–and Anne broke contact to sip her soda.

"The wine's not very good," said Rachel as she put her wineglass on the bar.

"I wouldn't know. But I'm surprised. They usually go all out for these things. Are you some kind of wine connoisseur?"

Rachel shook her head. "Hardly. I just know what I like. I guess I never acquired much of a taste for beer or hard stuff."

She was so formal, so proper, that Anne realized she must be terribly uncomfortable herself. And Anne wasn't helping any. It wasn't Rachel's fault that she was so beautiful. Anne decided then and there that she would try to befriend her, at least not push her away too emphatically. Make it easy on the kid, although exactly how much of a kid she was remained a bit of a mystery. Rachel's age was hard to figure–certainly older than her classmates, but considerably younger than Anne's thirty-seven years.

"Look, how about we try to have lunch later this week?" Anne suggested. "You know, our summer sibling welcome-to-the-firm lunch. Say, Thursday?"

Rachel's face lit up again, but then immediately iced over with formality, as if she were embarrassed at exposing herself, letting an emotion seep through.

"That would be very nice. Thank you."

"I'll have my secretary set it up. Might as well take advantage of the lavish lunches Farnsworth Crowley's famous for forcing on us. And you never know when you'll get another chance to escape the office in the middle of the day."

Anne got to the Reservoir a few minutes early and started in on some stretching to loosen the kinks in her legs. If only she'd been able to get to the pool last night, she wouldn't have felt the need for a run this morning, but the party had dragged on far too late, due mostly to Parker's incorrigible intercession. He meant well, but his constant matchmaking was growing very old.

The truth was, she didn't like to admit that he might be right about her reluctance to plunge spread-eagle into things. Most days it was easy to lose herself in her work and forget that living could offer anything other than stimulating intellectual challenges. And the time and energy that her career demanded–no, tell the truth, that she willingly gave to her career, whether or not it was demanded–left very little for anything else.

She'd tried over the years, albeit halfheartedly. Her relationship during law school had been comfortable, at least for her, but she'd thrown herself into her studies so fully that she didn't even notice that Lorraine had been unhappy until they were way past the point of salvaging anything. And that magazine editor she'd met at the gay Ivy League group–she'd been a pleasant diversion for about eighteen months. But that was just it–she was really just a distraction, someone who periodically took her away from what Anne considered to be her real life, her work life. She couldn't help it if her career was a priority; it was simply the way she was. It was fulfilling, exciting, didn't argue with her, and was always there–what more could anyone ask?

Gallagher jogged up in a tasteful running outfit, looking as magnificent as ever. Anne didn't care enough about her own appearance to don anything other than running shorts and an old tee shirt.

"I'm glad you called," said Gallagher. "I was hoping I'd get in a run this week, and I hate coming into Central Park alone in the morning."

"I needed it today. I was stuck at this work thing too late to get to the pool yesterday." Anne finished her stretching. "Shall we?"

Gallagher started them off at a relaxed pace. The track around the Reservoir was well populated at this hour, all the yuppie exercise junkies clamoring for their fix before hitting the office for a fourteen-hour day. They passed a pair of beauty queens donning headphones, and settled in at a leisurely half-run–they'd save the sprints for the end.

"Besides," Anne tried to regulate her breathing, "I wanted to get out of the house before the morning news came on."

"You can always leave the TV off, you know." Gallagher had great breath control, able to run and talk without ever seeming to need extra air. Anne, with the shorter legs, had to work a little harder to keep up, and was saved from overtly gasping only by the fact that she was in such top form due to her swimming. Gallagher ran only once a week–how did she do it?

"I make a point of leaving it off," said Anne. "I know it's stupid, but just knowing the news is on makes me want to get out."

Gallagher laughed. "I got stuck on a new financing deal last night until ten. It never stops, as soon as I finish one project there are ten more lined up waiting for me. I think I'll just quit and become a teacher."

"You keep threatening, but you never do it. You'd be a great teacher. But what would the investment banking world do without you?"

"Survive somehow. I think Joel would prefer it too–he was really pissed off about last night."

"So what else is new." Ever since Gallagher had moved to New York two years ago to take this hot-shit position with one of the world's biggest investment banks, Anne had been hearing about Joel's grumblings. She was sure he just had an ego problem with the fact that Gallagher was so successful, made more money than he did, and had relocated the two of them because of her high-roller career. He seemed to have an ego problem about most things, in Anne's opinion. Despite his ambivalence about Gallagher's career, he also seemed to revel in it–Anne suspected that one of the reasons Gallagher continued working so hard at something she didn't particularly like was that Joel enjoyed the fruits of her success. He'd probably explode if she announced one day that she was leaving the firm to become a grade-school teacher.

Anne just couldn't understand why Gallagher stayed with him when she was so obviously unhappy. She said he was stable. Maybe that was true–it was certainly the longest relationship she'd known Gallagher to have had since high school–but at what cost? Maybe Gallagher was always this conflicted about her boyfriends. Anne wouldn't know–she'd never had the chance to get to know any of the others, the relationships were so brief.

Anne was careful never to voice her more negative views about Joel–at least not to Gallagher. Well, at least not very often. After all, they were engaged–this was the man her friend was going to marry–and Anne felt duty-bound to support her in the relationship, even if she really didn't think it was a good thing.

"I got a card about a big Milburn reunion at the end of July. Are you going?" Gallagher was so tactful about changing the subject. Some things never changed.

"I don't know. I was thinking of going up to my place on the Cape to chill out for a few days sometime around then. Work permitting, of course." Anne had bought the little condo in Provincetown four years ago, after the breakup with Ellen, the magazine editor, and had come to rely on it as a calm little sanctuary from the frenzy of her work life. She tried to get there every six weeks or so for a mental health break. It didn't always work out–her schedule was not so easy to plan.

"I wish I could have gone with you that time in January. It would have been nice to see it, it sounds so great the way you talk about it."

"It is. Especially off-season." Anne wished she could have come too. Very much so.

"I was just going through such a rough time with Joel. He would have had a fit if I'd just taken off with you like that."

Of course he would. Because Gallagher's not allowed to have a life apart from him. Anne kept her mouth shut.

"Mmm, smell that?" asked Anne. "What is it, honeysuckle?" Anne loved the park in late June, with the trees and bushes lining the Reservoir in full blossom. She loved how the runners' circuit along the track took them through wafts of different fragrances along the way.

"I think so. Or maybe cherry blossoms. Reminds me of the pond at Milburn."

Anne laughed. "Yeah, didn't you kill all the goldfish in that pond during the prom one year? When you dumped in a whole bottle of gin to get rid of it before one of the chaperones came by?"

"That was you, not me."

"Oh no, it was you all right," said Anne. "I remember it very well. You had on this floor-length blue dress." You looked incredible.

"Your memory is scary. Every lawyer I know has an amazing memory, but yours is really unbelievable."

"You only say that because I remember all your secrets."

She saw Gallagher smiling by her side. "That's what makes you so dangerous."

Anne laughed and ran on in companionable silence, enjoying the feel of her legs pumping and heart pounding steadily, enjoying the pleasure of having Gallagher beside her. Gallagher had once remarked that they could go years without seeing each other and then pick up right where they'd left off in the middle of a conversation. That's practically how it had been when she'd called that day two years ago to say she was moving to New York. They hadn't seen each other for, what was it, probably a year and a half, but they'd immediately fallen back into their friendship without missing a beat. The only time it faltered was when Joel was with them, but that was rare. He didn't appear to like Anne very much, and she certainly didn't like him. Gallagher seemed to sense it all and preferred to see Anne alone. Even now, they only saw each other once every few weeks–Gallagher usually did her running alone after work or with Joel–but they always picked up where they'd left off when they got together.

"Well, if you decide to go to the reunion, I can give you a lift," Gallagher said, and then paused for a minute. "Joel's not coming."

"Really? How come?"

"Oh, the usual. He thinks it's bourgeois or something. I think he just doesn't want to feel out of place, and that's fine with me. I'll have a better time without him."

"I understand how he can feel like that–Milburn's just one big clique."

"I know. But it's so stupid. He doesn't even make the effort, acts like my family and friends are these totally alien things that have nothing to do with me, as if he expects me to choose between him and everyone else all the time. I just don't understand what's the big deal. He acts like it's a competition or something."

Yep, that about sums it up. As long as Gallagher was opening up like this, Anne figured she might as well get one card out on the table. "And he doesn't particularly like me, I don't think."

Gallagher was quiet for a moment. "No, I don't think he does. But it's not you, it's me. I think it's that he doesn't like anyone who could be so important to me."

Yeah, well, he's a guy.

"I try not to talk about you too much. I've been with him for four years, and all he really knows about you is that we went to prep school together and now we live in the same city. But he's still threatened by you. I guess I can't blame him, though. You *are* important to me." She shook out her arms. "Ugh, I don't know. It just bothers me."

"Well, anytime he wants to get to know me, I'm here." Anne tried to make her voice light, amiable, but couldn't tell if it worked. "Of course, maybe he just isn't comfortable with lesbians." Let's see where that one goes.

"I don't think it's that. But he can be so weird about some things, so who knows?"

Anne was certain that Gallagher had never said anything to him about their high school flirtations. Hell, in all these years, she'd never mentioned it even when they were alone together. Or did the subject come up that night they went drinking in Ithaca, back when she was in college? She couldn't really remember, but probably not. Anne was pretty sure she had come out to Gallagher that night, told her about Rae, since Gallagher seemed to know by the next morning. But all Anne could really recall from that night was trying to remember the lyrics to some Iron Butterfly song, and laughing hysterically over a pool-hopping adventure they'd had one summer. Whatever else had been said, it was long since forgotten between them, had never happened. And Anne was certain that the burial of that whole weird phase in their relationship had a lot to do with the fact that they were still close today–what was it?–some twenty years later.

"Wow, you realize we've been friends for over twenty years?" Anne asked. It just popped out. Whenever she was with Gallagher, there always seemed to come some moment when she let her guard slip a notch, where the filter between her brain and her mouth became porous.

"Yeah, I know, I was thinking about that recently. How it's so good for me to have you in my life, someone who remembers me back when I was a fun person."

Anne laughed. "Oh, don't kid yourself. You were never fun."

Chapter Eight

"Don? It's Anne Henderson. What's going on?" she said as she cradled the phone with her neck and pulled a blank notepad onto her desk. She could dispense with the pleasantries with him. They'd known each other too long to waste time with polite inquiries about each other's families–especially since his wife had left him three years ago and, as he knew very well, Anne was happily single.

"Major shit, that's what. We've been sued by every major record label and most of their top artists. I want you to put together a team that can meet with us tomorrow around three o'clock."

"Send me the complaint."

"The messenger's on the way. Anne," his voice had an edge she didn't recognize–he actually sounded scared. What the hell was going on? "I really need your help on this. You know the business, you know the industry. This could kill us."

"Relax, we'll take care of it. Don, look, you want to get together today for lunch? I can do a quick assessment once I get the papers, and we can talk about it, maybe put your mind at ease somewhat. You sound like you could use a friend."

He sighed audibly. "I need a good lawyer too. Lucky for me you're both. But I've got meetings up the wazoo today with the board of directors. This is major, Anne. And you might think about tapping some of your bankruptcy people while you're at it. It may come to that."

Jesus! "Not if I can help it," she said, scribbling some notes. "I'll have Sue set up the meeting and confirm with your office. Take a deep breath, Don. Whatever it is, we'll handle it."

"Shit, I should have let Joey buy me out instead of the other way around."

Anne laughed. "Yeah, I can just see you as a ski bum."

"Beats the hell out of this. Anyway, rain check on that lunch. I gotta run."

"See you tomorrow."

Anne hung up the phone and alerted Sue to the impending arrival of a messenger from Morex–she should bring in the package immediately. After flipping through the new crop of message slips–how could they build up so fast? It was only nine in the morning–she walked over to Parker's office, noticing on the way that two of the new summers had been given offices down the hall from her. Rachel Evans was furiously typing at the computer in one of the offices, and Anne wondered how she'd gotten underway so quickly. Hadn't they just started this morning?

"I'm not responsible for anything I said last night under the influence," said Parker as Anne walked into his office. "Unless, of course, it was witty." Parker was seated behind his immaculate desk and looked like an advertisement for corporate America.

"Don't you do any work around here?" she asked. "My desk is buried in paper, and you don't even have a notepad on yours."

"I'm organized. And, of course, I palm off all my work to senior associates like you."

"Speaking of which, Morex has a new case that we're going to have to get up to speed on right away. They're sending the paperwork over now. I need a team–one midlevel, not Darryl, two juniors." She thought of Rachel a few doors down. "One of the juniors could be a summer associate, if necessary. Might be interesting for them."

Parker's grin was wolfish. "Any particular summer you have in mind?"

She frowned at him. "You pick. Just make sure it's someone who's capable. This is going to be big."

He was all business now. "I'll take care of it. When do you want a team meeting?"

"Get me the names by noon. I'll have Sue distribute the file and the team can meet around two."

"Why not Darryl?"

"He wants it too much, for all the wrong reasons. How about Grady?"

Parker checked his list of work assignments on the bulletin board beside his phone. Anne often made fun of his position as assignment partner, but she knew that it wasn't an easy task, and he carried it off with aplomb. The way he carried off everything else.

"Grady should be available," he said. "He's doing papers on a preliminary injunction right now, so it'll be a crunch for him for the next week, but hey, that's life in the big city."

"Grady's fine. You figure out the juniors. I don't care."

"Want some partner backup on this one?"

"You offering?"

"Only if you need it. I'm under water for the next few weeks."

"Let's see how it goes. I haven't even read the papers yet. Besides," Anne leaned on his desk with both hands, "I fully expect to be a partner myself by the time it ever goes to trial."

Parker laughed. "You'll be managing partner by then."

Sue knocked on her door at five past two. "You're late," she said.

"Shit. Tell Grady to start talking about research assignments. I'll be there in a minute." Anne put the complaint on top of the stack of papers and searched for the pad on which she'd scribbled some preliminary notes. Don was right–this was going to be a major lawsuit. It had career-maker written all over it, and it was hers. For now it looked manageable, but she was grateful for Parker's offer of assistance. She just might need to call in some reinforcements. She found the notepad, placed it on top of the stack she lifted from her desk, and marched down the hall. She'd forgotten to ask Sue who had been assigned to the team. It didn't matter.

Or maybe it did. She walked into the conference room to find Rachel seated next to what would have been Anne's seat at the head of the long table. Anne nodded to Grady and walked to the seat at the end opposite Rachel.

"Amanda, Grady, you've met Rachel, I assume?" They nodded. "Okay, let's get started. First off, I want to remind you guys about confidentiality. I know you've heard it before, but it bears repeating. Nothing, absolutely nothing about this case leaves this office. You don't take any papers home with you, you don't talk about it with friends outside the firm, you don't even talk about it on a phone outside the firm, including a cell phone.

"As you can see from the names in the caption, this is a very big deal, and it's bound to attract a lot of media attention. As soon as the firm's name appears on any of the papers in the court file, we're going to start getting press calls. If you get a call, don't even tell them the time of day–just transfer it to my office immediately." She smiled. "Sue's good at getting rid of the press. Oh, and that reminds me, Grady, get on the horn with the other side and get us an extension on our time to respond. Draft up a stip for my signature and we'll get it filed."

Grady was busy taking notes. Anne ignored Rachel and turned to Amanda on her right. "Amanda, I want you to get everything you can on the lawyers for the other side," she flipped through the complaint, "a guy named Bolton out of some Minneapolis firm. Have it on my desk by five today. And who's our judge?" She turned to the first page. "Marks? Pull all of his intellectual property decisions–trademark, copyright, licensing, the works. I'd like a detailed analysis of his cases an hour before the client meeting tomorrow. That means two o'clock sharp. If you find there are too many for you to handle, get Rachel to help. You two work it out." Anne noted with a little annoyance that Rachel hadn't taken a single note. She'd better have a good memory.

"Okay, Grady, we're ready for substantive defenses. What have you come up with so far?"

She turned the meeting over to Grady, who had done a good job of pre-liminarily identifying the weaknesses in the complaint and spotting issues that could provide the basis for a motion to dismiss, depending on what the research turned up. She had him dole out the research assignments, and noted with tacit approval the fact that he kept the hardest, least glamorous ones for himself. He had the makings of a fine senior lawyer–he was willing to pitch in and do his share, and had the requisite people skills to make his subordinates comfortable in working for him.

Once Grady had concluded his analysis and Anne was ready to adjourn the meeting, Rachel piped up from the other end of the table. Anne could see that she'd written less than a page of notes, and wondered if there may be a problem here.

"I have a question." Although Rachel's voice was clear and strong, her downcast eyes suggested a measure of deference. It was hard to tell if she was even aware of the fact that the most junior person at a meeting wasn't really expected to speak up. She looked at Anne then, apparently waiting for permission to proceed–or maybe just waiting for confirmation that she did indeed have the floor. Anne nodded.

"Well, isn't there a possibility of a counterclaim here? I mean, the complaint lists a bunch of things that these recording artists have done to stop Morex from providing online public domain music, not just the copyrighted stuff, before they brought this lawsuit. Morex has lots of subscribers–I went online a little while ago to check out their site myself. It seems to me that the record companies and bands are doing more than just trying to get out of their contracts. They're trying to shut down Morex altogether, and the things they've been doing have probably interfered with Morex's subscriptions."

"That's an excellent point," Anne said, truly impressed. Where did this kid come from? "Take a look at it and see what you can come up with. We'll raise it at the meeting tomorrow. I want you there."

Amanda looked like she'd swallowed a lemon, and Grady made some more notes on his pad.

"Anything else?" Anne asked. Silence. "Okay, we're out of here. Grady, can you come to my office?"

Anne waved away Sue and her fistful of message slips as she led Grady into her office and shut the door. "I wanted to talk to you privately about this case for a minute. Have a seat." She walked behind her desk, unloaded the stack of papers onto its surface, and moved to the window to open the blinds. Sue always closed them when Anne was out, to stop the sun from streaming through and heating up the office uncomfortably. Like every other enormous skyscraper in Manhattan, the building had hermetically sealed windows that could not open–probably to prevent suicides, Anne thought in her more frustrated moments–and the individual offices had no separate thermostats. As a result, the temperature in Anne's office throughout the day could fluctuate uncontrollably from a chilly sixty to a sweltering eighty. Anne hated not being able to open her windows–to smell real air, or just to cool off–but she had to admit that the views of Central Park, and that peek of the Hudson in the distance, made up for it. She liked her office.

Anne took a seat beside Grady on the visitor side of the desk, preferring the informality of a side-by-side discussion. Grady needed to loosen up a little.

"Grady, I asked for you to be put on this case, even though you may be jammed up over the next week with your preliminary injunction. This case is too important to let anything slide." She saw the eager denial he was about to throw in, and held up her hand. "And I know you wouldn't do that, but you'd kill yourself in the process. I want you alive for the duration. So if you're having any trouble getting it all done, let me know right away. I'm here to help. And to that end, I'm taking the jurisdictional issue off your hands right now. I'll do it. If there's more than either of us can handle, we'll expand the team if we have to. Okay?"

He nodded while writing a few more notes. "Sure. That'll be great."

She lounged back in the chair a little and wished for the millionth time that she could wear slacks to the office. The firm had not yet jumped on the "business casual" bandwagon, but many of the lawyers were pushing for it, including Anne. Several of the clients had adopted such a policy, and she always felt awkward attending meetings in their offices and being the only person in a suit. She was used to being the only woman–never even noticed it anymore–but being the only person in uncomfortable shoes was a real drag.

"I meant what I said about the press, too. You're going to have to be on top of that, since your name will probably be on some of the court filings too."

"I understand." He looked so stiff sitting there with his suit jacket still buttoned and the crease of his trousers still pristine.

"Relax a little, Grady. I picked you because I know you're going to do a great job. Now what are your thoughts about the rest of the team?"

He thought a minute before responding. "Amanda's solid. A little timid, maybe, but she gets the job done."

"I agree. Rachel's the wild card, I guess, but she seems bright." Very bright.

"She is. She's Harvard, near the top of the class. Brown undergrad. I'll keep my eye on her, but I think she's okay." He paused again and smiled, seeming to decide whether or not to offer something further. "And she's quite of fan of yours."

"What do you mean?" Anne wasn't sure she wanted to know.

"She was in my office the minute she got the call from Sue this morning, asking for copies of the file, and asking questions about you. You know, what you're like to work for, how you like things done. She's going to dot every 'i' and cross every 't' trying to impress you."

Anne laughed, glad that Grady was finally letting his hair down somewhat. "Well, we'll have to set the bar pretty high for her then. She had a good point about that counterclaim." Anne got up and went behind her desk. "I think she'll work out fine. But if you see any problems, bring them to my attention right away, okay?"

Anne got home late that night after reviewing the settlement papers in the Rattinger dispute. As Walter had predicted, Crocker had caved in around two, and had a draft of the settlement agreement faxed to her before five. She revised the terms of the releases, but overall the deal was mostly done, and she'd saved her client hundreds of thousands in protracted litigation fees, not to mention collected most of the two million it was seeking. Not bad for a week of work. A solid ninety-hour week, that is.

She greeted her cats, Muffin and Chop, and scooted past them as they tried to trip her on her way to the kitchen. Chop had been playing in his water dish again, and had tracked the spillage all over the floor. Typical. She wiped it up, popped some leftover chicken in the microwave, and went into the den to check her e-mail. Since she refused to watch the news, and rarely had time for any newspaper other than the daily law journal, her access to world events was limited to online headlines. And that's the way she liked it.

She scanned some headlines as she pulled off her commuting sneakers to remove her panty hose–what sadist invented these things, anyway?–and settled back to click through the junk e-mail. The message from Shirl was a welcome surprise.

> Annie, hope all's well in Sin City. I'll be in town week after next for the opening. We've been on the road for a month, and if the lighting designer would get her act together we might actually have something to see by the time we open. Friday at eight, at the Thalia. I'll put two tickets aside for you (that's a hint–bring a date). They'll be in your name at the box office. Maybe drinks (or a wake) afterwards? I'd better see you there. Love always.

It would be great to see Shirl. They hadn't gotten together in several years, and because of their insane hours, they rarely even got to speak on the phone. Thank God for e-mail. She whipped off a quick response and closed out her mailbox.

Who to bring? The list of prospects was long, but they were all just friends, and she'd have to put up with another lecture from Shirl on how she needed some romance in her life. There was that cute aerobics instructor at the gym–not that Anne had even taken her class. Anne hated group exercise, preferred the solitude of laps or the occasional run with a Walkman or a single companion–no, she really didn't know the aerobics teacher well enough to invite her. But isn't that the point of a date? She could practically hear the tone of Shirl's voice arguing with her. Forget it. She'd go alone and make up some excuse.

A Web headline caught her eye and she clicked on it. How could she have missed it before?

"Morex Communications was sued yesterday in the Southern District of New York by a group of the country's leading record labels and a galaxy of top recording artists, who seek to enjoin. . . ." It was all there, the whole thing. Not totally unexpected, but sooner than she would have liked.

The plaintiffs weren't commenting, of course. Part of their reason for bringing suit in the first place was to stop Morex from letting it out that many of the most popular music groups in the industry were actually using synthesized, compiled music that was composed, arranged, and even recorded not by human beings, but by a computer. It was a potential public relations nightmare for the recording industry–last year's exposure of the rap group that had been lip-syncing all of its vocals was nothing compared to the scandal that could erupt over this music compilation, and the record labels, not to mention the bands, were desperate to keep it a secret. Hence the injunction–they wanted to break their contracts with Morex, but their real aim was to shut down Morex completely to gag it. In the complaint, they'd kept the details of Morex's role in the manufacture of this music intentionally vague, precisely because they didn't want this information to be made a matter of public record. Instead, Morex is demonized, and the plaintiffs appear to be the victims of a corporate gorilla.

It got worse. She saw a reference to Farnsworth Crowley serving as counsel to Morex, and several lines later, she spotted her own name as well. Don must have said something. Shit, that meant the phone calls would be starting already–better give Sue a heads-up, and get the PR office on standby in case they needed to issue a statement, no matter how innocuous.

She'd never been lead attorney on a big press case before, had always been second-in-command and let the partner and the press office deal with things. On those few occasions when some less glamorous case attracted minor press, Sue had erected an impenetrable wall and the calls had quickly stopped. Sue might not be able to handle this one, though. She was mature, tough as nails and formidable in her quiet efficiency–but it might be best to just route everything through Jerry in Public Relations.

Anne returned to the kitchen to retrieve her dinner from the microwave. Chop had decided to play a little hockey with his dry food, but she ignored it for now. She pulled a ready-made salad from the fridge, and sat at the dining room table to go over some papers while feasting on hopelessly dried-out chicken and wilted lettuce. Lifestyles of the rich and famous.

Don Moore was on the phone first thing Thursday morning. She took the call on speakerphone as she changed from the sneakers she always wore to and from the office–it saved the wear and tear on her pumps, not to mention her feet.

"Hell of a meeting," he started. "I just wanted you to know the president of the board was impressed with you yesterday. He's scared, Anne. So am I."

"I know, Don. Did your tech managers get in touch with Grady to set up some fact finding? We'll get the extension on our time to respond to the complaint, but I want to assemble as many facts as possible, as quickly as we can, to know where our best points are."

"They're on it. I think their first meeting is lined up for later today. By the way, who was that blonde? She spoke up at the end."

"You mean a blonde besides me?"

"I don't think of you as a blonde. I think of you as a contract killer."

Anne laughed and pushed her bangs back from her forehead before picking up the receiver to take him off the speakerphone. "That's a new summer associate we've got here. Name's Rachel something." She was very well aware of the name, but didn't want to give Don any encouragement–he was always trying to remedy what he perceived as her lackluster love life, and she knew where his inquiries were heading.

"She's just a law student? Please don't tell me you're staffing some kid on this case that could ruin me."

"That's right, I want to see you go under, so I can finally go home at night instead of staying here until all hours."

He flipped into Jackie Gleason. "You're a riot Alice, a real riot." The fact that Don looked like the actor made his impersonation a real party favorite, back when Anne used to go to parties. When was that?

"Look, Don, is there something you wanted to talk about, or are you just calling to torment me? I bill at a higher rate for abuse."

His tone became more somber. "I really just wanted to apologize about that slip-up with the wire service. When they asked me to confirm you were the attorneys, I figured they already knew. I just didn't think."

"It's no big deal. Just took us by surprise a little, but we were going to be in the middle of it anyway, as soon as any papers were filed. Just keep your mouth shut in the future, or I may have to take out a contract on you."

"I know. 'Talk to my lawyer,' and 'No comment.' By the way, you available for lunch?"

"I think so." She checked her calendar. "Wait, no, I've got a summer associate lunch."

"Oh?" His voice practically purred. "The lovely blonde?"

"Can it, Don. You can't afford my rates for that discussion. I'll talk to you later."

"I hope you like Italian," said Anne as she and Rachel sat down. "This place is good, but I mostly chose it because it's close."

"It's fine with me. Do you recommend anything in particular?" Rachel really had a magnificent voice. Anne wondered if she'd done any acting.

"It's all good. Take your pick."

Anne already knew what she would order–antipasto and grilled vegetables with sauce–but she studied the menu anyway to avoid looking at her lunch partner. Rachel made her uncomfortable, and it wasn't just because she was gorgeous. She had an air of command about her, a calm that exuded self-assurance and centeredness–it was a little disconcerting, especially in one so young. Just get through this lunch and it'll be fine, Anne told herself.

After they ordered and the waiter brought their drinks–Diet Coke for Anne, regular Coke for Rachel–Rachel commented on her selection and asked if she were vegetarian.

"No. I was in college for a while, wasn't everyone? But no, I just don't like to eat anything heavy in the middle of the day. And I try to swim most evenings, when I can get out of the office for a while, so I don't want to feel too weighted down."

They got off on a conversation about exercise–Rachel was a runner–and somehow the talk segued to the topic of prep schools. It turned out that Rachel had attended a prestigious girls' school in the midwest somewhere–Minneapolis or Chicago–before college at Brown. She bristled at Anne's reference to her undergrad school as "potted ivy," but didn't take any real offense. The fact was, they'd tread remarkably similar paths.

"So did you go to law school straight from Cornell?" asked Rachel.

"No, I stayed to do graduate work in theatre. Well, actually, it wasn't just the MFA. I stayed because I was in a relationship and didn't feel like leaving." At least that was the story she'd told herself. She'd met Marian in a show during her senior undergraduate year, after a depressing series of two-month affairs that she'd been anxious to exit after the first two weeks. She'd really thought that, with Marian, maybe this one could work–they'd become friends first, good friends, and had spent at least the first year of their relationship in a pink fog of sex and laughter. Anne still didn't know exactly when it had started to crumble, but she knew how, and it had a lot to do with the fact that Anne kept a part of herself on hold, as if she were standing in the wings while her life-show was performed onstage by everyone else.

She couldn't really blame Marian for taking up with that director from Auburn, and although it had been painful, she knew even at the time that it had also been inevitable. Neither of them had had any idea about how to be in a relationship, no idea about how to negotiate that fine line between taking care of each other's feelings and taking care of themselves. Marian was a bittersweet memory at this point–in many ways, they'd cut their teeth on each other. She was a kindergarten teacher in Kentucky these days, and they exchanged Christmas cards each year.

"What's an MFA?" asked Rachel.

"Master of Fine Arts. For acting."

"Wow, you're an actress?"

"Not any more."

"But what made you go into law after the theatre?"

"I don't know. I like it better. It lets me use more of my mind." And less of my heart.

They somehow returned to the subject of their prep schools, and Anne realized that Rachel was one of her few work acquaintances with whom she shared the peculiar, defining experience of an all-girls' school. Their revelation on this score went far to dissipate the initial discomfort Anne had felt, and Rachel's too. The conversation from that point on was relaxed, even enjoyable, as they traded horror stories from their youths, and Anne saw some of Rachel's severe midwestern reserve begin to dissolve. She was thoroughly engaging once she threw off her normally glacial exterior. Even charming. Anne couldn't help but acknowledge to herself the attraction she was beginning to feel, even though she was adamant that she'd never act on it. At another time, had they met under different circumstances–she didn't let herself think about it.

The arrival of the entrees launched the discussion into international cuisine, and Anne learned that Rachel had spent considerable time abroad during college. They laughed between bites as they exchanged anecdotes from Europe, where Rachel had studied music.

"So that's why your voice is so controlled," Anne observed. "You're a singer."

"My voice?"

"Yes. You have a great speaking voice. No one's ever told you that?"

"No."

"Well, you do, and I've been trying to figure out whether it's trained or natural."

"I never thought about it before."

"You should. It can be a real asset."

"I'll remember that." She stared at Anne for a little too long, her violet eyes just a little too unblinking, and Anne looked down, uncomfortable again. Her vegetables were almost gone. Change the subject.

"I think I'll order coffee," Anne said. "Want some?"

"Sure."

Anne called over the waiter to order it, and made sure that he would bring milk for it. "I started to get an ulcer in college," she explained after the waiter had left, "and the doctor said it was from too much black coffee. He said to stop drinking coffee altogether, but the best I could do was a compromise–lots of milk."

"Well," Rachel confessed, "I'm even less of a purist. I take it with sugar too."

"So tell me," Anne continued, "did you have any trouble finding a place to live in New York for the summer?"

"No, I'm living with my boyfriend. Tom has a two-bedroom, so it worked out well."

Boyfriend? Anne felt a cold wave splash over the hint of attraction she had momentarily felt. She could have sworn that Rachel was gay. Amazing. Oh well, Anne inwardly shrugged, feeling a mixture of disappointment and relief.

"Well, that was lucky for you," Anne said. "Lucky you didn't hook up with a California firm."

"I'm not going to practice anywhere but in New York."

"You sound pretty certain."

"I am. I know exactly what I want." She said it with such quiet determination that Anne didn't doubt it for a second.

The waiter returned with their coffee, and they were silent for a minute as they each doctored their cup. "So tell me," Rachel asked after her first sip, "are you married?" She quickly caught herself, realizing the inappropriateness of such a question in this era of heightened political correctness. "I only ask because I'm wondering about how women handle the whole work-family thing. I mean. . . ."

She looked like such a scared rabbit, Anne had to laugh. Besides, it was time to deliver her little coming-out line, which she always found was best dispatched as soon as possible in her work relationships. Coming out was a neverending process, it seemed.

"Don't worry about it. And no, I'm not married. I'm gay. As most people know, and you'll certainly hear about soon enough."

Anne checked Rachel's expression carefully and found it completely unmoved by this news. Good thing—the slightest hesitation on her part would have closed the lid on their friendship right there.

"How is the firm about that?" Rachel asked. "I mean, have you had any problems with anyone or any negative reactions?"

Ah, she's gauging the political climate of the firm. Okay.

"No, it's fine. They wave me around whenever they want to create the impression that it's a cool, liberal place. I don't mind, really—in some ways, it is."

That steered the discussion into the overall environment of the firm for women, and Anne was pleasantly surprised to hear Rachel identify herself as a feminist.

"I thought that was a dirty word these days," said Anne. "Especially for your generation."

"Why? How old do you think I am?"

Anne smiled. "You're not going to sue me if I answer that question? Okay, I'd say about twenty-five."

Rachel beamed. Her face was extraordinary. "I'll have you know I'm twenty-eight, and I earned every one of these wrinkles."

"I don't see any wrinkles."

She laughed. "The lights are dim in here. And I'm not leaving until after dark."

"Well," Anne put her credit card on the check tray, "you'll be staying here alone. I've got to get back. Do you realize it's nearly two-thirty?"

"You're kidding. I'm sorry."

"Don't be. I can't remember the last time I had such a nice time on one of these stupid lunches. I'm usually sitting across from some kid who's asking me questions about Civil Procedure."

Rachel laughed. "I'll have to think of some questions for the next time." Her face assumed a modicum of its former reserve as she continued, "And you know, I had fun too. I never thought . . . well, I just can't believe we have so much in common. I figured this would be a really stiff, formal thing. But you're–you're nothing like I thought you'd be."

Anne smiled as she signed the receipt. "Oh no, is that good or bad?"

Rachel's smile was almost coy. "I haven't decided yet."

The warm camaraderie of the past two hours inside the restaurant extended outside to the street, where they commenced a leisurely stroll back to the office. The humidity was low, the temperature a comfortable seventy, the sky a crystalline blue–but it all suddenly collapsed, imploding like a dead sun into a black hole, when Anne's gaze shifted down the street and locked onto the sight of a short brunette woman, not five yards away, walking toward her with a crooked smile and bottomless green eyes that sucked out her soul.

* * *

Thirteen. Flip. Push-off.

Who the *fuck* does she think she is? What the *fuck* gives her the right? Anne timed her strokes for each "fuck," cutting through the water like a hot knife through butter. There was no doubt she'd tracked her down, notwithstanding her feigned surprise at bumping into her on the street like that. She was just too diligent a reporter, and had an army of assistants out there looking under rocks for the scoop of the day. And how dare she give Rachel that little smirk when she'd introduced them? Rachel may not have caught it–she was too enthralled at meeting the famous Rae Sheldon–but Anne sure as hell had seen it, and felt an instantaneous protectiveness. How the *fuck* dare she?

The idiot in the next lane was pulling the usual middle-aged guy schtick, and Anne was in no mood for it. She'd expected it the minute she'd gotten into the lane a little while ago–he was one of those forty-something balding guys who thought he still had the physique from his long-gone glory days on the high school football field, and thought the pool was a good place to show it off. The salivating look he'd given Anne when she'd entered the water was wiped off his face within four laps, when she'd easily passed him at her three-quarter speed and utterly ignored his pathetic attempt to pace her. Next would always come phase two–he'd switch to a breast stroke, which allowed him more surface time for breathing and, since it was a slower stroke than freestyle, provided an excuse for the fact that she breezed by him.

Eventually, even the breast stroke would tire him, so he'd turn to phase three of the ego-salvaging routine–standing at the end of the lane to catch his breath for a few minutes and, once he felt recovered and strong, pushing off just as she was coming in for a turn, to get a head start on her heading into her next lap in a vain attempt to outdistance her. It was the most severe breach of pool etiquette, but these guys were always dilettantes who hadn't a clue that their ill-timed push-off with legs flopping all over the lane was not only rude, it was dangerous for anyone in a neighboring lane who could be caught with a foot to the face in the middle of a flip-turn. Anne's anger flared as she dodged his stray foot, so she poured on the steam and sailed past him so swiftly, with such power and fury, that by the time he'd finally returned to the shallow end of the pool, she'd passed him not just once but twice. Sure enough, as she startled him with her flip, she saw with satisfaction that he appeared to have had enough humiliation for one workout, and left the lane with his tail–and undoubtedly tiny penis–shriveled between his legs. Anne got a perverse pleasure out of blowing these guys away–she might be only five-three, but the pool was a great equalizer, and she was master of this domain.

Her impatience with the guy next to her only fueled her anger at Rae. That smarmy kiss–fortunately, on the cheek, since Anne had deliberately turned her face just before impact–she let it linger just a little too long for a friendly greeting. And the way she'd looked up into Anne's eyes, a single arched eyebrow and a searching look, as if wondering if Anne were going to slap her. But Anne was way beyond that, the heartrending and rage that had once enveloped her left long ago in the past and by now paved over, or eroded, by fifteen years of ice, grit, and living.

"Honey, you look fantastic," Rae had said excitedly. "I can't believe it's you!" Rae had played her part superbly. But then, of the two of them, she had always been the better actress.

"What are you doing in New York?" Anne asked. "I thought you were based in D.C." Anne knew very well what she was doing here.

"A newsmagazine the network's planning for prime time. Supposed to launch in the fall." Rae reached up to brush something off Anne's shoulder, although Anne was sure nothing was there. It was just a ploy for contact, intimacy. Get your hands the *fuck* off me, she thought. "And, of course, there are always a couple of stories to track down in New York." She kept her eyes on Anne, completely ignoring Rachel, which was probably for the best. Anne knew exactly which New York story this little staged coincidence was designed to unearth. Not on your life, bitch. Not on your *fucking* life.

"Well, you look great too," Anne said. It was expected of her, she had to say it. Besides, Rae did look great. Of course, Anne had seen her face over the years, as had everyone else in the country who owned a television set. It was unavoidable—in addition to the network news and occasional stints on the morning show, her face was always on the cover of some magazine or other, always popping up on a late-night talk show. Always exuding professional calm and a mass-appeal warmth during any newsworthy national event. And now a prime-time show too? Anne would have to throw out her TV.

Twenty-four. Flip. Push-off.

"I Will Survive" popped into Anne's head, playing over and over in the aft of her consciousness while she took out her anger on the churning water. The song held such poignant power for her twenty-year-old's heart when she'd danced her feet off at that London "sappho disco" in Earl's Court, literally screaming the words of the song in a circle with her friends, who hated Rae at that point even though Anne was still unwilling to give her up. Now it just served as an ironic reminder of how young she had once been, and a good beat to swim to. She relished the resistance of the water, attacked it. Maybe I should take up boxing too.

"I'm going to be in town off and on for the next few months," Rae had said. "We should really have dinner some night. I'd love to catch up with you."

Like hell. "Sure."

"You're not in the book." She looked down, then up again coyly, trying to make it appear as a confession. "I've looked."

Was Anne supposed to be flattered? "I'm unlisted," she said. "You can get me at my office. Farnsworth Crowley."

"I know. You're quite the power broker these days, aren't you?" The crooked smile—she was starting it again, as if she were still twenty-one and Anne were still a besotted idiot. As if they had never had that screaming confrontation on the Ithaca Commons that summer afternoon eighteen

years ago. As if all the hateful things Anne had said that day were just a
joke.

"Rae, I've got to get back to the office. You take care of yourself, okay?"
As if she would *ever* consider doing otherwise.

"I'm going to call you. Next week."

You won't reach me, my dear. Of that I'm certain.

Rachel had been completely star-struck by the whole encounter, and
pressed Anne with questions during the remainder of their walk back to the
office. Anne had dismissed her inquiries with monosyllables, and Rachel
had eventually gotten the hint.

"I'm sorry if I'm being nosy," Rachel said. "It's just that I never knew
anyone who was such close friends with a celebrity."

"We're not close." Just say it, maybe that will shut her up. "We were lovers. A long time ago. I don't know her anymore."

"Oh my God, Rae Sheldon is a lesbian? I thought she was married to
some big Hollywood producer."

"The head of the network." Please, didn't everyone in America have to
live through that disgusting spectacle five years ago? It was in *every* newspaper and magazine in the country. "And she's not a lesbian. Believe me,
she's definitely not a lesbian."

Fifty-two. Flip. Push-off.

Breath good, anger good. Her arms were timber—she could go another
mile if she had the time. Nothing like the gasping hyperventilation from her
smoking days. Kicking the nicotine had taken five long years, and every
day she'd cursed herself for the asshole she had been at having started it in
the first place. Just another little toxic residue from Rae. Well, at least getting Rae out of her system hadn't taken that long. She rarely ever thought
about her anymore—hadn't for years, as if the entire dark chapter were
nothing but a dream that leaves a thread of feeling more than any specific
details that can be recalled in the light of day.

Fifty-three. Not bad—thirty minutes on the dot.

Chapter Nine

"Shirl, you remember my friend Gallagher? I know she came to a class once at Cornell but," Anne thought about it for a second, "I don't know if you met any time other than that."

Shirl's smile was warm as ever as she greeted Gallagher. "I'm sure we've met," she said, clasping Gallagher's hand between both of hers, "but you've got to forgive me if I don't remember that class. I'm lucky if I can remember whether I had dinner last night."

Shirl hadn't changed much over the years–had really just become more of herself. Short hair now graying a little at the temples, but the same exuberance, the same sparks flashing from her eyes to the beat of her quickly clicking mind. The word on the street was that this would be her breakthrough hit, and it was about time. She'd been plugging away, directing good but little-noticed pieces at practically every major regional theatre in the country. Anne was happy for her, and nervous for her–she was long overdue for some serious recognition, and tonight the pressure was on.

Gallagher looked stunning, as usual. Thank God Joel was out of town for the weekend on some research project for something or other. Anne didn't care enough to pay attention when Gallagher had explained it yesterday–she was just so glad that Gallagher would be free.

"I'm really looking forward to the show," Gallagher was saying to Shirl. She's so Milburn, Anne thought. "Thank you so much for the seats."

"Purely self-interest," said Shirl. "I want the critics to hear a full house packed with friends." Her eyes twinkled as she continued. "And don't thank me until you see the show."

The seats were good–the Louis-seats in the front center balcony, so named for the French monarch-cum-theatre patron who occupied the best seat in the house to actually watch the play, as opposed to the most visible seat in a side box which afforded a terrible view of the stage but a great platform from which to be seen.

It was always a little sad for Anne to go to the theatre these days, as much as she loved it–she'd feel on the edge of a nostalgic little funk whenever she heard an orchestra tuning or saw the lowered curtain billow from some activity on the other side. The magic was about to begin, and she wasn't part of it, only an observer. She didn't regret her decision to leave the theatre, had known all along that all the talent in the world couldn't guarantee success, and she didn't believe she was all that talented to begin with. And she truly loved her work in the law–still performing in some ways, only she wrote her own dialogue–but now and then, especially when she sat in a full house just before the lights went down, she missed her life in the theatre.

By intermission it was clear that Shirl had a monster hit on her hands. Most of the critics seemed to be staying for Act II–and that was unusual, since they all had deadlines and usually cut out at intermission to write their reviews. Shirl was nowhere to be seen during the break–probably backstage with the actors–so Anne and Gallagher spent the interval sharing a Diet Coke and enjoying the warm July night air on the sidewalk outside.

"I'm really glad you could make it tonight," said Anne.

"Me too. Not just because it's great to see you, which it is."

"Twice in the same month. We've got to stop meeting like this."

"I also needed a break from Joel. I'm really glad he's away."

"Why? What's going on?" Gallagher didn't usually share her negative feelings about Joel, although Anne instinctively knew she had them.

"He's pushing me to move in with him. It's really getting bad. And the more he pushes, the more I just want to run away."

"Well, you are engaged," Anne said. "You're going to be living with him eventually." They hadn't set a date yet–also Gallagher's doing.

"I don't know. I'm beginning to wonder if I should go through with it at all. We have nothing in common, I can't talk to him about anything that's important to me. He always turns it into something that's on his mind. Sometimes I don't even know if I like him."

Anne wasn't going to touch this one with a ten-foot pole, although she was dying to. Gallagher was just going to have to sort it out for herself, without any encouragement from Anne. Anne knew that if she seemed to be at all endorsing the idea of leaving Joel, it could come back to bite her later. She'd just have to wait it out, and hope that Gallagher figured out for herself that Joel was totally wrong for her.

"Well, I'm certainly no expert on relationships," said Anne. "God knows."

Gallagher looked surprised by that. "You've had relationships that seemed to be happy. Certainly more than me."

" 'Seemed' is the operative word. You know, I've never been with anyone more than three years."

"I really respect that about you. You know yourself, and you don't hang around when it's not right for you." Gallagher twirled her hair for a minute. "Like that woman in the play. She's in such an impossible situation, but she's rising above it with this inner strength, like it's elevating her over all the smoke and debris so she can see what really matters, what she really wants." She paused before continuing quietly. "That's how I see you."

Anne felt a little claw snag her heart. What that speech would have done to her twenty years ago. Keep it light. "It's nice to have a friend who sees admirable things in me, even if they don't exist."

Gallagher looked her in the eye with a small smile, almost sad. "They're there."

Change the subject.

"So what are you going to do?" asked Anne.

"I don't know. Keep trying to figure out what to do, what I want, I guess. I must sound like an idiot."

Anne hated it when Gallagher got down on herself like this. "I think you sound like an intelligent, thoughtful person who realizes the enormity of a decision she's about to make. I wouldn't expect anything less of you."

The lights flashed, signaling the end of intermission. Gallagher took her hand to walk them back inside. "We're going out afterwards, right?"

* * *

"Defendant respectfully submits this Memorandum of Law. . . ." Anne read the opening paragraph for the third time before finally focussing on it and making a few notations. It was a challenge getting her head into work this morning. First there had been Don's hysterical call wondering when he would see a draft of the brief they'd decided to file, moving to dismiss the complaint. She'd been telling him for years to hire an in-house counsel so he could stop trying to involve himself in the nuts and bolts of the job performed by the company's outside lawyers. He wasn't a lawyer, and needed time-consuming explanations for everything. A lawyer on his staff would save him–and Anne–a lot of bother.

Then there had been Parker's cryptic suggestion this morning that they have lunch "to discuss some things." God knows what that's about, but she didn't like the look on his face. And to top it off, Sue had hit her with two messages from Rae as soon as she'd walked in the door today. Anne had successfully dodged the calls for two weeks, but Rae hadn't achieved her success by giving up easily.

Lurking in the back of it all was a constant replay of last Friday night with Gallagher, demanding attention like a hangnail that would surely bleed if she picked at it–but she couldn't resist. She was worried about Gallagher, and worried for herself as well, because Gallagher's subtle hints, constant touches, coy remarks–they all echoed just a little too much of another time, and threatened to force open a door that Anne had long since closed.

Anne was sure that Gallagher was not doing it consciously. She would have no way of knowing how Anne had once felt about her, and would have no reason to think that Anne would experience her attentions as anything other than a well-developed intimacy between good friends. It was all in Anne's head, she knew it, and yet Anne could not imagine why after all this time Gallagher's presence should trigger these inappropriate thoughts, certainly unbidden, as if strands of a long-forgotten melody had suddenly popped into her mind and would not quit playing. Background music, underlying everything, the words still elusive but the pulse and tones undeniably recalled, nostalgic, evocative.

The tavern Shirl and her lover Grace had suggested that night was a quiet little spot in the West Village. Shirl hated to party with the cast after an opening–she needed quiet time and human contact to unwind and await the reviews.

"Well, I know I must have hit the big time," Shirl announced after they'd crowded into the small booth. "Rae Sheldon contacted me this week." Shirl's look left no doubt about how she felt about Rae. "I got the messages but didn't call her back."

"Yes," said Anne. "Seems she's in town for some prime-time thing they're developing." Anne took a sip of her seltzer and felt Gallagher's eyes on her.

"You've seen her?" asked Gallagher, her tone almost a challenge. She made no bones about her views on Rae–understandably, since she'd borne the brunt of Anne's despair right after their breakup. Still, it was so long ago, it hardly mattered now.

"Not exactly," explained Anne. "I ran into her on the street, or she ran into me."

Shirl laughed. "I'll bet that was fun."

"Barrel of laughs. I was very cordial."

Shirl filled in Grace, minus some of the gorier details–Shirl always treaded lightly on the subject of Rae–and Anne felt a comforting warmth as Gallagher placed her arm across Anne's shoulders. Gallagher turned to Anne while Shirl and Grace were distracted, her voice low.

"What was it like?" she asked, her eyes searching.

"Awkward," said Anne. "Weird. All I could think was, How could I have been so nuts about this person? Anyway, I was in a hurry, so we didn't really talk at all."

Shirl caught that last comment as she lit a cigar. "I tried to warn you about her," she said with a smile.

"As you take every opportunity to remind me."

They'd enjoyed themselves that night, but when Shirl and Grace had decided to head back to their hotel after the papers came out around one—the reviews were glowing, as Anne knew they would be—Gallagher had asked if Anne could stay a while longer.

"I like it here," she said. "And it's been so long since I had a night out with the girls. I just don't want to call it a night yet."

"Fine by me," said Anne, enjoying the fact that Gallagher had remained beside her in the booth even after Shirl and Grace had left. It had been a long time since she'd had a night out with the girls too.

And as if they were seventeen again, they'd closed the bar. It had been wonderful, laughing over nothing, gossiping over the sturm and drang of the various Milburn friends strewn around the country. Late in the wee hours, after a particularly raucous recollection of a rafting trip they'd once taken down the Susquehanna, Gallagher had touched upon the subject that Anne had thought long laid to rest. It hadn't seemed remarkable at the time, just an offhand comment that Gallagher thought she would probably have been better off had she turned out to be a lesbian, since her mother seemed to dislike every man she dated. What stood out in Anne's mind now, as she looked back on it, was the way Gallagher's hand had been resting on Anne's leg, the easy pressure as she'd moved her hand back and forth over the light khaki fabric, all the while explaining that she'd never been so comfortable, had so much fun, with anyone else in her life.

Anne had nodded and said she felt the same way. That rafting trip back when they were teenagers was a case in point—although they'd started out with a group of six girls, Anne and Gallagher had somehow become separated from the group, and had spent the rest of the afternoon sunbathing on rocks and scaring each other with imagined scenes from *Deliverance* as they'd paddled through the errant tributary on which they'd become lost. Anne had been almost disappointed when the tributary had finally rejoined the main river and they'd spotted the rest of their group near the landing beach.

Of course, most of the splendor of that afternoon had been due to Anne's delight in simply being alone with this person she had adored. There was a simple, pure pleasure in the fact of Gallagher's company, a pleasure that Anne had experienced again and again over the years, untarnished by impossible imaginings or schoolgirl fantasies. Just the enchantment of being with a beloved friend who made her laugh and feel good about herself. Especially these days, when so much of her life was weighted down with heavy responsibilities, where so much rested on her ability to manage inordinate pressure, a friend like Gallagher was a lifeline.

Gallagher hadn't left it there, however. As Anne recalled their after-theatre conversation in the light of day, she wondered where Gallagher had been going with her observation that the two of them should really have started a relationship years ago. Probably nowhere–she was just comfortable letting her mind wander when she was with Anne. Still, it was puzzling that she'd come out and said something like "Can you imagine what Rhonda Dougherty would have done if we'd told her we were lovers?"

Anne had laughed till she cried–it was too funny. The idea of the most prim and proper, irrepressibly social gadfly in all of Milburn being faced with not one but two lesbians at the school. "If she didn't drop dead of a heart attack," said Anne, wiping the tears from her eyes, "she'd probably have run off to get a rabies shot and then begged her mother to yank her out of school!"

"Is she still that way, do you think? Little Miss Milburn?"

Anne shook her head. "I haven't seen her since graduation. She gave me a dirty look after my valedictory speech, and that was it."

Gallagher smiled with remembrance. "That was a great speech. I remember thinking I couldn't believe that someone I knew, just a kid like me, could be such a wonderful public speaker. Didn't you get a standing ovation? I know I jumped up."

"I don't remember. But I'm sure Rhonda didn't stand up. It galled her to no end that I was first in the class and she was second."

"Tell me about it. Her sister Debbie was on the tennis team with me, and loved to mention how anyone could get an A by choosing easy electives, but it took a real scholar to take Advanced Physics in high school."

"Yeah, as if I chose Sociology in my senior year just to beat out Rhonda. Give me a break. No one was more surprised than me when I ended up first. I didn't even know I was in the running until one of the teachers congratulated me."

"I wasn't surprised," said Gallagher as she subtly increased the pressure on Anne's leg. "You're probably the smartest person I know. I love that about you."

Anne smirked and sipped her seltzer. "You must know some pretty stupid people."

Gallagher had been quiet for a moment. "You know," she'd finally said, "I don't think we've ever been single at the same time? One or the other of us has always been in a relationship, ever since we met."

Anne had to think about it. "Yeah, I guess that's true. You were single when I was with Ellen. And before that–what was his name, after Lorraine and I broke up? You were with him that whole time I was single."

"Doug."

"Right, the infamous Doug. How could I forget? And the whole time after Rae and Marian, you were with Dennis."

Gallagher gave her a sad smile. "So we never really had a chance, did we?"

Anne laughed at the absurdity of it. "Well, I think maybe the fact that you're into guys had something to do with that, too. And remember the Lesbian Prime Directive."

"What's that?"

"Never, never get involved with a straight woman. I seem to remember wanting to have that tattooed on my chest after I got back from Europe."

Gallagher had laughed with her. It had seemed at the time nothing more than the kind of casual nonsense they'd been exchanging for years. But this morning, with the sun streaming through her blinds while she reviewed the Morex brief, she wondered momentarily what had prompted that bi-zarre turn in the conversation, and smiled at the thought of it–how that conversation, seeded with Gallagher's suggestive little germs, would have sprouted into impossible possibilities in Anne's fertile imagination of twenty years ago.

The brief was better than she expected, and she'd nearly reached the end when she looked up and saw Parker standing in her doorway.

"Ready?"

"Jesus, what time is it?" She checked her watch.

"Almost one. Can you get out?"

"Sure." She put the brief aside and grabbed her purse. She hated carry-ing a purse. "Lead the way."

"I thought we could just get a sandwich downstairs and sit in the park," he said as they walked toward the elevators. "It's a nice day."

Parker was no nature-lover. It could mean only one thing–he wanted to talk candidly about something that he didn't want overheard. Curiosity piqued, Anne followed him in silence.

Once they seated themselves on a bench by one of the lakes in Central Park, Parker took a huge bite and swallowed before launching in.

"Anne, I wanted to ask you about Darryl. Is there some problem be-tween you two?"

Anne had no idea what he was talking about, and said so.

"Well," said Parker, "I'm hearing some things that are a little disturbing, and I wanted your view of the situation before I talk to him."

"What things?" Anne hadn't worked with Darryl in ages, and had barely even seen him since that party last month for the summer associates. She was mystified.

"He's making some noises about you. And Rachel Evans." He let it drop there, let it sink in.

Anne felt a burst of anger ignite in her chest. "What the hell–you mean a relationship? Is that what you're getting at?"

"Not me, Anne. Him. You know I'm the last person who would question you, or any relationship you might have."

"That's, that's . . ." she couldn't find the words. She couldn't even think, it was so ludicrous. Start again. "There's nothing between me and Rachel. Period. As you of all people should certainly know. And as for Darryl, I can only assume he's pissed off that he's not on the Morex case, so he's resorting to a little dyke-baiting. Now what are you going to do about it?" Anne couldn't remember having ever been so furious. At least not about something work-related. This was her sanctuary, her escape from life, and Darryl was shitting all over it. She was ready to kill.

"Settle down. And I'm not going to do anything for now. I'm sure it'll blow over, and disciplining Darryl will only make it more of an issue than it should be."

"Or it might just look a little too hypocritical, coming from you," she shot back. Parker's dalliances with certain subordinates were well known.

"That's not fair, Anne. I'm thinking of you."

"That's bullshit. If you were thinking of me you'd cut this little shit off at the knees." She couldn't believe he was going to sit back and do nothing.

"Exactly what is between you and Rachel?"

This was unbelievable. They were friends, that's all. Yes, they were spending a lot of time together, and that in itself was unusual for Anne, who never really socialized with people from work—except, she realized, a few male friends. But shit, she was enjoying getting to know Rachel. Unlike most of her other colleagues, Rachel was someone she probably could have been friends with even if they didn't work together. It was true that they didn't have the excuse of being summer "sisters" anymore, since Alice Gray had returned from Denver and had assumed her big sister role with Rachel—so Anne's many lunches with Rachel probably looked out of the ordinary. Especially since Anne had basically ignored her own little sister Emily since the beginning of the summer. Still, it was nice becoming friends, and Anne didn't intend to stop.

She also had to admit to herself that she was more than a little attracted to Rachel, and enjoyed Rachel's occasional flirtations with her. She would never let it go anywhere, even if Rachel were actually serious–which she probably wasn't–but the flirtation was harmless and added a little zing to her long hours in the office. She didn't intend to tell Parker that, however–Anne's private feelings were none of his business.

"We're friends. That's it. What, I'm not supposed to have any female friends because I'm a lesbian?"

"All I'm saying is, you two have become pretty chummy. She's always in your office, or you're in hers. People notice. And that's not like you, Anne."

He was right, of course. They were in and out of each other's offices all day, usually just to shoot the shit–rarely was it work-related, although early on they'd started pretending that it was. That was part of the fun, part of the flirtation. They'd begin a conversation with some comment about the Morex case, and within a sentence or two digress onto some tangent from which they wouldn't emerge until someone else came in or the phone rang. Their conversations were far ranging and often racy. Light–a pleasant break from the heaviness of her work, even when Rachel talked about her occasional boyfriend troubles with Tom and dropped not-too-subtle hints about her growing interest in experimenting someday with a woman. And if Rachel too often let her eyes linger on Anne's for a few seconds longer than necessary, longer than was comfortable–well, no one else needed to know about that. Anne certainly wasn't encouraging it. It meant nothing, and Anne knew better than to let anything happen between them.

"Why did you have her attend that Morex meeting?" Parker asked.

How did he even know about that? Darryl.

"Are you asking me to justify the way I'm running this case?" Anne demanded.

"No, not–"

"Because I'll be happy to, but if you really have a concern about Rachel participating, then just take her off the case."

"Anne, that's not necessary. I was just asking. You've got to admit it's unusual to have a summer associate attend an important client meeting. Not even Amanda went."

This was getting to be too much. "It's also unusual to have a summer associate raise a substantive issue that needs to be discussed with the client. An issue that neither Grady nor I had hit on, by the way. It was her idea, and a good one–I thought she should be the one to raise it with the client." She took a deep breath and tried to quell her anger. "Now are there any other questions? Because if you've got a problem with my handling of this case, take Rachel off it and put yourself on." She knew he'd never do that–he didn't want the responsibility. She didn't want Rachel removed, either. It would look bad for Rachel to be taken off a case so abruptly. And besides liking Rachel, Anne liked her work. She did a phenomenal job, and didn't deserve the talk that would inevitably follow in the wake of such a move.

He laughed and flashed her some his charm. "No way, this one's your baby to the end. And don't take Rachel off, either. Just be careful, that's all. You know how the rumor mill runs around here. I don't want to see you get caught up in it."

"What are you going to do about Darryl? I don't want him on any more of my matters. None."

"I'm not going to do anything for now. I'll just keep my eye out for him, and you do the same. Watch your back."

She sniffed as she crumpled her sandwich wrapper. "No shit."

When Anne returned to the office after lunch, Sue literally threw up a roadblock with her body, waving pink message slips in her face.

"Come on in," said Anne as she squeezed past Sue and practically threw her purse into her bottom desk drawer. Sue was immune to her foul mood–she'd seen it all before.

"Don Moore says it's urgent," said Sue. "And he specifically told me to tell you he really means it, you have to call him at once. He also told me to get you an airline ticket and book you a hotel in Minneapolis for tonight."

"Shit. What else?"

"Rae Sheldon called again." Sue was unimpressed.

"Throw it away. If she calls again, tell her I'm out of town."

"Way ahead of you–I already did."

"Good. Anything else?"

"Grady and Rachel want to see you. Something about some documents they found."

"Okay, tell Grady I'll see him in five minutes, and Rachel after that. What time's my flight?"

"Two hours from now."

Plenty of time. She kept a packed bag in the office for such emergencies. "Get me Don on the phone, and arrange for a car to get me to the airport. Don't cut it close. I'll be in rush-hour traffic."

Whatever Don's emergency was, it had to be big–in all their years of working together, he'd never insisted she go somewhere on a moment's notice like this. When Sue buzzed her with the call, she picked it up on the first ring.

"Don, what's up?"

"We've got a ten a.m. meeting in Minneapolis tomorrow with plaintiffs and their counsel. All very hush-hush, very mysterious."

"What happened?"

"Got me. I got a call from Sylvan Records around noon, the president no less. Says he's got some information that my lawyer's going to want to see, and we can handle it in a meeting or we can do it the hard way and see it in their papers responding to our motion. How the hell do they even know we're making a motion?"

"No idea–it's probably just an educated guess. What exactly did he say he had?"

"Papers. Just papers. What the hell is he talking about? We haven't even done any discovery yet–what kind of papers could he have?"

Anne's head was spinning. She reached for the aspirin bottle in her desk drawer and popped the top.

"I don't have a clue. But if you think it's worth a trip to Minneapolis to find out now, I'll be there. Are we on the same flight?"

"Yeah. Four forty-five, TWA."

"We'll talk on the plane. I'll see you at the airport."

She hung up before asking which airport, LaGuardia or Kennedy. Sue would know–thank God for her. Grady knocked at her door as she swallowed the aspirin dry.

"I'm leaving in twenty minutes for Minneapolis," she said as he walked in. "Some meeting the plaintiffs called. Normally I'd have you there, but I want you to hold down the fort here while I'm gone, and get the brief finalized." She handed her markup to him. "Now what did you need to discuss?"

He had a peculiar look on his face as he handed her a small stack of papers and sat in the chair facing her desk. Anne looked at the pages, which appeared to be Morex interoffice memos.

"What's this?"

Grady cleared his throat. "Well, basically, it's some correspondence and memos in which Morex outlines its plans to tie up the recording industry in knots and extort money from them."

"What?!"

"Well, not in so many words. But it's pretty clear."

"Slow down, back up."

"Okay." He took a deep breath. "The idea seems to be that Morex would program certain identifiers into their source code for their composition files, the arrangements and compositions and synthesized vocals, all of it. It seems to be an invisible little fingerprint here and there that can identify the music as a Morex product."

"So?"

"So, there are some unsigned file memos in there dealing with the legality of using those fingerprints to track all the recordings produced in the industry. Morex seems to have been planning to demand a premium from the industry with the threat that they'll blow the cover off the whole computerized compiling scheme unless the record companies pay up."

"Jesus."

"Any idea if they went through with this?"

"Nope. But I'll see Don at the airport in a little while, and he'll have an entire flight to explain it to me." Anne paused. "Any chance the plaintiffs have seen this?"

"I don't see how. I only just found it yesterday, when Rachel and I were going through the Morex files to organize the stuff we'll need for the case."

"Well, start thinking about how we can avoid producing this stuff when we get into discovery. Something like this in the wrong hands could kill Morex worse than the lawsuit itself. Start putting together a draft confidentiality agreement, too. The plaintiffs won't want the details of this case exposed to the press, and I certainly don't want something that looks like an extortion plot by Morex to get out either."

"Won't that take away some of our leverage?"

"Probably. But it might be necessary anyway."

Anne looked up to see Rachel standing in the doorway. She looked great in that dark green suit, like something out of a TV lawyer show.

"Okay," said Anne, "let me talk to Rachel. I'll see you when I get back, and Sue will know how to reach me if you need me."

Anne pulled off her pumps as Grady left and Rachel took his place. She smiled with frank amusement at Anne's quick movements.

"Going somewhere?" she asked.

"Minneapolis. Lucky me." Anne took her sneakers from under the desk and started to put them on.

"Sounds like fun. But I think you'll need someone to enjoy it with. Someone who can show you around." She stared at Anne a little too long–the color of her eyes a tantalizing almost-blue, almost-purple–and smiled invitingly. "Someone who can recommend the best restaurants, that kind of thing."

The thought struck Anne that Rachel's flirtations were getting more obvious. And as much as Anne had grown to enjoy it, now was not the time. Especially after what Parker had said.

"I'm sure that's true," Anne said, "but if you're offering, we'll have to get into trouble in Minneapolis another time. This one's a solo, and I'm leaving in a few minutes."

Rachel looked disappointed, but didn't break eye contact. "Grady told you about the memos we found?"

Anne finished tying her shoes. "Yes, and I'll discuss them with Don Moore on the plane. I just wanted you to know that it's not a slight against you or anything that I'm not taking you with me. You're an important part of the team, but Grady and Amanda are staying, and you should too." Rachel looked incredibly fetching as she pushed back the blonde strands that hung in her eyes, and Anne couldn't resist lightening the mood with a little innocent flirtation herself. "Besides, can you imagine what people would say if I whisked you away to Minneapolis and corrupted you?"

Rachel smiled slowly and arched one eyebrow with an air of sophistication that suddenly reminded Anne of Rae, the slick moves she'd already perfected by age twenty-one to seduce anyone who crossed her path. This game suddenly wasn't as much fun anymore. But Rachel pressed on.

"How do you know it wouldn't be me corrupting you?"

Anne laughed at that. "Believe me, I've been corrupted by the best, while you were still in diapers."

Rachel left her eyes locked on Anne–she really must not realize how disconcerting that is. "Well," Rachel said, "I can always corrupt you here in New York." She got up to leave. "In fact, I think I'll make that my goal for the rest of the summer."

Anne stood and collected her travel bag from the corner closet. "You keep talking like that and you'll get us both fired."

Rachel laughed and was turning to leave when Anne's voice stopped her in the doorway. "By the way, Sue will have my phone number if you need anything. I should be back tomorrow night. Or Wednesday at the latest."

"Have a nice trip."

Chapter Ten

Anne returned to the hotel around eight to change out of her business suit and try to sort through the day. Their meeting with the plaintiffs and their counsel had been a nightmare. Somehow they'd gotten their hands on the extortion memos and letters from Morex, and were threatening the legal equivalent of nuclear holocaust if Morex didn't come to its knees. Don had been adamant on the flight in–he and the Morex board had never contemplated the plans outlined in those memos, and had known nothing about it.

Don figured it must have been the machinations of a small group of senior engineers, a cartel that had formed several years ago within the tech ranks and demanded a host of options and incentives. Don had fired them, but not before they'd issued certain cryptic threats about sabotaging the company. These memos, and the fingerprints they'd coded into the source code, had probably been a time bomb ticking away, and wherever those engineers were now, they were probably drinking a toast to the detonation.

A swarthy man named Jim Bolton was the lead lawyer for the plaintiffs, and had led the meeting for the assembled recording industry representatives and musicians. Anne had assumed that the papers they were about to throw on the table were the documents that Grady and Rachel had found, so she had come prepared with a series of legal maneuvers with which to counterpunch–threats of court orders to compel expedited examination of the lawyers, to determine how they'd gotten their hands on these internal memos; protective orders; maybe criminal prosecution, since it seemed that they were stolen. Don assumed that one or more of the former Morex engineers was working with the plaintiffs.

However they'd come by the documents, the sad fact remained that the plaintiffs were now in the driver's seat and armed with something that could destroy Morex–financially, and in the public eye. Worse, some Morex executives, including Don, could face serious penalties, maybe prosecution.

Right after the meeting, Anne had called Dave Francis, one of the white-collar crime partners at Farnsworth, and he was expected to arrive late to-night and attend tomorrow afternoon's session with the plaintiffs. They had a little over sixteen hours to devise a plan, or the whole thing would blow up in their faces. After ordering a hamburger and salad to be brought up to her room, she'd left Don in the hotel restaurant with instructions to get a good night's sleep tonight. There was little else she could do until they met with Dave first thing in the morning.

The phone rang as she was putting on her worn jeans–her standard hanging-out-in-a-hotel-room garb. A movie on HBO was blaring in the background, so she turned it down as she reached for the phone.

"Anne Henderson." Shit, she automatically identified herself when she answered the phone in business mode, and only after the fact realized how dangerous that was at a hotel. Oh, well.

"Anne? It's Rachel. Hi."

"Hi, what's up?" She checked her watch. "You're not still at the office, are you?"

"Sure. You work me like a dog," Rachel said with a laugh. "Anyway, I thought I'd take advantage of the client account to talk to you long distance. How's it going?"

Anne sat on the bed and leaned back against the headboard. "Not good. The plaintiffs have copies of those documents you found, and they're threatening everything under the sun. Morex never implemented the plan so far as anybody knows, but that hardly matters at this point."

"If it wasn't a Morex plan, whose was it?"

"We're not sure, but probably some tech guys who wanted to hold up the company for some money a few years ago. They seem to have planted them when they didn't get their way. Don figures they're working for the plaintiffs now. They probably have a deal to get a piece of whatever the plaintiffs recover. If you can't get it through the front door, you try siphoning it through the back."

"Wow. What are you going to do?"

"Beats me. Dave Francis will be here tomorrow, and we'll figure something out."

"So you've knocked off for the night? It isn't even eight-thirty out there."

"Yeah, I have a gorgeous brunette meeting me in my room in a little while."

"Uh huh. Well, that should take all of five minutes."

"Bitch," Anne laughed.

"Seriously, I can tell you about some fun stuff to do, as long as you have a free night in my hometown."

"What? I thought you were from Chicago."

"Nope. Twin Cities. And I'm a Gemini, too."

"Which twin am I talking to right now?"

"The one who's pissed off that she's stuck in this office while you're cavorting with a gorgeous brunette."

"Get over it, or I'll assign you more work."

Rachel's deep, enchanting laugh trickled over the wire. She was fun, she really was.

"Okay, fair enough. What I really called about was, I have two tickets to the symphony next Friday. Want to go?"

"What about Tom?"

"He hates the symphony. I'd rather go with you."

Anne smiled. It was a nice idea, and being with Rachel was a pleasure. It was like having another Milburn classmate in the city. But she'd have to say no this time.

"I'm going out of town next weekend, I can't. I really wish I could, though—will you promise to ask me again?"

Rachel huffed in that distinctive way she had, like a parent exhibiting tremendous patience with a recalcitrant child. "Well—only if you promise to take me on your next business trip. Where are you going next weekend?"

"A big reunion at my prep school. I got talked into it. I don't really want to go, but now I have to."

"If I'd known it was so easy to talk you into things, I would have tried it a long time ago."

Now it was Anne's turn to huff. "Don't get any ideas. I still have some say on your future at Farnsworth. A future that's rapidly diminishing, by the way."

"Well, I'll just have to think of something good to change your mind," Rachel said almost seductively.

"God, let's hope the firm doesn't record these conversations. We'd never be able to explain them."

Come to think of it, Anne realized, it was possible. Although she was unaware of the firm ever having done so, she knew that the attorneys' phones were all equipped with the capacity to record a phone conversation, or even the ambient sound in the office where the phone was located. Many people assumed the "Mic" button on the phone enabled the speakerphone, but in fact it triggered the recording device. In New York, it was perfectly legal for one of the participants in a conversation to record it, even if the others on the line didn't know about it, and Anne knew of several attorneys who preferred to record phone and office conversations rather than take detailed notes.

Rachel indulged in some more of that throaty laugh that Anne loved. "This is nothing compared to some of our discussions in your office. Or mine."

"That's true." And it was. They often got onto highly risqué topics during their frequent closed-door conversations. Anne always knew when something outrageous was about to come out of Rachel's mouth. She'd get that "just you wait" look on her face and close the door for privacy before launching into a topic that would eventually make Anne blush.

"Believe me," Rachel continued, "I haven't even gotten warmed up yet!"

Anne was sure that was true as well–and something warned her not to mention that Rachel had the ability to record their conversations. Probably paranoid, but still. . . .

"Enough," Anne announced. "Time for me to hang up. My brunette's waiting."

"Okay. See you whenever you decide to grace us with your presence."

Anne was still smiling to herself as she hung up and reached for the remote to turn up the HBO movie, when she heard a knock at the door. Probably her hamburger. She opened the door without checking the peephole, and stared at Rae.

"Aren't you going to invite me in?"

No. "What are you doing here?"

Rae walked past her into the room. She was dressed to kill, as usual—perfectly tailored suit to show off her still-incredible shape, silk blouse with a plunging neckline suggesting more of a bosom than Anne knew she had. Anne pulled her eyes away—but not before Rae caught her looking and let a slow smile creep across her lips.

"You're a hard woman to track down. Didn't you get my message?"

Anne looked over to the nightstand and saw the light flashing on the phone. Why hadn't she seen it before? Shit.

"I said, what are you doing here?"

"I thought as long as we're in the same hotel we should have a drink together."

Anne still stood by the open doorway, unmoving. Unmoved.

"I mean, what are you doing in Minneapolis?"

"I have a meeting," Rae said as she looked Anne up and down in frank appraisal. "You look as great as ever. Still swimming, I gather?"

"Rae, it's really not a good time."

Rae walked to her, pulled her hand from the doorknob, and pushed the door closed. "We can order room service."

"Forget it. I'm going to bed."

Rae gave her the crooked smile. "We can do that too." Anne was re-lieved to note that it didn't work–maybe Rae had lost her touch. Or maybe Anne had just grown up.

"I've got a lot on my mind and I'm really not up for whatever game you're playing. So if you don't mind–"

Rae took another step closer to Anne–Anne could see the tiny wrinkles at her eyes, the fine lines that were etched from her nose to the sides of her mouth. Lines that would be laugh lines on anyone else. It was the same awesome face, only older. More certain. More dangerous.

"Shh," said Rae as she put her finger to Anne's lips, and Anne hated herself for feeling a flicker of desire spark at the touch. It would be so easy, just this once.

"No." Anne stepped away as if scalded. "I mean it, I want you to go. I don't know what you think you're doing here, but I don't want any part of it." She turned and faced Rae from several feet away. "Please. Now."

Rae stared at her and bit the inside of her lower lip. Hadn't she gotten over that habit by now? It was still adorable. "I'll go on one condition," she said carefully.

"What?" Anne really didn't want to know.

"You have one drink with me. Downstairs in the bar, nice and public."

"I don't drink."

Rae was amused at that. "You've got to be kidding. Well, you can have whatever you want, but I'm drinking bourbon. Deal?"

"One drink and you'll go away and leave me alone?"

Rae gave her a look that Anne had never seen before, at least not on Rae's face–desire, combined with something that looked like hurt. "If that's what you want," she said softly, "yes, I promise."

Don immediately launched into her before she could even sit down at their breakfast meeting. "Was that Rae Sheldon I saw you with last night?" Anne was glad that Dave Francis hadn't joined them yet.

"Yes. She's an old friend from college."

"Well, I don't want to be hearing about this case on the news tonight." He was looking at her strangely, as if he didn't trust her.

Anne looked at him in disbelief. "You know me better than that, Don. The case never even came up."

Which was odd–Anne had been certain that Rae had tracked her down precisely so that she could sniff around the Morex case, but she hadn't even mentioned it. The hottest legal news story of the year, maybe the decade, and Rae never even asked about it.

"Still," he grumbled, "it looks pretty strange having a big reporter like that talking to my lawyer. I don't like it–something doesn't feel right."

"I agree. She surprised me, I didn't even know she was in town. She says she saw me in the lobby and got my room number from the desk clerk. Turns out she's here for some broadcast affiliate meeting." Anne didn't totally buy it, still suspected that Rae had had her minions staking out the airport or something as soon as she'd learned Anne was leaving town. But Rae had insisted it was just a coincidence. Even if Rae had planned it all, it had been a wasted trip–she got nothing.

Rae had behaved herself in the bar last night–miraculously. Because Anne wasn't about to change her clothes in front of Rae, she'd stayed in her old jeans and polo shirt to head downstairs. Rae had kept her hands to herself and led them to a table in the back of the dark piano bar, far removed from the music and other patrons. She'd pushed the ashtray toward Anne, and cocked her eyebrow in her classic way when Anne informed her she'd quit smoking twelve years ago.

"Good for you. I always knew you had more will power than anyone I know."

"I wouldn't say that," Anne replied. "It took me an awfully long time to finally get away from you."

Rae looked surprised at Anne's forthright approach. That's right, Rae, I'm not twenty anymore. I'm not afraid to tell you exactly what I think.

"I guess we both did a lot of stupid things back then."

"I know I did. You seemed fairly smart, though. You did exactly as you pleased."

Whatever Rae was going to say was interrupted by the waiter, who took Anne's order for a seltzer and Rae's order for a bourbon on the rocks. Rae pulled out a Vantage and lit it. "Will the smoke bother you?"

"I'm over that, too."

Rae laughed softly and curled the end of her cigarette against the side of the ashtray. "You're not going to make this easy, are you?"

Anne just looked at her, wishing it was over.

"Okay, look." She stretched her neck from side to side, seemingly to work out a kink, and looked down at her cigarette. "I've thought a lot about you, especially since I ran into you on the street." She looked up at Anne, gauged the determinedly noncommittal look on her face, and continued. "Actually, for a long time before that, too. I know you don't want to hear this, but I want to say it anyway."

She paused. Anne wasn't going to offer her any help or encouragement.

"I know it ended badly between us, and it was all my doing. I don't have any excuses for how I acted, so I won't bore you with any."

This was not going anywhere that Anne could have guessed. She continued to stare at Rae, her stomach churning and the initial anger giving way to cold indifference. Rae was still so beautiful, but at a remove, as if on TV or in a photograph. There was nothing real about it.

"But I think I understand some of what I put you through, and I wanted you to know that. I've had a little experience with that myself in the past few years." She appeared to tear up, or maybe it was just the light. Anyway, her voice betrayed only a hint of quiver as she plowed on, a real pro. "My marriage has been over for years. Serves me right, I guess. But every time Bob takes up with some new woman, I think about how you must have felt."

"I'm sure I wasn't the only one."

Rae looked at her, unblinking. "You were the one that mattered."

Anne shook her head as the waiter placed their drinks on the table. "Rae, that's ridiculous. We were babies. You can't compare what we had in college to a marriage of however-many years. I appreciate your concern–kind of late for that, but I appreciate it anyway–but still, it's crazy to see your marriage problems as some kind of cosmic payback."

"I don't really–although I do think I'm getting what I deserve. I'm not saying this very well, I know. All I really want you to know is that I'm sorry." She took a sip of her bourbon, and Anne thought about how unmoved she was by the whole scene, completely untouched even though she'd so often imagined something along these lines, fantasized about it with cruel delight in those first years after Europe. "I look back on it now and I really believe they were some of the happiest times of my life. And I shit all over it."

"Yes, you did. But that was a long time ago. It's time to get over it. I did."

Rae smiled softly, her face so reminiscent of the one Anne had loved. "Are you seeing anyone now? That blonde I saw you with?"

Anne couldn't help but chuckle. Typical Rae. "No, I'm single right now. Happily so."

Rae tried out the crooked smile again, but it evaporated when Anne didn't respond. Her bag of tricks was running low. "You know, ever since I saw you on the street, I can't stop thinking about you. You're even more gorgeous than when we were in college." Anne didn't want to hear any more of this, but couldn't seem to make herself interrupt Rae. "I keep thinking about how it was back then, how incredible we were together. Remember that time in Bath? I thought the innkeepers were going to ask us to leave."

Anne remembered it very well–just one of the many dazzling sexual binges they'd consummated in between Rae's dalliances. That was one thing that had never changed, never let up, no matter how deep the hurt that Rae had inflicted–or maybe because of it–they had always been highly combustible in bed, two unstable elements combined in a nuclear reactor of charged emotion, frenetic energy, and white-hot desire. She didn't like where this discussion was heading.

"I'd rather not stroll down memory lane, if you don't mind."

"It's never been like that with anyone since," said Rae. "I know it hasn't for you, either."

She knew no such thing. Although it was true, Anne knew she was just fishing. "I'm sorry if your marriage isn't working out," Anne said. "I really am. But I'm very content with where I'm at these days, and my sex life is none of your business."

Rae took a puff and blew it in her face—not obviously, but just enough. "Content? Come on, counselor, that's a pretty careful word."

"I've learned to be careful over the years. I learned that lesson quite a while ago."

"Don't you ever wonder if it could be like that again? Safe, no commitments, just incredible sex on your own terms?"

"Those wouldn't be my terms," Anne said, shaking her head. "You just don't get it, do you? It's only incredible for me if there *is* a commitment. That's what's safe. Something where love is involved. And reciprocated."

"I loved you," Rae said, her voice uncharacteristically soft. "You know that."

Anne smiled ruefully. How could she have found anything desirable in this woman? "I guess you did in your way. But it's certainly not what I needed then. Or now." Or ever.

"I guess that means I can't entice you upstairs? For old times' sake?"

Anne put a five-dollar bill on the table and stood up. "It's been nice seeing you again, Rae. But don't call me, okay? We have a deal."

Rae took her hand and held it gently. Her touch meant nothing, the momentary desire Anne had felt upstairs thankfully gone. Rae looked at her openly, honestly—perhaps for the first time in her life. "I'd really like to see you sometime. No games, no seduction. Just . . . friends. Do you think that we can manage that?"

I doubt it, Anne thought. But Rae was a powerful woman, and somewhere in the back of her mind, Anne knew not to make a complete enemy of her, not to close this door. At least not yet.

"Tell you what," said Anne. "I'll call you if I want to get together, okay? Meanwhile, why don't you work on your marriage and stop trying to sleep with women? You're giving lesbians a bad name."

Rae had squeezed her hand then and laughed. Maybe Anne would be willing to see her again, in ten years or so.

Anne still didn't know what to make of Rae's unexpected appearance, or her strange come-on last night, but assured Don that the Morex story did not appear to have been on the reporter's mind.

Dave Francis joined the breakfast meeting in the hotel's private dining room just after Anne and Don had ordered. He looked tired. "Flight delays in Chicago," he said. "I didn't get in until around two. Now here's what I propose."

Dave outlined a series of maneuvers for keeping the plaintiffs at bay at least until a ruling on the soon-to-be-filed motion to dismiss. And he recommended a firm of private investigators to get to the bottom of the leak out of Morex. Someone was trying to sabotage this case, and even if it were the former engineers, Morex needed to get to the bottom of it to assess where the next missiles would be coming from–because they all assumed that this first series of documents was just the beginning of an arsenal that the plaintiffs intended to launch. It was a sideshow, totally unrelated to the merits of the lawsuit itself, but it threatened to overshadow everything and become the main event.

The last suggestion Dave made before they wound up the meeting was a strategic masterpiece. "If all else fails, we'll have no choice but to take the wind out of their sails by going public with this news first, and make everything else public as well. The facts underlying the lawsuit, the whole story about the computerized music–all of it."

Don was apoplectic, his eyes bulging and veins popping at the mere thought. "But that's exactly what they want! That stuff gets out, both sides are sunk."

"Not necessarily," Dave said as he looked to Anne, who nodded in agreement. He was a smart guy. "If we break the story first," he explained, "and I mean really break it, a huge splash, then we tailor it the way that suits our purposes, and the plaintiffs are the ones who are caught with their pants down. They're the ones who have been making millions by palming off digitalized compositions and vocals when the public thought it was buying performances by live human beings. And they're the ones who have been stealing internal corporate documents. We're the innocent victims of corporate espionage and an unscrupulous recording industry. Believe me, they'll be playing PR catch-up for the rest of the case."

"What does all that have to do with the lawsuit?"

"Nothing," Anne chimed in. "At that point, the lawsuit's almost irrelevant–it's a public relations war, and Morex comes out on top. Or at least no worse off than the record companies–and that may be as much as we can hope for at that point."

Don sighed and picked up the check, ready to face their scheduled showdown with the plaintiffs. "I hope you guys know what you're doing."

Anne's taxi pulled up in front of the small hotel around ten on the following Friday night. She'd had to turn down Gallagher's offer of a ride to Philadelphia, since she was stuck in the office putting out brushfires until well after Gallagher's noon departure deadline. When Anne had called to tell her she'd be taking the train down later that evening, Gallagher seemed to have detected some of her reluctance to go at all, and made her promise that they'd meet up at the reunion luncheon the next day as planned.

"You know, my parents are going to be insulted that you're not staying with them," Gallagher had said that afternoon on the phone. "My mother had her heart set on seeing you."

"She'll see me, don't worry. She's a Milburn alum, so I'll see her at the reunion."

"You know what I mean."

"I know, but I'm sure she got more than her fill of me way back when. I figure I used up my welcome a long time ago."

The truth was, Anne was always a little uncomfortable seeing Gallagher's mother, ever since that miserable summer after her return from Europe. She'd been a crying fool taking up space in their home for two solid weeks, keeping her presence in the United States a secret from her parents the whole time–she just couldn't deal with coming out to them and explaining the whole sordid mess while drowning in the despair of her first broken heart. Although over the years Mrs. Davenport had always been gracious in assuring her it had been no trouble, Anne couldn't divorce her embarrassing memory of those two weeks from her subsequent visits to the house. Mrs. Davenport had been so wonderful to her during those two weeks–far more understanding than her own mother had proved to be–that Anne simply couldn't make herself impose on their hospitality again.

Besides, this little hotel was so charming. Almost an old-style bed and breakfast, with deep-pile carpeting and antique furnishings tastefully appointed about the individually decorated rooms. Even since Anne's parents had moved to the Berkshires several years ago, she had always enjoyed staying here when she was in Philadelphia on business.

The concierge handed her a message slip as she checked in–she was amused to see that Gallagher had called twice during the evening. Anne ordered a sandwich and a Diet Coke to be sent up to her room, and followed the bellboy into the quaint wood-paneled elevator. All she wanted to do was eat dinner, take a hot bath, and sleep–preferably through to Sunday.

When Anne got into her room, she went straight for the phone. She knew the number by heart, of course, having called it several times a day throughout most of her adolescence, and Gallagher answered on the first ring.

"Okay, you can go to bed now," Anne said. "I'm here."

"I was worrying you'd changed your mind."

"I did, several times. But I'm here anyway. How was the drive?"

"Lonely. I've really got to talk to you about something."

"Okay, shoot."

"Not now. You're still going to the luncheon tomorrow, aren't you?"

"Yes. But the tables are probably divided up by class. I doubt if we'll sit together."

"Well, try to find me afterwards, okay?"

"Okay. I've got some news for you, too."

"Oh?"

"You'll never guess who I saw at the hotel in Minneapolis last week."

Gallagher was quiet for a minute, and Anne smiled at the suspense as she stretched out on the four-poster bed.

"Not Rae," Gallagher said, her tone making it sound like a dirty word. Anne laughed—she got such a kick out of Gallagher's unvarnished disdain for Rae.

"In the flesh."

"You didn't sleep with her, did you?"

"Gallagher, it was a figure of speech. Of course I didn't sleep with her. You know, you're the second person in two weeks to accuse me of sleeping with a straight woman."

"Oh? Who was the other?"

"Just my friend Parker, seeing things that aren't there. Practically accused me of carrying on with one of the summer associates."

"Why?"

"Because some idiot is spreading rumors. It's like I can't be seen talking to a woman without everyone thinking the worst."

"Who is she?"

"Who? Oh, the summer? This friend of mine at work, you've heard me mention her I'm sure, Rachel Evans? She's great—you'd like her. A real Milburn type."

"I resent that," Gallagher said, and Anne could picture her smile at the other end of the line.

"You know what I mean. She went to an all-girls' school and, I don't know, we just click. You know how that is."

"Is she pretty?"

Gallagher was in a weird mood tonight. "Yes, she is. What does that have to do with it?"

"Nothing. I was just curious."

"Anyway, if I were getting laid half as much as everyone seems to think I am, I'd be walking around with a smile on my face seven days a week."

"I hate that phrase."

Anne laughed. "God, you're so Milburn."

"So what did Rae want?"

"Believe it or not, she wanted to apologize. Sort of."

"You're kidding."

"Nope. At least that's what she talked about. But I suspect there was something more to it."

"I'll bet." The irony practically dripped off her words.

"No, not sex." Anne didn't want to bring up Rae's off-the-wall proposition, partly because she knew Gallagher would never let her hear the end of it, and partly because it was just a red herring–she didn't fool herself into thinking that Rae had any real sexual desire for her. Rae used sex like any other tool, to get something else, and the only thing that Rae could be gunning for now was the Morex story. "I think she wants the inside track on a big case I'm on."

Gallagher never asked Anne about her cases except in the most general way–intuitively respecting the confidential nature of Anne's work, just as Anne respected the confidentiality of Gallagher's.

"Well, if she thinks she can get some pillow talk out of you, she obviously doesn't know you very well."

"I wish you'd tell my client that. He saw us in the bar together and laid into me the next morning about talking to the press." She still felt a gnawing little glitch at the thought of Don questioning her like that. Trouble always seemed to materialize in the wake of Rae.

"You set him straight?"

"Pretty much. He's just paranoid about this case. Everyone is. But I think I was able to put his mind at ease. He's known me a long time."

"No one's known you as long as I have, you know."

Anne smiled. "God knows that's true. So, my ancient, older-than-dirt friend, what do you say we try to work in a run in the afternoon tomorrow? If my office leaves me alone, that is."

"You didn't bring any work with you, did you?"

"I don't have to. It seems to follow me wherever I go."

"Okay, we have a while before the dinner-dance. Unless you'd rather go rafting?"

Anne left that one untouched. "A run would be nice. Around the hockey field, like old times. You can tell me all your deep dark secrets."

Gallagher's laugh felt like a warm sunbeam through a part in the drapes. "You already know all my secrets, and I know yours."

Chapter Eleven

Anne got to the luncheon a little late, even though she'd been at the school for over an hour, having left the hotel after an early-morning swim to stroll around the extensive school grounds, soaking up some sun and memories. As usual, she'd lost track of the time once her thoughts digressed to the Morex case. The plaintiffs seemed to have cooled their heels as a result of Dave's threat of court intervention, and everyone had agreed to a short truce–but it was only a matter of time before the shit would hit the fan. The private investigators had been looking into the case for over a week now. Anne just hoped they would turn up something fast. Anne made sure her cell phone was on, and headed across the back lawn where the luncheon was already underway beneath a huge lawn tent.

She spotted Gallagher at the Class of '78 table right away, positively glowing as she sat with her classmates and listened to the swarm of conversation buzzing about her head. Gallagher looked up almost immediately, as if she felt Anne's eyes upon her, and beamed a radiant smile that nearly took Anne's breath away. It must have been the Milburn setting, the nostalgia of the moment in seeing the groups assembled by class–Anne felt a sudden rush of those old feelings from her childhood, and blushed at Gallagher's smile. A smile that seemed to beg for rescue. Time to find her own class, where she belonged.

Just her luck, a place appeared to have been saved right beside her old nemesis, Rhonda Dougherty. Now Hunter, Anne reminded herself. Who could forget the announcement of that wedding back in the early eighties? Anne's mother had sent her the half-page article out of the paper–the union of two of the most socially prominent Philadelphia families, utterly predictable. Anne had used the folded clipping as a coaster until it had eventually disintegrated.

"Why, Anne Henderson," Rhonda squealed. "I can't believe it!" Rhonda was being cordial today, it seemed. Wait until she'd had a few.

Her hair was up in an impossible-looking bun that made her look like a relic from the 1890s, and although her makeup was about an inch too thick, it still failed to mask the bags under her eyes.

"Hi, Rhonda," said Anne. "It's been a long time."

"You remember Sandy and Blair, don't you?" Rhonda asked, relishing her role as self-appointed hostess for the table. As if Anne hadn't spent six years in class with these women.

"Sandy," said Anne, ignoring Rhonda, "I hear your architecture firm is responsible for that wonderful new hotel downtown. I'll have to stay there on my next business trip." That's right, Rhonda, I not only remember them–I know something about the lives they've lived in the past twenty years.

"Yes, that was my project," said Sandy, seeming pleased at the recognition. "Well, me and about ten other people, of course."

"Blair," Anne continued as she turned to the woman beside Sandy, "you're teaching here in the pre-school, aren't you?"

Blair was already on her second mimosa–Anne saw the empty first glass–and appeared to be quite relaxed. It was going to be a long lunch.

"Yup. Five years now. You're not sending me any little brats to watch over, are you?"

Rhonda spoke up before Anne could respond. "Anne doesn't live in town, honey. She's a New Yorker now."

Let's liven this up a bit. Rhonda would certainly know that Anne was a lesbian–it had undoubtedly been hot news burning up the Milburn wires back when Anne had come out–but Anne decided to make the point anyway, for no other reason than she hated the ersatz camaraderie and wanted to be provocative. And, of course, she wanted to watch Rhonda choke on her own spit. It was one of the perks of being gay–the well-timed coming out.

"Actually, Blair," Anne said coolly, "I'm a lesbian. I don't have any children. Yet."

She saw out of the corner of her eye that Rhonda's jaw was practically on the white linen tablecloth, and continued to look at Blair, whose beet red face was an unveiled mixture of shock and embarrassment.

"No, I–I don't believe I knew that," Blair garbled. She couldn't get that mimosa to her mouth fast enough.

"Oh, get over it," Sandy interjected. "Of course you did. You too, Rhonda, we heard about that years ago." She turned her attention to Anne and smiled. "We have a couple of gay architects at our firm. Have you had any problems with your office? People know, don't they?"

So that was it. Sandy would play open-minded urban sophisticate and pitch Rhonda and Blair into the roles of small-town hicks. Philadelphia may be a large city, but Milburn was its own little universe, and was about as small-town and small-minded as you could get. Anne poured herself a glass of water and looked around for one of the student hostesses to bring her a Diet Coke.

"Sure, people know," Anne said. "And the firm's fine. Being gay actually helps, in a way. It keeps the men from hitting on me, except for the real sickos, and it gives me the image of ball-busting bitch. That's a real asset for a lawyer."

Sandy laughed with genuine pleasure. "You'd be a ball-busting bitch no matter who you sleep with. Remember that time in English class, when we got into a huge fight over that e.e. cummings poem?"

Rescued from further agitation by Sandy's deft manipulation of the conversation, the four of them spent the next hour or so in relative comfort–recalling past hijinks, catching up on one another's lives, showing pictures of half-grown children, and eventually listening to a series of welcoming and self-congratulatory remarks from the headmistress and director of the Upper School, generously sprinkled with not-so-subtle pleas for alumnae dollars. Rhonda and Blair were just shy of plastered by the time the plates of smoked salmon were cleared away for dessert. They seemed to become more palatable when they were drunk–or at least more relaxed–so Anne found herself almost enjoying their company. Miraculously, she didn't think once about the Morex case.

The buzz of conversation elevated as soon as the welcome speeches concluded, and Blair was just ordering another mimosa when Anne saw Gallagher rise from her seat several tables away. Anne had unconsciously kept her eyes in the general direction of Gallagher's table throughout the lunch–saw her laughing with Missy Foster, her old friend from the tennis team. She'd kept half an eye open for an available seat at Gallagher's table, any opportunity to join them for a minute. But she might as well have been back in the huge stadium-seating study hall, senior year, looking down on the rows of desks arranged by class in front of the top-most tier of seniors, searching for any chance to steal away unobtrusively to one of the desks neighboring Gallagher's for a quick exchange of a few insignificant words with her, and disappointed that one or the other of them was always so occupied by their respective friends that they hardly ever got the chance to spend even a few private minutes together in school.

Anne barely heard Rhonda's story about the audacity of Redwood Prep having refused to admit her son into the Middle School–she was too distracted by the sight of Gallagher in that lovely yellow dress walking toward the main building with Missy's arm around her shoulder. Probably a bathroom break. Still, the sun seemed to have gone behind some clouds for the moment.

"Our family has given so much money to that school, for generations," Rhonda was saying. "My father went there, and so did Calvert and his father, not to mention my own two brothers." Rhonda was practically seething. Not that she gave two shits about the quality of education her son was being denied–Anne was sure that Rhonda's sole concern was the social slap in the face she perceived from Redwood's rejection. Anne was secretly glad–it was about time these schools started erecting some academic standards for admission. Milburn had done so for years–that was the only reason Anne had been admitted and given a scholarship–but Milburn was the exception among the historically closed ranks of the city's best prep schools. Maybe the twentieth century was finally starting to dawn in the Main Line, now that it was almost over.

Blair and Sandy murmured some condolences in Rhonda's direction, and Anne kept her thoughts to herself as she raised her cup to the hostess pouring coffee.

"Anne," said Sandy, "I don't know how you can resist this peach tart." Sandy didn't seem to mind speaking with her mouth full. It was a refreshing gaffe in an otherwise etiquette-conscious afternoon.

"No thanks, I'm too full from all that salmon," Anne lied. No sense inviting more critical analysis of her habits by confessing that she tried to avoid sugar.

"Do you still swim?" Sandy asked, and Anne was touched that she had remembered this detail from Anne's life. Anne and Sandy hadn't really run in the same circles in high school, had always been little more than long-time acquaintances.

"Yes, whenever I can get to the pool. It's not easy. And I run in Central Park now and then with Gallagher."

"Central Park?" Rhonda was horrified–so much so that she didn't appear to know, or care, that a huge crumb of peach tart was stuck in the heavy red lipstick on her lower lip. "Isn't that dangerous?"

Anne laughed at the absurdity–she always got a kick out of the nightmare image of New York held by the rest of the country. "Yeah, but I carry an Uzi with me. It's a good upper body workout."

"I can't believe you still hang out with Gallagher," said Blair, nearly slurring her words by now. "I never understood why you had to make friends with kids from other classes."

"Well, Gallagher's hardly a kid." She was an accomplished, intelligent, painfully beautiful woman that anyone in their right mind would jump at the chance of knowing. But Anne wasn't about to get into that old debate–not with these people. Anne just shrugged and sipped her coffee.

"You know," said Sandy, "I think it's great you two have kept up after all this time." Her look was almost wistful. "I wish I had some old friends like that still in my life. I'm so busy with work and the kids, I hardly have time to see any friends at all."

Anne felt a hand on her shoulder just then, and instantly tracked a tingling sensation down her back.

"Having a good time?"

Anne looked up into Gallagher's eyes, the color of melted Hershey bars, and smiled. The cavalry was here.

"We were just talking about you," Sandy piped up. "You look sensational. Why am I the only one who's aged in the past twenty years?"

Gallagher slipped into the empty seat beside Anne–when had it been vacated? Anne hadn't even noticed–and left her arm across Anne's shoulders. It felt too good, and Anne was afraid for a second that she'd blush.

"Nothing scandalous, I hope," Gallagher said. She was a natural in this setting, so Anne just sat back and went along for the ride.

Rhonda felt the need to inject herself into the conversation that had briefly excluded her. She leaned forward to speak from Anne's other side. "Well, just a tad. Anne was telling us how you two get together to go running in Central Park."

Gallagher stroked her hand softly on Anne's back–or maybe Anne was just imagining it–and gave them a little smile. "Not nearly enough," Gallagher said. "Anne's so busy with work, I can never drag her out of that office."

"Well, you're not exactly living the life of leisure," Anne said as she turned to face Gallagher. Her stomach clenched for an instant as her eyes lingered on that face. Her complexion was so nicely set off by that yellow dress. And her hair was getting longer too, almost touching her shoulders. Anne loved Gallagher's hair when it was long–tight brown curls just barely tamed into submission. Gallagher returned her gaze for an awkward moment, until Anne broke eye contact to reach for her coffee cup.

"What do you do, Gallagher?" Blair asked, not yet too drunk to overlook the social niceties.

"I'm an investment banker."

Knowing that Gallagher would never tout her own achievements, Anne felt the need to do so. "Gallagher's one of those power brokers they make movies about. She buys and sells companies."

"I thought you were going to be a teacher or something, like me," said Blair. "I'm teaching in pre-school here." Not everything is about you, Blair, Anne thought. And Gallagher couldn't be like you if she tried.

"I keep thinking about doing that," Gallagher replied. "Maybe some-day."

"Are you married?" Rhonda's favorite topic of conversation, after her kids.

"No."

"Wait," Blair said, "you're engaged, aren't you? I'm sure I heard that somewhere."

The hand subtly massaging Anne's back appeared to stop—was it really there at all?

"Not any more," Gallagher said softly. "That's off now."

What?! Anne looked at Gallagher, who shifted her gaze from Rhonda to meet Anne's eyes full on. Now wasn't the time, her look said, and Anne fought to suppress the hundreds of questions that sprang to her lips.

"I'm so sorry to hear that," Sandy said with understanding. She seemed to sense there was a story here, but was too polite to probe.

"Don't be," Gallagher shrugged. "I called it off."

"Why on earth would you do such a thing?" Rhonda's tone suggested she'd just been told that Gallagher was moving to Nepal.

Gallagher returned her eyes to Anne, who was silently trying to absorb what she was hearing. Her voice was soft, as if intended only for Anne's stunned ears. "A lot of reasons, but I guess they all boil down to the fact that he's not the person for me. And I wasn't willing to go on pretending that he is."

Blair smelled blood. "Ooh, sounds like there's someone else in the pic-ture. Come on, tell."

Gallagher smiled at Anne, the blush so bright, so poignant on that strik-ing face that Anne couldn't peel her eyes away if she'd wanted to. But Anne was drowning in the chocolate-brown eyes and didn't want to stop.

"Blair, you're terrible," chided Sandy. "Now leave Gallagher alone." Thank you, Sandy. I didn't want to hear about some other guy in Gallagher's life right now. Not ever.

Gallagher removed her hand from Anne's back, or had it been on the back of her chair all along? It must have been on the back of the darted blue silk blouse that Anne had worn especially because it brought out the little bit of blue in her eyes. Anne felt the ghost of Gallagher's hand once it was gone. Just a slight chill where the warmth had been.

It was a mistake to come, a mistake to think that she could be with Gallagher in this setting and not be inundated with the feelings and memo-ries of their past. Memories are just phantoms, she told herself, just some-thing recalled from long ago, without form or substance. They're not real and they can't hurt you. Didn't her evening with Rae prove that? But for some reason these memories were feeling very real, as if they'd been there all along, dormant, now beginning to awaken from a long hibernation and threatening to jeopardize the most important relationship–friendship–in her life. Get out of here.

"It's been great seeing all of you," Anne said as she stood up and re-trieved her purse from the back of the chair.

"Yes," said Gallagher, who was on her feet in a flash, towering over Anne at her side. "We're going to have a little run this afternoon before the dinner-dance tonight. Work off some of that salmon."

Damn, that's right, she'd forgotten. She could always claim a work emergency and get out of the rest of the weekend, get back to her cocoon in New York.

"You two are just too healthy for my blood," snorted Rhonda. "I'm go-ing to take the champagne tour of the new wing, and then a nice long nap." Rhonda didn't look like she needed any more champagne–but with any luck, she'd sleep through the entire dinner-dance. Anne and Gallagher exchanged quick goodbyes with the group before Gallagher grabbed her hand, practically wrenching her from the tableside and out onto the great lawn toward the main building.

As soon as they were away from the highest concentration of milling alums who were scattered in twos and threes across the back lawn, Gallagher increased the pressure on her hand.

"I wanted to tell you before," she said apologetically, "but you were out of town, and then so wrapped up at the office–I didn't get the chance."

"When did it happen?" Anne asked. She wanted to ask how it had happened, but didn't want to hear about this other guy–and she was sure there was one, something about Gallagher's manner when Blair had asked.

"Two weeks ago. Right after our night out at the theatre, in fact. Joel came back early."

Don't tell me he found you with someone else. I don't want to hear it.

"We got into an argument," Gallagher continued. "Well, not really, it was more of a continuation of a discussion we'd been having for months. And I just decided, that's it. I really didn't care enough to keep fighting anymore. I didn't care enough about him, or the relationship, or the wedding, or any of it. It just wasn't worth it."

This isn't making sense at all. "I don't get it. You just woke up one morning and decided to call it off?"

Gallagher was looking off into the distance, and the soft breeze blew some brown curls across her face. Anne wanted to brush them away, but didn't.

"In a way. It's more like I woke up one morning with a clear mind. I realized what I'd been feeling for a long time, and not feeling. I always sort of knew–I was fighting with myself more than him, I guess. I think I just gave in more than gave up." She turned to look at Anne as they reached the sidewalk that would take them around the main building and into the parking lot in front. "You can't believe the relief I felt. I know it's a cliché, but it's really true. It was like this incredible weight was lifted off me. I was happy, really happy, for the first time in I-don't-know-how-long."

And she looked happy, looked lighter somehow. She seemed to stand taller, walk with more bounce in her step. Her face was softer too, as if some barely discernible stress lines had been airbrushed out of the picture. The overall effect was magnetic, and Anne felt it powerfully.

"Are you saying you don't love him anymore?"

Gallagher sighed a little and pushed the hair away from her face. They were nearing the parking lot. "I guess I do, in a way. But not in that special way that makes people get married. It was never like that. It was always more of a friendship than something romantic. Like looking at a picture of a love affair, rather than living in it or feeling it. I guess I thought that was enough, that I could make that work."

Gallagher was quiet for a moment before continuing, seeming to choose her words carefully. "But that's not enough. It couldn't be. And the more I pushed myself to feel something that wasn't there, the more miserable I was. How could I marry him when nothing about it was right?" Her voice got quiet, although no one else was around to hear. "I think I know what's right for me–I guess I've known it all along–and he's not it."

The heaviness that had been lifted from Gallagher suddenly found a home in Anne's chest. There was someone else after all. And although Anne should be happy for her friend, all she really felt like doing was crying. Don't say anything. Just walk–there's the car–don't think about the warmth of Gallagher's hand, just get back to the hotel and leave.

"I guess you know exactly what I'm talking about," Gallagher said after a few more steps. "I remember you saying just about the same thing that night we went out drinking in Ithaca." Anne looked at her, puzzled. "When you told me about Rae."

Anne couldn't remember anything she'd said that night, but shook her head anyway. There may be some comparisons between her own coming out and Gallagher's revelation that she shouldn't marry Joel, but there were distinct differences. Anne couldn't bring herself to point them out at this particular moment, though–she was too annoyed with herself for getting caught up in a maelstrom of old feelings that had no place here. This was Gallagher's issue, not hers. And Gallagher needed her to just be a friend right now.

"I don't know what to say," offered Anne, trying to keep her voice under control—so much so that she knew she sounded cold, indifferent. Better that than to burst into tears. "To tell you the truth, I don't remember much from that night."

Gallagher stopped a few feet from the car and turned to Anne, still holding her hand, her grip a vise. Gallagher's face betrayed a mixture of excitement and caution. Even a little fear. "Annie, don't you get what I'm trying to tell you?"

Anne just stared at her, wondering where the conversation had taken a sudden left turn into confusion. Everything in Gallagher's manner told her that she should get it, that Gallagher was patiently waiting for it to sink in. But Anne didn't want to get it, didn't want to play a guessing game with Gallagher that could only end with a discussion about some new man in Gallagher's life. Anne stared into the brown eyes that peered at her from that matchless face—a face that she knew better than her own—unable to make sense of the insistent ringing of something that kept intruding into her consciousness. Something like a phone. It was a phone, her cell phone, and she pulled it out of her purse on automatic pilot.

"Anne Henderson," she said dully. Was that her voice?

"Anne, it's Don."

"Don?" She was underwater, moving in slow motion. And Gallagher was standing in front of her, still holding something that resembled her hand.

"Yeah, look, I'm sorry to bother you, I know you're away, but I'm faxing you something at your hotel. You've got to take a look at it right away. It's from the PI's. Where are you?"

Don's frantic tone switched her into gear. "I'm at my school reunion." She covered the phone and mouthed to Gallagher, "It's a client."

Don kept talking. "How far are you from the hotel?"

"I can be at the hotel in–" she looked at Gallagher, who nodded and started to walk briskly to the driver side of the car, "twenty minutes. What's happened?"

"They've discovered where the copies were made. It was at Morex–recently. Something about after-images on the photocopiers tipped them off."

Shit, that meant it was an inside job, not the engineers, who hadn't had access to the Morex offices for several years. It put a whole new spin on the corporate espionage.

Gallagher drove her back to the hotel with Anne talking to Don the whole way. Anne had no idea if she'd make it to the dinner that night–it would depend on what she found in the PI's report and what she would be able to accomplish by phone in the next few hours. She may even have to leave for New York tonight. Gallagher was understanding, and tried to hide her disappointment. Anne left her at the car with a promise to call either way.

Two faxes and four hours of phone calls later, Anne wasn't much further in her understanding of the Morex situation. They'd narrowed the list of people with access to those files, but it was still a sizeable number, and would require background and bank-account checks on all fifteen of them. Given that it was a weekend, there were very few people at work, so the PI's were presently on the Morex premises searching the offices for leads.

When she finally got around to retrieving her voice-mail messages from her office in New York, Anne was pleased to hear Joey's voice. She still didn't know if she'd have to leave for New York tonight–wouldn't know for another hour or so, when the PI's were expected to report in–so she decided to take the time now to return Joey's call.

"How's my favorite ski bum?" Anne asked when Joey answered the phone.

"Yo, Anne, good to hear from you!"

"You called me."

"Right." He was as crazy as ever. Once he'd sold his interest in the company to Don, he'd effectively retired on his millions, and had become even more eccentric. At least he wore shoes now. She still loved him. "Where are you?" he asked. "Don said you're away this weekend."

"You've been talking to Don?" What for?

"Yeah, he called a few days ago to complain about this lawsuit and see what I could remember about those engineers who'd tried to hold us up."

"And?"

He laughed. "You've got to be kidding. I can't even remember my own name."

"Well, it doesn't matter anyway. It doesn't look like they're responsible for what Don's worried about."

"You're being as mysterious as he is–he wouldn't say why he wanted to know."

"Lawyer stuff."

"Whatever. Anyway, he sounded awfully upset, so I thought I'd come to New York and let him buy me dinner. You too, I'll take as many free meals as I can get."

"Hey, that's great. When are you coming?"

"Next week. Maybe Tuesday or Wednesday?"

"Perfect. But I assume this trip isn't totally altruistic. What's her name, and is she over eighteen?"

Joey gave her a snort. "What, I can't just be in a generous mood?"

"Spill it."

"Okay, I admit it, I've got a box at the Mets game for Thursday. But really, there's no woman in the picture."

"Baseball? Come on."

"Really. I've been single for over a year. Almost two."

"I find that hard to believe," Anne teased. Ever since Joey and Jane had divorced ten years ago, he'd had a neverending series of increasingly brief relationships with younger and younger women.

"Honest. The last one was just too weird. I figured I'd take some time out from all that for a while."

"Who was the last?" Anne asked. She remembered Joey mentioning her, but didn't think she'd ever met her. Anne recalled that she had been a bit older than his usual conquests, too, already a few years out of college.

"Elizabeth. You would have liked her. She was a law student, or about to be."

"Great. No wonder she was weird."

"No, she wasn't weird. It's just how it ended that was so bizarre. She just took off. She said she was leaving for school, but it was so sudden, you know, everything was great and then she was just gone."

"Must have been your charm." The light on her phone started to flash. "Listen, I have to go. But I'll see you in New York next week. Call me when you get in, okay?"

"Okay."

The message wasn't from the PI's, it was from Parker. What else could go wrong? She called him back right away.

"What are you doing in the office on a Saturday?" she asked when he picked up on the first ring.

"Cleaning up your messes, of course. Look, I just wanted to give you a heads-up about something before you get in on Monday. You know, any chance to ruin your weekend."

"Gee, thanks. What?" Although his voice was light, she didn't like the sound of it.

"Can you think of any reason why Darryl would be in the Morex war room?"

An iceberg formed in the pit of her stomach and started to spread its frozen tentacles throughout her chest. The war room was a small office that had been taken over by the Morex team for review of documents and team meetings. One or more associates on the team could be found there at nearly any time, day or night, poring through the files. Her voice was steel as she considered the possibilities. "None at all."

"Well, I was walking by a little while ago, and there he was. Alone."

"What was he doing?"

"Nothing. Just standing by the table. But when I said hi, he seemed a little uncomfortable, and left right away."

Anne sighed heavily. Parker knew as well as she did that Darryl had no business in there, that his presence there suggested the inconceivable–that he was involving himself in the Morex case, and might even be responsible for the document leak. She couldn't begin to imagine the consequences if it were true.

"Lock that room and get a key to the team," Anne said. "Who's at the office now?"

"Amanda and Rachel."

"Okay, I'll call Grady at home and tell him to get a key from you. Meanwhile, keep an eye on Darryl."

"You want me to talk to him?"

"No, I'll handle it Monday morning. But I'm going to have the investigators look into him too between now and then."

"Do you really think that's necessary?"

"Parker, I don't like this any better than you do. But if he's responsible for what's been going on, we have to know about it. Right away."

"The firm could take a big hit on this if you're right."

"Tell me about it," she sighed. She'd personally take a bigger hit, and he knew that too.

Anne's taxi pulled up outside Milburn Academy shortly after nine. She'd seriously considered not going at all, but there was nothing she could accomplish by going back to New York at this point, and although the dinner portion of the evening was probably over, she might enjoy the dance. Get her mind off the impending doom that awaited her on Monday morning.

Because it was becoming clear that the Morex files had not been transmitted to the plaintiffs by any current Morex employees. The PI's had been thorough in a relatively short amount of time–nothing incriminating had turned up in any of the offices, nothing in the phone records or bank accounts to suggest anything out of the ordinary. Computers were wonderful things.

But that left only one possibility, and Anne had the PI's working all day tomorrow on it–the Morex lawyers had to be involved. They'd start with an investigation of Darryl, but in an abundance of caution, Anne had instructed them to look into the team members themselves, including Anne, just to shore up evidence excluding the team from any complicity. She'd need that kind of evidence when she confronted Darryl.

It was too late to call Gallagher by the time she'd finally hung up from her last call–surely Gallagher would have already left for the dinner–so Anne jumped into the shower and then threw on the cream-colored silk slacks, white blouse, and pearls that she'd brought for the night. She barely recognized her excited, slightly sunned face in the mirror as she ran a brush through her golden hair. Not that it mattered anyway–who could she dress up for at this gathering?

The alumnae association had kept the large tent erected on the back lawn, and since lunchtime had laid down a dance floor in the middle, with an orchestra podium off to the side. A five-piece dance band was playing some swing from the forties. Something for the old-timers–there would be no rock and roll tonight, which was just as well. Anne was in no mood for it.

She strolled to the crowded bar at the far side of the tent to order a Diet Coke, and scanned the crowd for familiar faces. Naturally, the groups appeared to be congregated largely by class, and she spotted Mr. and Mrs. Davenport at a table with a group of older couples, the women probably Mrs. Davenport's classmates from '46. Anne was just about to approach their table to say hello when she caught sight of a few of her own classmates, several with bored-looking husbands in tow, gathered near the dance floor. She decided to make her way over to the younger group first to say hi. Gallagher was nowhere in sight.

Anne saw that Sandy, Rhonda, and the ubiquitous Blair, each apparently dateless, were laughing uncontrollably with a group of several couples over some remark by Brooke, one of Anne's fellow altos from the Glee Club. Many of them appeared to be wobbling on their feet already, from either hysteria or inebriation.

"Well, so many of us are dateless tonight," she heard Brooke saying as she joined them, "we're going to have to dance with each other!" Brooke seemed to find the observation incredibly witty, and was too drunk to notice Sandy's frown. Rhonda and Blair exchanged a look before Rhonda turned to acknowledge Anne.

"Oh, Anne doesn't have a problem with that, do you, Anne?" said Rhonda. Anne forced herself not to roll her eyes, and merely smiled as she greeted everyone, deliberately pushing aside the conviction that she should not have come tonight. After a moment, the band struck up "In the Mood," and several of the assembled women paired off for the dance floor, with husbands or each other, leaving Anne with Rhonda, Brooke, and Blair.

Anne decided the moment was opportune to remove herself gracefully and wander over to the Davenports' table, but when she turned from the group she spotted Gallagher seated with several classmates on the other side of the dance floor. Gallagher caught her eye, smiled, and left her companions mid-sentence to rise and nod toward Anne, who stood rooted to the floor for a moment, heart suddenly leaping in her chest. All at once, it was twenty years ago, the Spring Dance, and Anne was a confused, lovesick teenager struck dumb by the overpowering beauty of the woman who was walking toward her–a woman whose playful smile was directed only at Anne. A woman whose graceful, mesmerizing gait acted as a magnetic charge, pulling Anne in the direction of the dance floor. Anne automatically put one foot in front of the other in the direction of Gallagher. They met in the middle of the dance floor and, without a word, fell into the steps they'd perfected years before, in Gallagher's basement, listening to her father's old records.

"I didn't think you'd come," Gallagher said, beaming a sunrise smile.

"I wasn't sure myself until a little while ago." Anne cautioned herself not to stare too closely. Gallagher was breathtaking tonight, her hair begging to have fingers run through it, her incredible shoulders and back exposed in a burgundy halter that came together in a tantalizing V at her cleavage, her long athletic legs shown to perfection in the seamless eggshell slacks. Her entire body seemed to be bathed in an intense, vibrating aura that called to Anne powerfully.

"You look fantastic," Gallagher said. I do? Even with this silly grin plastered on my face? Anne feared her sudden blush was betraying every secret in her heart, and looked away.

"You do too," Anne mumbled.

"Everything taken care of at work?"

She nodded, not wanting to think about work. Not now. Gallagher gently tightened her hand at Anne's hip. "Good, then you're all mine tonight." I'm all yours every night. That's the problem. Change the subject.

"Did I miss much at the dinner?" Anne asked, and then laughed at the look that Gallagher gave her, conveying just how ridiculous the question was. They smiled at each other again, as if sharing a private joke. It was amazing how some things were never forgotten—like dance steps she hadn't attempted in decades. Like feelings she'd thought were completely buried. They danced through the song as if born to it.

The band segued into "Dancing in the Dark," its rich melody sending the already enchanted evening into a deeper, more textured realm. Anne couldn't help but think of a night many years ago when she and Gallagher had watched Fred Astaire and Cyd Charisse fall in love to these chords. A night they'd spent side by side on Anne's living-room sofa watching *The Band Wagon*, Anne acutely aware of Gallagher's rapture at the sensuous dance onscreen, Gallagher's leg pressed against hers. An evening that was deeply moving as only a sixteen-year-old can experience it, watching a glorious Hollywood love story while sitting beside her beloved.

Suddenly, it was just too much for Anne, who felt herself beginning to surrender to the feelings that this nostalgia-laden night was evoking, the feelings that Gallagher's mere presence inspired. She knew that she should just leave the dance floor as the love song began, knew that it was crazy to answer Gallagher's beckoning look by stepping closer into the arms that were urging her to dance.

She looked into Gallagher's face—and felt a rush of desire so intense that she almost shuddered. Gallagher's look was too alluring, too tempting. Gallagher didn't seem to care what the others would think, and Anne couldn't think straight at all—her judgment impaired by unbidden memories of long-dormant dreams and a sudden, relentless thundering between her legs as she felt Gallagher's arms encircle her in a full-body slow-dance embrace. What the hell, fuck Milburn. She was powerless to resist.

Anne stepped into the dance and gingerly moved her hands up Gallagher's slender bare arms to wrap them around the back of that long swan neck. The skin was so incredibly smooth, Anne could have happily spent the rest of the night, the rest of the century, just running her hands along those arms. She was drawn into Gallagher's irresistible spell, melted into it as she felt the heat, the tantalizing friction of their bodies pressed together. This dance would fuck with Anne's mind for weeks, she knew it, but she didn't care. The only thing that mattered was that she was back in the delectable arms that she'd craved for so many years.

"Think we're causing a scandal by dancing like this?" Gallagher whispered as she stared mischievously into Anne's eyes, seeming to enjoy the provocative display—just as she had at the Rhino a hundred years or so ago. But the difference was, this time she knew she was dancing with a lesbian, and everyone else knew it too.

Anne tried to ignore the pounding of her heart, tried to forget about her swollen insistent throbbing, and turned her head to lay it, just barely, on

Gallagher's shoulder. "It'll probably be written up in the *Alumnae News*," Anne said, careful not to show her shortness of breath.

Gallagher laughed. " 'Lesbians Take Over Milburn Reunion.' I love it." Yeah, well, it won't be you they'll hold responsible. Oh, well.

"You know," Gallagher said in a low velvet voice right beside her ear, "I've never forgotten that night we went out to that gay bar. When we went dancing."

Me either. "Oh?"

Against her better judgment, Anne lifted her head to peer into Gallagher's face, and saw there a look of such intensity that Anne's mind was momentarily wiped blank. She knew she should avert her eyes, but could not. She also knew that she shouldn't run her hands across the silky back of Gallagher's neck, but she was doing it before she could stop herself, and watched in delirious fascination as Gallagher bit her lower lip slowly, seductively, half-closing those deep brown eyes in a display of obvious and sensuous pleasure. Those lips, mere inches from Anne's, curled into an almost-smile, so perfect to kiss. What was she thinking? That underwater sensation threatened to come back. Only this time it was a tidal wave, tsunami, ready to break over her head and topple her underneath.

The song ended and Gallagher broke the spell as she stepped back a fraction and slid one arm around Anne's waist to lead her off the dance floor. "Come with me," she whispered. "And don't bring your cell phone." The thought of resisting never entered Anne's mind. Without another word, she let Gallagher lead her out onto the lawn, away from the crowd, over to the grove of cherry trees surrounding the pond. She hadn't brought her cell phone tonight, or purse, or anything but I.D. and a few dollars in her pocket. She was free to dance, free to roam among the tables, free to go wherever Gallagher would take her.

They stood in the shadows, shielded from the night sky by the fragrant branches of cherry trees, and stared at the lily pads floating on top of the pond. Gallagher left her arm around Anne, and Anne tried to get her heart rate down and cool the molten lava that had poured out between her legs.

It was no use–she was not going to quell her excitement at this point unless she got away from Gallagher altogether, and that was out of the question. Instead, she leaned into Gallagher's side, slipped her own arm around Gallagher's slender waist, and enjoyed the peaceful quiet of the night. They hadn't had a moment like this in years–not since that cast party, their walk in the garden. She turned her head to look at Gallagher, wondering if she was recalling the same scene, wondering if she remembered it at all. Wondering if Gallagher had any inkling of the overwhelming effect her presence was having on Anne–had always had, especially when they were alone together on a dark night. Gallagher lifted her hand just then, and brushed the golden bangs from Anne's brow–it was such a sweet gesture, so loving, that Anne suddenly felt herself tear up. The magic of their dance, the thrill at her touch, the unspeakable longing, were all somehow heart-breaking.

"Now that I'm finally here," Gallagher said softly, looking into her eyes, "I can't seem to say what I want to say." Gallagher's expression was almost pleading. "You're going to have to help me."

What does she want me to do? If it were anyone else, Anne wouldn't think twice about it. She'd recognize the scene, the undeniably electric tension, for exactly what it was–she'd know the rules, and she'd throw herself into it wholeheartedly. But as desperately as she wanted Gallagher at this moment, as intensely as every cell in her body was responding to her slightest touch, she just couldn't do it–couldn't take the chance that it was all in her head, that she was experiencing it all by herself, caught up in a flood of self-induced feelings from the past. Because this was Gallagher, her straight friend, her closest, oldest friend. The stakes were unimaginably high, and her perception of everything was simply too distorted by the years upon years of longing, much as she'd tried to deny it.

"I can't do that, Gallagher," Anne said, her voice barely audible. "You're too important to me. I–I can't let myself guess at what you're trying to say."

Gallagher reached up with her free hand and wiped away the tear that had somehow slipped down Anne's cheek. When had that happened? Whatever Anne had just said, it seemed to have given Gallagher the courage she'd needed, if only for a moment. But that's all it took–Gallagher traced the wet tear streak down Anne's face, then leaned in and kissed it slowly. Anne could not hold back the small sigh that escaped her at that first feather touch of Gallagher's lips, and steadied herself against the tsunami that hovered now, ready to crash and sweep her away. It was no use–it didn't matter, none of it mattered.

Anne instinctively moved her hands up to Gallagher's shoulders, driven by an overwhelming need to press herself to Gallagher, to feel the length of Gallagher against her. Gallagher pulled back from kissing her cheek just long enough to search Anne's eyes–and seemed to find what she was looking for, a naked desire that Anne knew she was now unashamedly radiating–the kiss on the cheek having melted the last of Anne's resolve not to give in to the colossal pull of Gallagher's invitation. Anne watched in fascination as Gallagher's smile transformed into something so delicious, so blatantly erotic, that Anne's already rapid pulse flipped into overdrive. She was on the edge, felt herself pulled to the brink of something terrifying and enormous, as Gallagher's hand slowly started to move around to the back of Anne's head, her fingers laced lovingly through Anne's hair. Gallagher gently coaxed Anne's head the few remaining inches it took. As Anne closed her eyes, she felt the warm, soft press of Gallagher's lips against her own, and let the universe swallow her.

Anne was lost in the waves, drowning in the tidal flow of emotions that had been held so long at bay. The glowing embers of desire they'd been tending for the past hour suddenly ignited at the press of their lips into a flaming, all-consuming rage. Within seconds, Gallagher's tongue was in her mouth, probing and searching every inch of tongue, every crevice, with such insistence, such increasing speed, that Anne felt its effect as immediately as if it were working its magic directly on her hammering clit. The kiss that had lasted only seconds in her dreams now stretched into minutes, and the crushing strength of her lock on Gallagher was matched pound for pound by the power of Gallagher's stronghold. Anne pressed herself into Gallagher's body, her chest, pelvis, thighs all moving, grinding, begging for contact. She felt Gallagher's leg deftly nudge its way between her own, and oh God, Anne knew if she straddled that thigh, even just a bit, she would come for sure.

Anne pulled way from the kiss to catch her breath, and nearly died all over again at the sight of Gallagher's disheveled, heavy-lidded look, arousal steaming off her. A small seductive smile played on Gallagher's slightly swollen lips.

"You're taking me back to your hotel with you, aren't you?" Gallagher said, her voice strewn with gravel, thick with desire. Anne had never heard anything more powerful, and felt her legs weaken momentarily–dizzy from the surge of yearning that instantly flooded her every pore.

"Are you sure?" was all that Anne could think to say as she searched Gallagher's eyes. She wasn't thinking very clearly, it was happening so quickly–an adrenaline and hormone high that was clogging every pathway to her brain except for her most basic sensory receptors. No cognitive function, just raw feeling. She was alive, resonating with unfulfilled need.

A whisper of uncertainty clouded Gallagher's face for a heartbeat. "Don't you want to?" she asked cautiously.

"More than anything," Anne said, tightening her arms. "I'm dying for you."

Gallagher smiled and stroked Anne's face as if it were a delicate work of art. She spoke softly, her voice a smooth gloss overlaying the exposed, static urgency vibrating between them. "Then what else do I have to do to throw myself at you?"

Anne heard herself moan–she could take it no longer–and hungrily reached for Gallagher's face again, kissing her boldly, deeply, immediately rekindling the white-hot combustion that had not really abated at all, feeding the flames with each thrust of her desperate tongue, the passion and heartache of twenty restrained years blossoming in an outpouring of tears and unmitigated want. She felt Gallagher's hands slip from around her back and begin massaging her breasts, and her taut nipples strained through the silk blouse in response, screaming to capture every exquisite sensation from those masterful fingers. Anne ran her hands across Gallagher's shoulders, through her hair, and shamelessly pressed herself ever further, ever deeper into the body that was engulfing her, enveloping her in a raging torrent of incendiary need. This couldn't go on, not here–they were dangerously close to the point of no return, and another moan from Gallagher, another press from her leg, would make it impossible to stop.

"Well, what have we here?"

Gallagher's hand froze and immediately shot away from Anne's blouse as she broke the hermetic seal of their lips and pulled out of the embrace, leaving Anne's head spinning in the yearning aftermath. Anne felt as if a part of her own body had been severed for an instant, and turned in the direction of Gallagher's panicked gaze–where she saw Rhonda and Blair standing a few yards away, staring at them.

"Don't you two think that's a little inappropriate here?" Rhonda said, a malicious gleam in her eye.

"No," said Gallagher quickly, her voice catching slightly in her throat. "It's not what you think."

It's not? Why was Gallagher backing away with her eyes bulging like that? Why were those hands that had just massaged Anne's breasts to near climax now straightening her hair as if she were preparing for a debutante party?

"Come on, Rhonda. Let's go," said Blair, tugging on Rhonda to pull her toward the tent. Anne's mind didn't register the snicker Rhonda delivered as a parting shot–she was too focused on the glacier that had descended over Gallagher's face, crushing everything in its path and burying those beloved features under a mountain of ice.

"Gallagher?" Anne said, taking a tentative step forward. Gallagher recoiled instantly, and Anne felt it as acutely as a slap.

"Don't," said Gallagher, looking about wildly for a place to rest her eyes, anywhere but on Anne. "I–I can't talk right now." She took another step backwards, as if anticipating Anne's movement toward her–but Anne didn't move, rooted as she was to this spot under cherry blossoms that would never look the same to her, trying to make sense of what was happening. In the silence, Anne experienced the enormity of the rejection–and the end of their friendship–in simultaneous blows to the gut.

"Don't you think we should talk about this?" asked Anne quietly, searching Gallagher's face for direction, some sign to acknowledge the passion they'd just abandoned.

Anne's question seemed to switch Gallagher into gear. "No," she said emphatically. "I have to go. I'm sorry." Gallagher's usual grace had curiously left her–she practically stumbled in her haste to get away.

Watching Gallagher's retreating back, Anne felt the world shut down with the cooling of her wet desire. She stood under the cherry trees for a few blank moments before setting out toward the main building, where she called for a cab. It picked her up after ten minutes of utter nothing. Within one hour she had checked out of her hotel room and boarded the train for New York.

Chapter Twelve

Darryl was in her office on Monday morning at nine sharp, looking scared but defiant. Anne had asked Parker to attend the meeting as well–she wanted a witness. There was no telling where this meeting would end up, but one thing was certain: Darryl had some serious explaining to do. Especially in light of her early morning chat with Rachel, who had accosted Anne as soon as she'd arrived at eight. Although Anne was used to Rachel's visits first thing in the morning, the look on Rachel's face today told her that something was wrong–she'd closed the door and taken a seat across from Anne without any of their usual warm-up banter, and after a moment had cautiously launched into her story: apparently Darryl was hitting on her, getting downright offensive in pestering her for a date, and she was beginning to feel uncomfortable working in the same department with him.

Anne was outraged, but Rachel had insisted that she didn't want to lodge a formal complaint–she was approaching Anne as a friend, seeking guidance only. Anne explained that something would have to be done, and probably would be, because the firm took very seriously any reports of potentially harassing conduct. Rachel had shrugged, and seemed willing to let it drop at that.

"So did you have a nice time at your reunion?" Rachel asked casually, her expression softening with the change of topic. She seemed to pick up immediately on Anne's strained expression. "What's wrong?"

"No, it was horrible." Anne didn't want to get into it, she wanted to focus on work and forget the whole thing. She knew that was impossible, but she'd be damned if she'd dwell on it during working hours. She'd be damned if she'd cry in front of Rachel, or anyone else.

Rachel's voice was soft and full of concern. Her violet eyes searched Anne's, and Anne couldn't bear one of her too-long gazes just then, so she'd looked away.

"Look," said Rachel gently, "if you want to talk about it, I'm here."

"I appreciate it. Thanks. But I'm fine." She wasn't, and Rachel probably knew it, but she needed to refocus on work.

"Oh, I know you're fine. But come by later anyway, okay? After all, I'm not doing anything but slaving away for you, and that can always be interrupted." This was one morning that Anne was in no mood to entertain Rachel's increasingly bold flirtations. After this weekend, Anne doubted she'd ever again play with any come-ons, especially from curious straight thrill-seekers. That door was forever closed. Anne had returned Rachel's engaging smile with a half-hearted nod, and turned her attention to the papers on her desk in a gesture of frank dismissal. Rachel had gotten the hint, and left Anne with just a few minutes to prepare for her showdown with Darryl. By the time he was seated in front of her, Anne felt ready to improvise as needed.

"Darryl, do you know why you're here?" Let's cut right to the chase.

"Not really, no." His look dared her to challenge him. She was only too happy to oblige.

"We've had a serious breach of security in the Morex case. And you were recently seen in the Morex war room, where you had no business." Less is more. She decided to let him chew on that a while. His cocky attitude didn't budge an inch, so she fed him a little more line. "Our private investigators have determined that the breach was not accomplished by any Morex personnel, past or present." Pause. "They're now investigating the attorneys. Is there anything you'd like to tell me before I receive their report?"

His quick, frightened glance at Parker was the only glitch in an otherwise seamless performance. But it was enough. She had him.

"Well, it looks like you guys have already formed your own opinions, so there's nothing really for me to say. Until the investigators finish their work and you come apologize to me, that is."

Parker uncrossed his legs and leaned his elbows on his knees in a posture of friend and confidante. "We haven't made up our minds about anything," said Parker. "But in fairness to you, if you've got any explanation for what's been going on, we want to give you the chance to say it here."

"I don't have any idea about any security breach. No matter what you believe, I'm not involved. I wasn't doing anything in the Morex war room when Parker saw me the other day. I had been talking to Rachel, and she'd just left for a minute–she said she'd be right back–so I was waiting for her. I don't see what's the big deal."

Let's blast him with one he's not expecting. "They maybe you can tell us why you're spreading rumors about me and Rachel," said Anne. The look that paralyzed his face was worth the wait. She had seen that look often, many years ago. Stagefright.

"I–I don't . . ."

Anne flipped through pages on a notepad. "Let's see, the first one was about a month ago, late June. Several more two weeks ago. Last week you really seem to have picked up steam." In fact, the notepad had nothing but doodles on it, but Anne kept it shielded from Darryl's view.

"Okay, look," he said, "maybe I said something. And I'm sorry about that. But it's completely inappropriate, and you know it. I was just saying what everyone else was thinking." He was warming to the subject, starting to speak more forcefully. It was the first time Anne had actually seen him behave as a lawyer instead of an ass-kissing sycophant. "In fact, I'm considering bringing a sex-discrimination suit against the firm. Preferential treatment to your little girlfriend, while the guys like me are getting shut out of work on your cases."

She would enjoy wiping that smug look off his face. She started slowly, with the measured cadence that she usually saved for summations. "Darryl, listen to me carefully. First of all, it's not true. There's nothing but a friendship between me and Rachel, no matter what your obviously troubled little mind has conjured. Second, you'd better have a lot of money behind you, because the counterclaim I'll assert for defamation will be beyond anything you can afford on your soon-to-be nonexistent salary.

And third, you may be facing your own sexual harassment suit, if it's true that you've been hitting on Rachel and refusing to take no for an answer."

The smugness wavered just a bit, but didn't totally disappear. "I'd say you've got your facts screwed up," he said. "It's Rachel who came on to me, but when I asked her out she turned me down. That's when I found out about the two of you–she told me herself."

What? Anne stared at him for a moment as she processed this information. He had to be lying. But why would he make up something like this? Anne proceeded carefully, with the soft killer voice that told all listeners to beware. "You've got sixty seconds to explain exactly what you're talking about before I have security escort you out of the building."

Darryl sat upright, on the edge of the chair, and looked Anne square in the eye. "She told me all about it. When I asked her out, she didn't say no at first–she kept putting me off, saying she was involved with someone else, but she'd consider it. Finally she just said no, and I dropped it–and that's when she told me it was you she's involved with, not that guy she's living with. She said that you've been having an affair almost since the summer started."

Parker jumped in. "And when did she supposedly say this?" he asked, animated by this development.

"Lots of times," Darryl answered. "Most recently, just this Saturday, before you walked by the war room."

Anne couldn't move on to the 'when' just yet–she was still stuck on the 'what.' "Wait, back up," she said. "Are you sure she meant a sexual affair? Think clearly, what exactly did she say?"

"Yes, a sexual affair. She said you were lovers. She even talked about how hot you were in bed." He looked embarrassed for a second. "Sorry." Anne shrugged. "Look," he continued, almost pleading, "I don't care what you do in your private life, I really don't. But when it's in the office like this, it's just not fair."

Anne shook her head. "Darryl, I'll say it again–it's not true. None of it. We're friends, that's it." She looked at Parker. "But this is raising an issue that we're going to have to think about." She returned her gaze to Darryl, who seemed to have lost most of his bluster and was waiting for her to pass judgment. "Darryl, I don't want you to say a word about this conversation to anyone. No one, got that? You may find yourself in the middle of a lawsuit yet, but as a witness, not a party."

He looked confused. "What's going to happen–what am I supposed to do?"

"Just do your work for now," she said. "You're not fired. We're going to have to get to the bottom of this, but I don't think there will be any repercussions for you if you're telling me the truth. And stay away from Rachel for now."

He looked contrite as he left her office, and Anne almost felt sorry for him. But she didn't have time to think about it. She had to call the investigators.

Don was in her office by eleven on Wednesday to await the report from the investigators, which for some reason was taking longer than they'd expected. Something about the investigation had required them to travel out of town, and they were due back any minute.

As they waited, Don filled her in on his dinner with Joey last night. Joey was still playing with a jazz band when he felt like it, and otherwise spent his time surfing in Hawaii and skiing in Lake Tahoe. He'd be coming by for lunch around noon, but Anne didn't know if she would be able to leave the office by then–it depended on when the PI's arrived, and what they'd found.

"Where are your people now? I don't want them in the vicinity if the news is bad," said Don, whose pacing in front of Anne's desk was becoming annoying. He seemed to have aged in the past month, and Anne felt too sorry for him to tell him to sit down.

"I've got the entire team on research projects in the Library two floors down. They'll be there the rest of the day, and all day tomorrow too."

"Good." He sighed, and ran his hands across his substantial girth. "I can't take much more of this, you know."

"I know. It's almost over." And it was. The plaintiffs had called yesterday with a renewed threat, claiming they had additional documentation of this supposed extortion conspiracy, and would be reaching out to the Justice Department if Morex didn't come to its knees within forty-eight hours. It was just more of the same–Anne herself had already seen the documents to which they were probably referring–but the call had at least alerted Anne to the fact that the leak was continuing, and therefore had given the investigators an opportunity to narrow their search.

Dave Francis had met with Anne until well into the night last night. Even if the plaintiffs' counsel were uninvolved in the security breaches, and were merely the recipients of documents illegally obtained by someone else, the lawyers themselves were now involved in a serious ethical violation under the Code of Professional Conduct, because they had threatened criminal prosecution in order to gain a negotiating advantage in the civil case. The plaintiffs' lawyers could be disbarred, plain and simple, and Dave therefore saw their call as providing a significant tactical opportunity for Morex. He also felt it was time to pull the trigger on their public relations plan–a one-two punch to both the plaintiffs and their lawyers. He'd asked Anne last night if she had any media contacts.

"As a matter of fact, I do," she said, hesitating only a second before mentioning Rae. If it was the Morex story she was after, she would have it. And if it wasn't–well, she'd have to do it anyway. She owed Anne.

Anne had called the network and left a message around midnight last night. She had no idea where Rae was, or when she'd get the message–and was amazed when her phone rang at two in the morning.

"I knew you'd still be at the office." The sultry voice was laced with invitation. Forget it.

"I need you to do something," said Anne. "You know about the Morex case?"

"Yes." Rae was suddenly all business. Bingo.

"Well, it's yours. We'll give you an exclusive with the CEO, and his at-torneys. But there's a catch."

"Naturally. What?"

"You have to do it tomorrow, and give us the tape with final approval for broadcasting it."

Rae paused for a moment. "Why do I feel like you're trying to use me?"

Anne laughed. "Because I am. I'll explain it to you later, but only if it's off the record. You have nothing to lose, and maybe you get to expose the biggest recording industry story of the year."

Rae didn't spend more than a second thinking about it. "I'll be at your office, with a crew, at two tomorrow afternoon."

"We can have the tape?"

"After editing and voice-overs, yes."

When Joey arrived a little before noon, he threw himself on the sofa in Anne's office, and flipped through some books he found on the bookcase beside it, while Anne and Don went to the war room to continue discussing the case. They couldn't discuss it in front of Joey since he was no longer with the company–it would be a waiver of the attorney-client privilege, and the whole discussion could end up being evidence in the lawsuit. Anne and Don returned to her office after a short while, upon being informed by Sue that the investigators were back in town and on their way over.

"Ready for lunch? I'm starving," Joey said as he leafed through the firm's Pig Book–the directory of all of the attorneys and summer associates at Farnsworth Crowley, including a picture and bio of each.

"Not yet," said Anne, noticing the Pig Book in his hands. "What are you doing, looking for dates?"

"Hey, don't blame me. Some of the lawyers here are attractive. This Lindsay Brock–what's she like?"

"Married, and it's an old picture. Put that away, will you?"

"Oh come on, I'm just–Jesus!"

"Forget it, Joey. I'm definitely not introducing you to any of my colleagues."

"No." He got up, agitated. "It's Elizabeth."

"What? Who's Elizabeth?" Anne walked over to where he was standing, but he wouldn't let go of the directory, and continued to stare at the page.

"My Elizabeth. The law student. Elizabeth Evans."

Anne looked at the page that contained the picture and bio. Elizabeth Rachel Evans.

"You mean *that's* the woman you were involved with awhile ago? She's a summer associate here. And a friend of mine." Or she was–Anne still didn't know what to make of what Darryl had said. "But she goes by Rachel, not Elizabeth."

"She was Elizabeth when I knew her. This is so weird. Anne," he said, looking up at her, "she used to ask about you all the time."

Anne's breath caught in her throat. "You talked to her about me?"

"Yeah. I always thought it was kind of funny, you know? How she'd slip your name into a conversation and ask about you."

"Wait," she said, shaking her head, "I don't get it, how did my name come up?"

"It was nothing–we got into a talk one night about my college days. Early on, probably one of our first dates. And your name came up, of course. No big deal. But after that, she'd bring your name up now and then, just out of the blue."

The floor was dropping out of Anne's stomach. "How?"

"I don't know, it wasn't really noticeable or anything. It was just that, thinking about it now, it seemed like she'd turn the conversation on to a subject where your name would eventually come up, like a discussion of lawyers, or Cornell, or lesbians. You know, just stuff. It wasn't anything obvious she'd ask about, just stuff like have I heard from you, what are you doing, what firm are you working for. Different things like that."

Anne started to feel a small coil of anger begin to burn in her chest. "And you never bothered to tell me there was this total stranger asking about me?"

"It wasn't like that," Joey said, placating. "It was just here and there, over the course of months. I never really thought about it until now. I guess I figured she was just interested because she was going to be a lawyer too. And, maybe, you know, she had a little thing for girls–sorry, women." He turned back to the page. "Man, this is just too weird."

Don looked bewildered. "Well, I guess that's a hell of a coincidence."

Anne's voice was controlled, but her insides were churning. "I don't think it's a coincidence at all."

Sue knocked at the door and announced that the investigators had arrived.

"Joey, we'll be back in a little while. Don't leave this office. Don't even go to the bathroom. Sorry, but you've got to stay right here, with the door closed, and I think we'll be able to explain what's been going on shortly."

"What about attorney-client privilege? I thought I wasn't supposed to get involved."

"I'm afraid you may already be involved."

Rae showed up with her crew at two on the dot, and Anne was ready for her. The past two hours had been a whirlwind, and her head was spinning as Sue ushered Rae and the entourage into the main conference room for the interview with Don and Dave Francis. Rae's professional demeanor was flawless, with the exception of a moment when she overheard Sue informing Anne that Gallagher had left another message. The killer look that Anne shot at her erased Rae's amused sneer and cut short any snide comment she was about to deliver. Anne had avoided Gallagher's calls for three days now, and wasn't about to let any of that turmoil interfere with her focus now. Nor could she concentrate on the information the investigators had uncovered about Rachel. It would come out in the interview, and Dave would handle it. Only after the interview was over, and the tape locked securely in her drawer tonight, could she turn her attention to the problem of Rachel.

Sue had done a superb job of keeping news of the interview from sweeping the firm. Anne didn't want Rachel alerted to the fact that anything like this was going on, until Anne had formulated a plan on how to deal with her. Dave arrived with copies of the agreement that Anne had drafted to memorialize the terms under which the interview would be conducted, and Rae quickly scanned it before signing. Don was ready, everything was in place, and Anne stood to the side beside Parker as Rae sat down with Don and Dave.

It worked out beautifully. Don described the nature of Morex's agreements with the record companies, and the way in which the various recording artists had relied upon computerized compositions, arrangements, performances–even vocals–to grind out chart-topping hits. He was relaxed and amiable, just a guy doing business with a computer, and his low-key way of explaining it all was informative and understandable.

The real coup came from Dave, however, once Rae got into her questions about the lawsuit. There was no doubt about the criminality on the part of the record companies and their counsel, and Dave was forceful without being histrionic–documents had been stolen, a corporate spy had been planted, and the whole lawsuit appeared to have been engineered as part of a grand scheme to destroy Morex so that the record companies could take it over. The scheme appeared to have been hatched as long as two years ago, when an individual connected with the plaintiffs' counsel had begun laying the groundwork and eventually arranged to come work for the law firm that has traditionally represented Morex, in order to feed information to the plaintiffs. When Rae asked about how Morex and Farnsworth Crowley were going to deal with the espionage, Dave deftly sidestepped the question by pointing out that, unlike the plaintiffs' counsel, Farnsworth would not threaten criminal prosecution to settle the case. The information may well be turned over to the Justice Department, but that was up to the feds, and it was totally unrelated to the lawsuit.

After the interview was over, Don was visibly upbeat, and Anne felt a wave of relief. His good spirits would go far in the negotiations they still had to undertake with the plaintiffs tomorrow. He and Dave were scheduled to get on a plane later tonight.

Rae pulled Anne aside as the camera and sound crew were packing up. "Anne," she said privately, her tone confidential, "I know what's going on here, and it's okay with me–though I'll probably have a lot of explaining to do back at the studio."

"How long will it take to do the edits and voice-overs?"

"A few hours. I'll messenger the tape over to you around five."

"Okay."

"And Anne," she said as she reached for Anne's hand and cocked an eyebrow, "I hope you know that I'd like to see you sometime when it's not just about business. There's got to be a way for us to get past everything that happened and get together now and then. Just to talk, maybe try to be friends. Do you think that's possible?"

Anne smiled and gave a noncommittal shrug. "I really don't know."

Rae sighed. "Well, it's a hell of a story, anyway. I just hope I get to run it." She gave Anne the crooked smile, but it was without guile.

"You'll know in twenty-four hours."

Rae gave her hand a squeeze. "For what it's worth, I hope it helps. Even if I don't get to run it."

Anne casually strolled into Rachel's office at precisely one o'clock on Thursday, and took her customary seat in a relaxed posture that indicated she was just there to shoot the shit. She'd been up most of the night working out the strategy for this confrontation and Dave's meeting in Minneapolis that would immediately follow, and it was timed to the second: Sue was setting up the VCR in Anne's office at this moment, and Rachel would not be out of Anne's presence for a second once Anne's cards were on the table–she would have no chance to warn the lawyers in Minneapolis about what was coming. Don and Dave were already in Minneapolis with the duplicate of the tape they'd made after taking a look at the final product last night. They would meet with the plaintiffs' lawyers in one hour.

The information discovered by the investigators was good, but not good enough. It mostly consisted of strung-together suppositions and a few hard facts that could conceivably be explained away as coincidence. As Dave had explained it, the only sure-fire way to pull off the confrontation in Minneapolis would be to get a full-blown confession from one of the players–the whole story. And the only player available was Rachel. Unfortunately, Rachel was herself a master at deception, and Anne had to hope that, notwithstanding her deviousness, Rachel's youth and ego would come into play enough to allow Anne to trap her. Anne was going to have to employ every device in her MFA bag of tricks to make it work.

After about five minutes of light bullshit, Anne checked her watch and said she needed to stop by her office to get a file that she was expecting.

"It shouldn't take long, but why don't you come with me? We can continue this fascinating conversation there."

"Behind closed doors?" asked Rachel provocatively.

Anne smiled. "But of course."

Rachel gave her a blatantly suggestive grin and rose to walk beside Anne down the hall. "Rachel," said Anne, seemingly for Sue's benefit as they approached her office, "I need to give you an update on where we stand in the Morex case. Come on in." Rachel gave Anne a sidelong glance and followed her into Anne's office, shutting the door behind them.

"Okay," said Rachel coyly. "Now that you've got me locked in your office, what are you going to do with me?"

Anne felt her skin crawl under her suit jacket, but smiled and walked over to her desk, where she called Sue on the speakerphone. "We don't want to be disturbed for a while, okay? Hold my calls."

Sue's voice came over the box, "Not even for Don?"

Rachel leveled Anne with a look of sheer predation and shook her head.

"I don't think so," said Anne. "Just take a message."

She clicked off the phone, and took a moment to return Rachel's seductive look with something she hoped was convincing. She was fairly sure it was—she'd prepped herself to get into character for a full hour before walking into Rachel's office.

"You don't really want to talk about Morex, do you?" said Rachel as she ambled over to Anne's desk and slowly took a seat in front of it, crossing her legs to optimum advantage.

"Not especially. Tell me, did you go to the symphony on Friday after all?"

"No," she ran her hands through her short hair. "It wouldn't have been the same without you."

Anne laughed. "Oh, come on, don't tell me the symphony was just an excuse to see me. We see each other practically every day."

Rachel's stare was bold. "Let's stop kidding each other. You know what I'm talking about."

Anne leaned back in her chair. "Tell me."

"I'm talking about spending time with you outside of the office. I'm talking about a date."

Anne laughed again, and it required no acting. She was having fun. "You seem to forget that you're straight. And I'm not."

"I haven't forgotten a thing."

"So you want to go out on a date with a lesbian, is that it?"

Rachel shook her head. "I want to go out on a date with you. Whether or not you're gay. Whether or not I am."

"And then what?"

"And then we see what happens."

"But what do you want to happen?" Let her hang herself. Just give her some rope a little at a time.

Rachel paused and locked her eyes on Anne's, her expression deadly serious. "I want the same thing you want."

"Oh? What do I want?"

"You want to sleep with me," Rachel said casually. She recrossed her legs and leaned on Anne's desk.

"Just because I'm a lesbian? That means I automatically want to sleep with you?"

Rachel looked at her as if patronizing a small child, cocking her head to the side. "Are you saying that you won't sleep with me?"

"I'm saying it's a very interesting proposal, but you'd better think about it some more." Anne picked up a pen and started twirling it in her hand. "I'm not in the habit of sleeping with straight women, and you're probably not in the habit of sleeping with any women."

Rachel lowered her lids slightly, and her smile was overtly seductive. Anne had to admit to herself that it was beginning to have an effect–she was a painfully attractive woman. Too bad she's a snake, Anne thought.

"I've never done it before, if that's what you're asking," Rachel said softly. "But I think it's a habit I could definitely acquire."

"Really? You've never slept with a woman before?"

"No," she confessed. Her smile broadened. "But I'd love to try. At the hands of a master, of course."

"And what about your future with Farnsworth Crowley? You know that would be jeopardized if it got out."

Rachel arched one eyebrow, in complete control of the situation. "Who's going to know?"

Time to move in. Anne smiled innocently as she landed the first blow. "Well, Darryl, for one."

Rachel couldn't hide the startled look that flashed across her face. "Darryl?"

"Sure. He's already spreading rumors about us."

Rachel dismissed it with a little snort. "He's just angry because I won't go out with him. I told you how he's been harassing me. No one would believe him."

Anne shook her head. "No, I think he's saying it because you told him that you and I were having an affair."

"Me?" she said, suddenly less sure of herself. "When did he say that?"

"Right around the time that you set him up to make it look like he was the one who was leaking documents in the Morex case."

Rachel sat up straight in her chair. The seductiveness had vanished, replaced by a look that didn't begin to penetrate Anne.

"I don't know what you're talking about," she said icily.

"By the way, how's your father?"

Now she was rattled. "My father?"

"Yes, Roger Evans. You know, the partner at that firm in Minneapolis representing the plaintiffs? I only ask because he's going to be called into a meeting out there, in–" Anne checked her watch, "–oh, about twenty-five minutes, and I hope he doesn't have a weak heart, because it's going to get pretty ugly for him."

Rachel stood up to leave. "I don't know what you think you're doing, but I don't have to listen to this."

"I'm afraid you do–you won't be allowed to leave this office for the next hour. In the meantime, you might want to take a little stroll down memory lane. Joey sends his regards."

That stopped her cold. She slowly sank back into the chair. "Joey?"

"It took awhile for us to put it all together. I have to hand it to you, you would have made a fine trial strategist. But they don't let convicted felons practice law, so I guess that's out." Someday Anne knew she would look back on this episode and feel a little ashamed at how much she had enjoyed watching this little shit deflate before her eyes. But not today. Rachel had threatened to destroy Anne, the firm, and a close friend–and come frighteningly close to doing it.

"Look," said Rachel, "I think there's been some misunderstanding." All the power and confidence had been bled from her voice.

"How about you kill a few minutes by taking a look at what will be airing on the network news tonight," suggested Anne, "and you can tell me where we got the story wrong, okay?"

Anne picked up the remote control that Sue had left on her desk, and switched on the TV that was set up on the other side of the office. Rae's face came on the screen, and Rachel watched in a horrified stupor as Rae delivered her introductory comments on the general background that Anne had provided.

"Turn it off!" Rachel demanded. "They can't broadcast that! That's, that's libel!"

Anne laughed and turned off the VCR. "You need some more law school. Libel is written, slander is spoken."

"You know what I mean. We'll sue you for every penny, and the network too."

"Nope. Guess you missed that class, huh? Truth is an absolute defense to defamation. And as for the network, there's a little thing called the First Amendment. Or didn't you take Constitutional Law either?"

The game was over, and Rachel knew it. She shook her head and ran her fingers through her hair. Her voice was dead. "What do you want?"

"I want you to tell me exactly how it was done–starting with your relationship with Joey. I want to hear it all, and then, if I decide you've told me the truth, we'll see. Anything less than full cooperation, and your face, together with your father's, is on every TV in the country tonight. I kind of like the picture in the Pig Book–that's the one I gave to Rae."

"What's it matter what I tell you? I can just deny it later. It'll be your word against mine."

Anne smiled. "You may be right–in which case, you have nothing to lose. But I'll know if you're lying," she held up a two-inch-thick sheaf of papers, "because I can check your story against our investigative report."

"If you've got a report, why would you need to hear it from me?"

Anne pulled out all the stops, and her performance was Oscar caliber. "I don't. This is for you. Call it a gesture of good faith. I don't want to see you nailed if I can help it, and if I can convince the firm that you're cooperating, that you've given us the complete story, then maybe I can protect you a little." She let her voice grow soft. "I care about you, Rachel, no matter what's happened."

It seemed to do the trick. Rachel started out slowly, in short clipped phrases, but she soon gathered steam and out it all came–how the Morex engineers had approached her father's firm two years ago to discuss the fact that they'd created a series of incriminating documents. They didn't have them–they'd been fired and excluded from the premises before they could retrieve them. But they had pinpointed exactly where the documents were filed at Morex, and could describe in detail the exact nature of the digital fingerprinting they planted into the source code. Rachel explained how her father, a tax lawyer, had initially been unaware of what his partners were planning, but had been drawn into the loop when he'd been called in to consult on a tax issue involving one of the record companies. How Rachel had been a paralegal at the firm at the time, planning to attend law school the following year, and it was actually her idea to see if she could infiltrate the offices of Farnsworth Crowley as a summer associate–two years down the line.

"But how did Joey fit into all of it?" asked Anne. She needed to cover all of the bases.

"He was an easy mark. I'd read about Morex buying him out back when it happened. It was all over the news, how he was this swinging bachelor, or divorcé, who was sort of into younger women. I had six months to kill before school started, and there were worse ways to spend it than surfing in Hawaii, so I went and found him. Getting involved was easy–he was a pushover. And great in bed."

Joey would be happy to hear that. Anne decided not to tell him.

"But why? Why get involved with him? He was no longer with the company."

Rachel was on a roll, happy to show off how clever she'd been. "That was the beauty of it. We called it deep background. He knew the company inside out, but since he was no longer there, it wouldn't raise any alarms at the company to have me hanging around Joey and asking questions, and no one would recognize me later if I popped up as a summer associate working on the lawsuit. The engineers had told us what to look for in the files, but what they knew about the company as a whole was limited. Joey knew the entire business, and could talk about the inner workings of the company. You know, pillow talk." She smiled amiably. "The fact that he was such close friends with you was a surprise, and a great opportunity–I got the inside scoop on the company and the lawyers at the same time." She was very pleased with herself.

"But it was a big gamble. Suppose Joey hadn't been interested in you?"

Rachel sniffed smugly, as if the thought were inconceivable.

"Or if you hadn't gotten an offer from Farnsworth?" pressed Anne.

Rachel's smile oozed confidence. "Not such a big gamble. I knew I'd do well at Harvard–every law firm in the country would bend over backwards to hire me. Even Farnsworth."

She was right, of course. With her credentials, she could have written her own ticket anywhere. Too bad–now she'd be lucky if she could stay out of jail.

"And us?" Anne had to ask, not really wanting to.

"Us?" Rachel asked, perplexed for a minute. Anne raised an eyebrow, a mixture of what she hoped was a combination of come-on and "oh, come on."

Rachel gave a little laugh. "Oh, that was just fun–and a way to make sure I stayed inside the loop on the Morex case."

"Hoping for more pillow talk?"

Rachel leaned her elbow on Anne's desk. Her beauty was a powerful sword, but here she appeared to be trying to use it as a shield instead. "It was worth a shot," she said. "And I still think it would have been fun."

"But why start rumors that there was something between us?"

"A little extra insurance. Something to protect myself if the shit hit the fan. It's your career on the line if we'd gotten involved–or if people thought we did—not mine. I'd just be an innocent law student who was seduced by a powerful attorney. Your credibility would be shot, and I'm golden." She smiled then, and Anne felt a shudder down her spine. "It still might work, you know. There are a lot of people here who believe it's true." She gave Anne a quick wink that nearly made her sick. "I just wish it were."

A few moments later, Sue escorted Rachel to the firm security office, while Anne stayed behind. She clicked off the phone's recording device, and called Minneapolis.

Chapter Thirteen

The drive up to Provincetown was always murder at the end of summer, even in the middle of the night. What was normally a five-hour shot up the coast off-season turned into a seven- or eight-hour crawl in bumper-to-bumper traffic, especially on a Friday night/Saturday morning. The worst part was the little one-lane Route 6 that ran the length of the Cape. Anne used the time to daydream, listen to Top 40, mull over the dramatic end to the Morex lawsuit–and push away all thoughts of Gallagher. She was saving her deepest thinking on that subject for solitary night walks on the beach.

Dave Francis and Don had called her from Minneapolis immediately after the meeting last week, and had given her a blow-by-blow of the whole thing. She wished she could have been there for the final kill, but her presence was unnecessary in Minneapolis, and was very much needed in New York. The confrontation with Rachel had to occur at roughly the same time, and she was the only one who could do it. Still, she would have given anything to see the look on Bolton's smarmy little face when Dave started the videotape of Rae's interview. According to Dave, the room had erupted in a flurry of insults, threats, and finger-pointing, all of which boiled down to Bolton's insistence that Morex and Farnsworth Crowley were crazy, had fabricated the entire thing, and could prove absolutely nothing. Dave had waited patiently for precisely that moment to turn on the audio tape of Rachel's confession, which Dave had downloaded after Anne had converted the file to digital and e-mailed it to him.

Once the room had settled down, with the plaintiffs glaring in disgust at their lawyers and everyone glaring at Dave and Don, Dave had calmly outlined what Morex was prepared to do. In Anne's view, it was an outrageously generous proposal, given the venality of the other side's conduct, but as Dave had pointed out, this was no place for retribution. Morex could extract its pound of flesh in the marketplace–not at the settlement table. It was generous, but it bought peace, and that was Don's primary objective at this point.

Anne had reviewed the settlement papers this week before leaving town. The plaintiffs would withdraw their claims with prejudice and hand Morex a sweeping general release. Morex would permit the record companies to buy out the remainder of their contracts for a ridiculously low sum, but Morex would not hand them releases from liability–thereby retaining the right to sue them in the future for their past misdeeds. Morex would also retain the proprietary intellectual property underlying all of the music that it had created, but gave the record companies a royalty-free license to it all in perpetuity. Morex agreed to destroy the algorithms that could be used to track the digital fingerprinting of the music, thus essentially letting the record companies and artists do whatever they wanted with the past recordings–integrate all or portions of the songs into subsequent recordings–and Morex would never know. It didn't matter–Don wanted no part of any fingerprint-tracking anyway.

Finally, the parties had signed an iron-clad confidentiality agreement, so that neither party could ever divulge the facts or claims underlying their dispute, or the contents of the settlement agreement, except in the context of sworn court pleadings or under compulsion of law. Since the plaintiffs could not sue Morex, this provision served to close the door on the record companies or artists ever disclosing the whole sordid story in the press or in a lawsuit against Morex–while Morex was free to do so if it ever exercised its right to sue the record companies. Morex kept one copy of the videotaped interview, and under the terms of Anne's deal with Rae, the network could not report the story without Morex's consent.

Although Dave never mentioned the issue of criminal prosecution, the wording of the confidentiality agreement also left Morex free to report the illegal activities of the plaintiffs and their attorneys to law enforcement–and under the law, Dave had no choice but to do so. If the Justice Department or the bar association instituted any formal proceedings against the plaintiffs or their attorneys, Morex would be able to provide all pertinent information under a subpoena. Dave told Anne just this past Wednesday that he'd had a long conversation with a former colleague in the U.S. Attorney's office, and believed that they'd be able to work out a quiet plea arrangement that would punish the criminal conduct of the key players without any media attention. The disbarment of the responsible plaintiffs' attorneys would be a quiet affair as well.

Anne pulled into the parking lot beside her little condo at around three a.m., and felt the weight of the past two months begin to lift as soon as she stepped out of her car and smelled the salt air blowing in from the harbor. Clean and brisk–was there even a hint of autumn in the air? This far north there was often a slight chill at night, even in mid-August. She toted her laptop and one small overnight bag into the apartment–she had plenty of clothes here already, and needed to bring only a few essentials from New York. Not bothering to unpack yet, she dumped her bag in the middle of the living-room floor and headed to the kitchen to make herself a cup of decaffeinated tea. When it was ready, she brought it out onto the deck overlooking the town and harbor, and sat back in one of the deck chairs to enjoy the stillness of the night for a little while before bed.

She didn't want to think about Gallagher, but could not stop her mind from the self-torture, the sheer masochism of reliving that night by the Milburn pond almost two weeks ago. She shuddered, either from the cool air, or from the flash image of Gallagher's terrified, frozen stare as she had backed out of their embrace. And then the words, the betrayal, the precision cut of that "I'm sorry" slicing through her abdomen as she played the scene over and over in her head. Maybe if she played it enough it would lose its power to hurt, its blade would eventually dull. But Anne knew better, knew that those words would haunt her, and hurt her, for a very long time–and that she would continue to inflict this pain on herself for no good reason until her mind found something else to occupy every waking moment. In about fifty years or so.

It was more than the collapse of what had never really begun, and more than the despair of knowing that she would never be with the one person that she knew, had probably always known, was the one great love of her life. She didn't even know if she believed in all that romantic crap, didn't know if people actually had just one great love–she only knew that that's how it felt, that Gallagher had been a constant solitary beacon to her heart for as long as she could remember. She could live with heartache and celibacy–she'd perfected it–but she didn't know if she could live without her most cherished friendship, a constant rock-solid anchor to which she'd always known she could turn. She loved Gallagher, that was clear now, loved everything about her, loved every way of being with her–as friend, confidante, schoolmate, soulmate. The loss of Gallagher in her life was stupendous, opening a gaping hole in nearly every facet of her existence, leaving nothing but a bleak, empty void that could never be filled.

There was no way they could ever be close again. Anne doubted they could even pretend to resume a friendship at this point–Anne certainly couldn't, not now, and for this reason she'd ignored the twice-daily phone messages from Gallagher for the past two weeks–but even if they could, it would never be the same. Whatever superficial acquaintanceship they might try, it wouldn't begin to approximate what Anne had lost, and would serve only as a painful reminder of what there had been, and what there could have been.

So I have no choice but to figure out a way to live my life, fill my days, without Gallagher, Anne thought. Should be easy–we've mostly just traded phone calls anyway, and only gotten together every now and then. It's not as if she were such a continual presence in my day-to-day life.

But she was. Even when they'd lived in separate cities, they'd been close. Each had always known the other was there. The connection was always present, ready to be called upon at any time. Now there was just dead air. And Anne was tempted to wrap herself in it, use the desolation as a buffer from the rest of the world, from anyone who might be in a position to hurt her like this again.

She was flipping over to the anger side of the anger-pain-numbness schizophrenia that had plagued her since the reunion. But this time the fury was directed at herself, not Gallagher. How stupid she had been, to fall into the same trap that had ensnared her twenty years ago–feeling things for someone she knew could never return her love. And what about the Lesbian Prime Directive–never get involved with a straight woman? Never even *think* about a straight woman. Gallagher may be a very different person from Rae, but the ending was still the same–Anne's battered heart hanging out there, blowing in the breeze.

Anne got back to the condo late on Saturday afternoon, after an exhilarating bike ride on the miles of paved trails through the sand dunes that lined the coast. At least she could keep her body in shape–maybe the mind would follow. Off-season she would swim her laps in the big hotel pool at the end of town, but it was crowded with guests at this time of year, so she had to content herself with the solitude of mountain-biking. It was better than nothing.

And it afforded her the endorphin high that always seemed to help her think. There was no great mystery about what had happened to Gallagher. It was what happened to *every* straight woman who stepped into something she couldn't handle. Anyone could feel attraction, desire. But it took a lesbian to know when it was a life-defining event, and it took a lesbian to have the courage to see it through. The rest was just bullshit–straight-girl games with something exciting, playing with fire, leaving hot coals and ash in the aftermath. Gallagher shouldn't have toyed with her like that, but the real fault was her own–she had *known* better.

And what on Earth was she supposed to say when Gallagher finally succeeded in reaching her on the phone? Laugh it off and pretend that it was nothing? Listen to her bullshit apology and go on as friends? Worse, suppose Gallagher still intended to explore some infinitesimal desire she may feel? Anne was clear on that score–it could never happen, not again. Much as *every* fiber of Anne's being was screaming for it, Anne simply could not let Gallagher touch her again, physically or emotionally.

So where did that leave her? As Anne had pumped the last few yards up to the top of the highest sand dune overlooking the water, she had resigned herself to the fact that she had no idea. She didn't have to decide today. Or this week. Maybe it wasn't even a decision for which she could prepare–maybe she'd know how to act when the time came, the next time she spoke to Gallagher. Maybe. Until then, she'd just have to sit with her feelings and not try to find a solution. Thinking about it just tied her in knots.

Back in the condo, she showered and changed into clothes for dinner. Much as she hated the idea of eating dinner in one of the many Provincetown restaurants every night, the solitude she craved gave way to common sense–she knew that if left to her own devices, in this mood she would never get around to preparing a nutritious meal for herself. She grabbed a light jacket and was preparing to head down Commercial Street when the phone rang. She was tempted to ignore it, but it might be the office.

"Anne? It's Parker."

"What's up?"

"I just wanted to check on you. Sue gave me your number."

"I'm fine."

"Well, you cut out of here so fast on Friday, and next thing I know Sue's telling me you're taking some time off. It's not like you."

"I know. I'm just beat. I hope it's not a problem." She didn't really care if it was. She needed a break, and had no intention of returning to the office until she was ready. It could be a week, a month–or never. She refused to think that far in advance.

"No, no problem. But I don't think I've ever seen you take more than a week of vacation the whole time I've known you. And even then, you're usually doing work for part of the time."

He seemed so concerned that Anne was tempted to tell him what was really wrong. But she just wasn't ready to talk about it, not even to Parker.

"I know. I guess the Morex mess just wiped me out."

"Okay. You know, I hear Harvard has expelled Rachel. They called for confirmation about the disciplinary action that's being taken against her. I guess the Bar Association contacted them. Anyway, she may or may not be prosecuted, but she'll certainly never practice law in this country."

Anne had no response to that–she didn't care what happened to Rachel Evans. Just another untrustworthy straight woman, as far as she was concerned. But mention of Rachel reminded her of something.

"Parker, did you ever talk with Darryl, explain it all to him? Let him know the firm's not taking any action against him?"

"Yes, but why? I thought you hated Darryl."

"I do. He's a total ass-kiss. But it's still not fair to let him think there's a cloud over his head."

"I spoke to him personally, and let him know that he was in the clear–except for the rumors he was spreading about you. I don't think he'll be gossiping about anybody again."

"Well, I guess that's good news for you."

Parker's laugh was warm. "Oh, I could use a few good rumors about me. Care to start any?"

"Not on your life, pal. I'm not having any heart-to-hearts with anyone in that office ever again!"

"Can't say that I blame you. And Anne"– his voice became tentative–"I want you to know I'm sorry about how I questioned you. About Rachel. It's my job, yes, but I should have realized it was all bullshit."

Anne appreciated the apology, but it made no difference, at least not right now. She didn't feel connected to Parker, or anyone else.

"Don't think about it," she said. "I understand."

"So." His voice brightened. "Picking up any hot beach babes in the Gay Mecca?"

Time to end this discussion. "I gotta go, Parker. Thanks for the call."

"Take care of yourself, okay? Keep me posted."

"We'll see. Bye."

As she hung up the phone, she heard footsteps on the deck outside. No doubt one of the neighbors with whom she'd become friendly over the years–maybe Doris, the seventy-year-old retired gym teacher who lived two doors down. Doris was nice–a real pisser, as Shirl would say–but Anne was not in the mood to socialize. She'd have to make an excuse and get out.

The knock on the door was timid, not the usual pounding that Doris delivered. When Anne opened the door, her breath caught in her throat and she felt her chest constrict, clamping down on her lungs and heart, squeezing them into marbles. She stared into the Hershey-bar eyes of Gallagher.

"Don't close the door on me," Gallagher said, her voice more forceful that her knock had been.

"What do you want?"

"I want to talk to you. But you won't return my calls."

"How did you get here? How did you even know I was here?" But she knew the answer already.

"Sue." Sue is dead meat.

"Well, I'm afraid you wasted a trip," Anne said. "I don't want to talk to you." It wasn't exactly true–she wanted to talk to her very much, but she couldn't. Physically couldn't. Her throat would dry up and she'd choke if she even tried.

"Then just listen. Will you listen to me?"

Anne sighed and shook her head. "I'm sorry, Gallagher, but no. I just can't." Anne looked hard at Gallagher. She was so beautiful. "I don't want to hear anything you have to say."

Gallagher angrily pushed past her into the condo, and turned to confront Anne from the middle of the living room. "No, you're not shutting me out. I know you too well–that's just like you. But I won't let it happen. You're going to listen to me, deal with me, whether you like it or not."

Against all reason, Anne smiled–nearly burst out laughing, in fact. She'd never seen Gallagher so angry, at least not at her, and for some reason it struck her as hilarious.

"God damn it, it's not funny!" said Gallagher. Her cheeks were flaming, her hair was wild. It was all too much for Anne, who couldn't help herself–she stifled a guffaw, but a giggle popped out.

"I'm sorry, Gallagher," she said, shaking her head. "And believe me, there isn't anything about this whole thing that I find funny either. I guess I'm just punchy from too little sleep." And too much crying.

"Close the door."

"No. I'm leaving to go eat dinner."

"Then I'm coming with you."

She couldn't exactly tie her down. Anne shrugged. "Do what you want."

Commercial Street was packed with sunburned tourists in shorts and tank tops–mostly gay couples, but an unusually high number of straight couples and families too. Anne had noticed the trend over the past several years. Unlike when she'd first started coming here in the early eighties, when the town was predominantly filled with lesbians, gay men, and artists of no particular persuasion, there was now an increasing percentage of straight people, young and old, who spent their vacations here at the tip of Cape Cod. Anne had always assumed that one or the other member of these couples was actually closeted, and had selected Provincetown for vacation precisely because it afforded such a wealth of cruising opportunities. But maybe not–maybe it was just a reflection of the country's general acceptance of gays, the increasing nonchalance with which straight people responded to the gay community. Sometimes Anne felt irritation at the encroachment of the straight world on her little gay haven–after all, they have the rest of the world available to them, why do they have to come here? But they were respectful–didn't gawk at the sight of two leather men kissing in front of Town Hall–and usually Anne accepted their presence with the same blasé attitude with which they accepted hers.

Usually, but not tonight. Anne glared bullets at each straight couple she passed in the clogged center of town. Gallagher was walking silently by her side–hadn't even commented on the fact that all of the pedestrians were holding up traffic by walking in the middle of the street instead of on the tiny sidewalks. Maybe Gallagher noticed the women with their arms around each other and the men holding hands, but maybe not. Anne was proud of her gay brothers and sisters, proud to show them off to Gallagher. See, there are some people in this world who have the courage of their convictions.

Anne stopped in front of the seafood bistro that required no reservations, and figured that it was still early enough for them to get a table without waiting in line. She was right, and after the owner, Sis, gave her a big hug in greeting, she was shown to a table overlooking the bay, with Gallagher following mutely behind.

As Gallagher took her seat across from her, Anne noticed the tee shirt and shorts that she was wearing. "You're going to be cold after dinner in that," Anne commented. "It gets breezy up here as soon as the sun sets."

"Does this mean you're talking to me yet?" Gallagher looked tentative.

"It means you'll be cold tonight."

They looked at the menu quietly, although Anne didn't need to read it–she'd get a lobster and salad, her traditional first-night-in-Provincetown dinner. While Gallagher ordered Portuguese soup and some baked cod, Anne tried to shake off the unreality of the whole scene–the two of them sitting here, where Anne had so often wished they could be, acting as if everything were normal.

"Here's what I propose," Gallagher said eventually. She had her business voice turned on–the dealmaker was about to move into action. "We agree to spend a civil evening together, talking about whatever we want. That can include everything I want to say to you, and everything I know you want to say to me. But the ground rules are, as soon as one of us wants to stop that particular discussion, we do. No questions asked. And we'll just see how it goes."

It was a sensible suggestion, but Anne wanted to disagree just because she was in a disagreeable mood. Still, after all these years, maybe she could give Gallagher the benefit of the doubt and at least try. She owed her that much. She fought with herself for a moment over the notion that she owed Gallagher anything at all–but quickly resolved it in deference to the years of friendship they'd shared. She'd agree, not for Gallagher's sake, but in honor of a friendship that was now gone.

"Okay. Deal. Pass the bread."

Gallagher's smile lit up the room, but she masked it almost at once, as if fearful that a too-eager attitude could sour the deal.

"You go first. What do you want to say to me?"

"I don't have anything to say to you, Gallagher. And that's what I have to say." No, I'm not going to make this easy for you.

Gallagher didn't miss a beat. "Okay, I'll go first. I want to say I'm sorry."

"Fine. Will you go home now?"

"And I want to tell you what happened to me that night. And what I've been going through since then."

"Don't bother. I know exactly what happened to you. And I don't give a shit what you've been going through, because as far as I'm concerned, you did it to yourself. And to me."

"Fair enough."

"And if I'm going to get through this meal without getting sick, we're going to have to end this discussion for now."

Gallagher nodded cooperatively. She had on her Milburn-polite face, and Anne knew she'd honor the ground rules. True enough, they said very little during dinner, and what few comments they did exchange were cordial. The superficiality of it all nearly got to Anne at one point, just as she cracked open a lobster claw and accidentally sliced open her thumb on the shell–the tears that welled up had nothing to do with her bleeding thumb, had everything to do with the impassable avalanche that separated her from the woman across the table. She sucked the blood from her thumb and furiously wiped a stray tear, hoping Gallagher hadn't seen it.

The sun was setting as they emerged back onto Commercial Street, and Gallagher suggested a walk through town. With nothing better to do, and too uncomfortable at the prospect of returning to the intimacy of the condo, Anne agreed. Gallagher stayed close by Anne's side, but knew better than to touch her. They waded through the dinner-bound couples–all of whom seemed disgustingly in love and oblivious to the world–and wandered slowly past the shops and nightclubs that were getting ready for the big evening rush. They strolled in their own separate cocoons of pain and frustration, each absorbed in her own thoughts. As they neared the extreme west end of town, where the businesses gradually gave way to charming little houses, Gallagher asked about the proximity of the beach.

"Well, the bay is right over there," Anne pointed past the houses fronting the harbor, "but the ocean is straight ahead and to the right, about a mile. Maybe less."

"Let's go see the ocean." Gallagher was looking at her. "Okay?"

Anne shrugged, and they continued their slow pace through the quiet residential streets in the deepening dusk. Anne heard a foghorn in the distance, and some disco music blaring from one of the houses several streets away. Pure Provincetown.

They reached the deserted road that ran alongside the tide pools and out to the beach, and walked quietly in the dark. The town at their backs, they had no streetlights here–only the sliver of moon barely visible as it rose just over the crest of the dune ahead of them. It would have been such a peaceful moment. If only.

"I want to tell you what's going on with me," Gallagher finally began. Her voice was gentle but insistent. "All right?"

The part of Anne that wanted to cover her ears and run as fast as she could relinquished its hold on her to something else. Probably masochism, but maybe it was just a desire to reach closure on this whole thing once and for all. Gallagher was an experienced and determined businesswoman– she would not give up until she'd had her say.

"Okay," Anne sighed.

Gallagher took a few moments before beginning. She was so lovely in the moonlight that Anne wanted to cry. Stop it.

"I freaked out at the reunion, plain and simple. Not because I was kissing you. I'd wanted to do that for so long that"–she took a deep breath and pushed a few errant curls from her face—"well, for a very long time. But the point is, it was Milburn, and everything that represents. I guess I hadn't really thought it through. I just—I just kissed you because I wanted to. And when they saw us, Rhonda and Blair, it was like I was back in high school and we'd gotten caught in something. All I could think was, it's going to get all over school, and my parents will find out, and everything."

"Yeah, well, that's what happens when people come out."

"Yes, but you came out on your terms, you picked the time and place. It sounds stupid, I know, but I never thought past that first kiss. Well, I did, but it was all wrapped up in you. I never thought about the outside world."

Anne looked down at the sand alongside the road and shrugged. "Okay, you messed up. You realized it's not for you. And you can make up some bullshit excuse for everyone and run back to your safe little straight life."

"No, that's not what I want, and you know it."

"Well, that's what you've got."

"No, it's not. I don't have that life anymore."

"What do you mean?" Anne wasn't sure what she was hearing, and forced herself to pay close attention, filter out the pounding in her ears.

"I went back to my parents that night and told them."

Anne stopped and stared at Gallagher, whose eyes were brimming with tears that barely clung to her long lashes and threatened to spill down those fiery cheeks any second. Anne wanted so badly to embrace her, to comfort her, but the world was tilting at a precarious angle, and she was on the edge of a very steep precipice. She dared not move for fear of tumbling into the abyss.

"What?" She continued to look into Gallagher's eyes, and felt the unearthly pull begin. But she had to be sure. "What are you saying?"

"Anne, I've been in love with you since I was fifteen years old. Maybe it took me forever to put it together, but it's true, it's who I am."

Anne shook her head—not in disbelief, but in wonder. How could this be?

"Gallagher–"

"No, listen to me. I love you. I don't know what it is to spend a single day not loving you." The too-full lashes finally gave way, and the tears started to stream down her windswept face. Gallagher brushed them away impatiently, her eyes blazing holes into Anne. "Don't try to tell me you don't feel the same way. I felt it that night. I can feel it now."

Gallagher took her by the arms and pulled her close, enveloping her in a hard embrace that was almost angry, as if she could squeeze Anne's reluctance out of her. The arms surrounding Anne were strong, sure, and would hold her if she fell. But she didn't fall. She stood on her own two feet, on solid ground, and looked up through her own tear-blurred eyes at the face she had adored for so many years, reeling from the power of Gallagher's words.

"I have to think," Anne said.

Gallagher smiled tenderly. "No. That's all you do. You spend your life safe on the sidelines, thinking. The real question here isn't what you think. It's what do you *want*?"

Anne buried her head against Gallagher's shoulder, breathed deeply of the delicious scent of her exposed neck. Maybe she was right, maybe the time for thinking was over, long past. What the hell.

"The same thing I wanted twenty years ago," Anne said softly, nearly crying. "I want you, Gallagher. I always have."

"Then be with me." Her voice was a whisper, her mouth right beside Anne's ear–urgent, pleading. "Please."

They made love that first time on the sand, in the lee of a secluded dune and nestled between patches of beach grass. Fumbling and frantic, still half-clothed as they surrendered to the frenzied climaxes that were ready to erupt as soon as they kissed, it was nothing like Anne had imagined it would be. When Anne slipped her hand through the wide pantsleg opening of Gallagher's shorts and pushed aside the drenched panties to touch her for the first time–astonished at how swollen she'd become so quickly, how thick her cream–Gallagher came immediately, screaming Anne's name in choked sobs, and Anne came at the same time, unable to hold back the earth-shattering waves and her own tearful cries. They took their time after that, slowly undressing each other in the moonlight and marveling at every inch of skin as it was exposed. She buried herself in Gallagher, reveled in her, drowned herself in the intoxicating tastes and smells and sensations of this woman, this lover, this soulmate who was loving her as she'd never been loved before, as she'd never allowed herself to be loved. Fully, thoroughly, completely.

Hours later, after they had rinsed themselves in the cold waves and re-dressed, they made their way back through town slowly, arms locked tight around each other, and began the inevitable process of reviewing, reciting, reliving their long history together, the tortured odyssey that had finally brought them to this point. Anne was surprised by some of it–the fact that Gallagher had told Joel the reason she was leaving him was that she was in love with Anne–but some of it, like Gallagher's thoughts and intentions at certain memorable moments in their past, just served to confirm what Anne had long suspected but hadn't dared hope. It would be a long conversation, likely to last for years.

December 31, 2000

The Monument overlooking the town and harbor of Provincetown was draped in strands of tiny string lights that splayed out at the bottom to create the conical illusion of a Christmas tree. Anne and Gallagher walked down a deserted Commercial Street that was Dickensian in its holiday ornamentation amid the snowdrifts. Braced against the cold in their heavy coats and mittens, they took their time and stopped alongside some of the more festively decorated shops on their way to the millennium ceremony at the base of the Monument.

"I still think the new millennium started last New Year," said Gallagher. "When the calendar switched over to 2000."

Anne smiled warmly at her lover. "We went over this last year. Since there wasn't a year zero, how could 2000 mark a new millennium?"

Gallagher nodded as they walked on. "I know. It just feels like this ceremony is a year too late. Everyone else in the world celebrated last year."

Anne laughed. "Provincetown has always done its own thing."

They passed the newsstand that was closing up for the night, and saw the magazine with Rae's face on the cover. Gallagher gave her a sidelong glance, and Anne shook her head with a smile.

"Don't say it."

"Oh, come on," Gallagher laughed, "just one wisecrack. I mean really, she's marrying the head of the biggest studio in Hollywood. You've got to admit, it's a little much. She won't stop until she's married the President of the United States."

Anne put her arm around Gallagher's waist, and felt the familiar arm circling her shoulder. "No," said Anne, "she won't stop until she *is* the President of the United States."

They stopped in front of a particularly ornate house draped in multi-colored lights tastefully arranged around the porch, windows and shrubs. Must be some gay guys.

Anne sighed. "I wish we could have another week. Every time we come up here I never want to leave."

"I know, me too," said Gallagher, giving her a gentle squeeze. "I miss Muffin and Chop, of course. I always do when we're away. But still, I wish we could stay. And I'm sorry that the school calendar is cutting our vacation short."

Anne looked up into her deep brown eyes and smiled. She would never tire of losing herself in those eyes. And right now, framed by those cheeks bright red from the cold, they were particularly gorgeous. When Gallagher leaned in just then to kiss her gently on the forehead, Anne's breath caught for a moment. They may have spent the last three hours making love, but Anne felt her excitement stir all over again. It hadn't been enough. As usual.

"It's not just your schedule, you know. Parker needs me to cover a court appearance for him next week." Ever since she and Parker had formed their own firm two years after Anne had made partner at Farnsworth Crowley, her workload had eased considerably, but it still got in the way of the rest of her life sometimes. Only occasionally, and only when she agreed to it. Gallagher was her priority, and Parker respected that. "Besides," Anne continued, "I would never complain about your teaching schedule. I'm just glad you're finally doing something you love. I don't care if we're in Provincetown or New York or Timbuktu, it's a vacation just being with you."

Gallagher shook her head and smiled. "Five years and I still can't get used to the incredible things you say to me."

"Well, I'll just have to keep on saying them then."

Gallagher squeezed her. It felt so good. "Please do."

"Hey, five years–you know, you're officially my longest relationship."

"I know," said Gallagher with a look that never failed to melt her. "And you're mine."

Anne returned her look tenfold. "Oh, I'm yours, all right."

Gallagher kissed her again, this time on the lips, and their passion briefly sparked once more until they pulled away and laughed.

Gallagher was staring into her eyes. "I can read your mood eyes."

Anne pressed her lips back against Gallagher's, and spoke softly through the kiss. "What am I feeling?"

"The same thing I am. But we'll never make it to the ceremony if we keep this up."

"You're right," said Anne as she pulled back and laid her head on Gallagher's shoulder. There would be plenty of time for that. There always was.

THE END

About the Author

Cameron Abbott is an attorney in New York City, where she litigates complex commercial disputes involving a variety of high-tech industries around the world. She also serves as an arbitrator in the securities industry, teaches as Adjunct Professor of Law at a law school located in New York, and has appeared as a television commentator on various legal issues.